The Twist

Richard Calder

D0782840

Four Walls Eight Windows

NEW YORK

I die because I do not die.

St. John of the Cross

© 2003 Richard Calder

Published in the United States by:
Four Walls Eight Windows
39 West 14th Street, room 503
New York, N.Y., 10011

Visit our website at http://www.4w8w.com
First printing December 2003.

Library of Congress Cataloging-in-Publication Data on file:

The Twist/Richard Calder
ISBN 1-56858-292-7

10 9 8 7 6 5 4 3 2 1

Typesetting by Jerusalem Typesetting

Printed in Canada

Chapter One
American Gothic

I looked out the window. The landscape *seemed* earthly. More or less, at least. But I was between worlds. Between Earth and Venus. Earthly things, here, had been subverted by the alien. And life, they said, was strange…

The desert rolled monotonously past as the stagecoach sped through deepening twilight, a reluctant breeze flowing through the open windows. The young woman turned her face to catch the inflow of cooling air; like me, looked out toward where Tombstone poked above the horizon, its glittering towers catching the rays of the dying sun; then closed her eyes and sighed. The sun was like neon. It resembled a morgue's strip lighting, the shadows cast by the towers like crisp, blackened bodies laid out on white tiles. The young woman, of course, also belonged laid out on tiles; but in a morgue far colder, far more anonymous than that suggested by a pale desert close to night. For she was Venusian. A necrobabe.

"The hangman had jerked the hood over my head," said the tall man who sat next to her, his gaze fixed upon my mother opposite. "There had been the sound of creaking boards, a commotion of gears and pulleys; and then my stomach had tried to punch its way through my palate and out the top of my skull. And when I fell through the trap that dark morning, ma'am, teeth gritted, sphincter braying, expecting the next second to impact on the hard turf of eternity, I tell you, it was that same moment"—he averted his gaze to make an amused evaluation of his travelling companion—"that *exact* moment when I first saw her. For this little girl is Miss Death herself, ma'am. Or, shall we say, Death's emissary. *My* death at least. A Death to whom I stand perpetually in awe."

The tall man redirected his attention at us, the family whom he had chosen to receive the burden of his revelation. My mother stared back at him, perplexed; my father tapped his walking cane upon the floor, his eyes alternately holding the stranger's own and then scouring the coach's interior, intimidated, plainly, by the stranger's appearance as much as by his words, but determined not to show it. I understood why my father might feel afraid; but I could not understand his disapprobation. The tall man and the young woman were the most marvellous people I had ever seen. They were *vastly* romantic. The man, dressed in black, was the quintessence of all the images of gunslingers that I had cut out and pasted in my scrapbook; and the woman, in her soiled bombazine and with her face of a depraved cherub—I wished I had been as pretty as her—was a creature from the other side of life, Miss Death indeed, a veritable angel of oblivion, one of those whom, back home, we referred to in whispered disbelief.

The fabulous pair had only joined us at the last stage; after unspoken acknowledgements, our party had lapsed into silence. My mother and father were muted, I think, more by an apprehension occasioned by the newcomers' alarming, but, to me, heart-crushingly exquisite physicality, than by any lack of the necessary social skills. But as we had approached Tombstone—our mutual taciturnity surely as much a trial as any explosion of garrulousness—the tall man had, caught up, perhaps, by a buoyancy of mood as he contemplated the delights of city life, been quite unable to forestall what seemed a ready disposition to oratory.

"For though I fell through space, ma'am—a black rush of cloying air, rain, fear and the rank smell of my loosened bowels greeting my clumsy dismount toward hell—the tug on my nape, the crush of windpipe, the burning of hemp upon the skin never came. Instead of all those clichés of horror that I had been haunted by during my nights in the pokey, I seemed to fall, without outrage to flesh or marrow, without interruption of thought—no border guards or bureaucracy to mark my transition from this country to the next—toward something my precociously cynical mind recoiled from as if it were another horror, the universe's last, best practical joke. A tunnel of light had opened up, a tunnel I could see as plainly as if I had been disencumbered of my hood."

"Are you telling us, sir, that you are a *felon*?" said my mother, with that tight-assed, Bostonian delivery of hers that was as mean-spirited as the nod she had begrudgingly awarded the couple when they had boarded some hours previously. My father tut-tutted; behind his eyes I detected that familiar compulsion of his to cut and run. One hand went to his breast, as if he were trying to calm his heart, or was about to take out his pocket handkerchief and gag the mouth that had made such a misery of his days; he would have had no wish to champion one who existed merely as a reminder of his life's disappointments. His shining armor, rusted, some score of years now, by a wretched climate of matrimony and debt, was locked securely in his modest personal armory; and at such times when his wife's mouth was likely to get him into trouble, he would be disinclined to remember where he had stashed the key. I looked at him askance, enjoying his discomfiture; I looked at his unspeakable, still outraged spouse. In truth, I would have enjoyed seeing both of them hurled into a life-threatening attack of conniptions.

The tall man suffered my mother's ice-matronly regard in silence. And then he grinned, displaying gold-capped incisors, a dandified fox who was happily toying with a fat hen.

"No ma'am," he said, careful to bring out the velveteen menace in his voice, the tone I myself adopted when, back home, playing Cowboys and Indians with my friends in the park, I reserved for myself the role of the villain, "I am telling you that I have been the recipient of a near-death experience. I am telling you of how I came to meet a being from another world."

"You survived a hanging," said my mother, with matter-of-fact disdain, "and found that you had brought a Venusian across the demarcation zone. Oh yes, I've heard such tales before. The magazines are full of real-life stories of people who've escaped near drowning, near evisceration, near broken necks, only to find they are unable to rid themselves of an un-welcome house guest from the other side. Haven't such things been responsible for the turpitude we find the West awash with today?" She shook her head and turned to my father. "If it wasn't enough that we have had to share our journey with an alien, it seems we have now an outlaw to contend with, too."

"Excuse *me*," said the young woman, her eyes still closed and her face evincing signs of an enervation that was surely as much emotional as it was somatic, "I didn't *choose* to be here. I would've been gone long ago if it hadn't been for the incompetence of that hangman." She opened the fan she held in her left hand and idly pampered herself with stirrings of dust-filled air. "Don't pander to these people any more, Mr. Twist. They ain't interested in our poor, doomed romance, and I ain't interested in their cockamamie lives."

"You are, as always, the gourmand. I take heed of your judgment," he said. Tombstone had rolled fully into view, like a *mise en scène* brought center stage by cunning theatrical machinery. I leant forward, my feet swinging above the floor

4

as the coach's suspension struggled to absorb the rigors of the trail, the heels of my Mary Janes tapping out a syncopated tattoo against one of the trunks that contained my family's possessions. I was glad that our journey was almost over; I would be glad to get a drink; and I would be as glad, almost, to see the last of the surrounding hills. People said it didn't do to be caught in the desert after nightfall. That was when the zanies came down from their cliff-top lairs, abseiling those dull bronze monoliths to suck at the roots of the saguaro cacti and, if chance should offer up a supplement to their diet, tracking down any human who might be stranded on the warped ash-white plains that stretched millions of miles west. But I would be less than glad to have to say farewell to the marvellous couple who had seared my imagination with a livid, indelible joy; who embodied the promise of something beyond the petty existence that was all that I had ever known, all that I had to look forward to.

The tall man had taken notice of how I stared at his scandalously pretty comrade, and his eyes had gone magnesium, igniting like distress flares. I flushed. "I beg your pardon, sir," I said. "I didn't mean any offence. It's just that I've never seen a Venusian before." The stranger relaxed, his grin becoming less feral, more avuncular. "Sir," I said, the excitement I felt at being in his presence negating my habitual chariness, "is it true that Venus is where *all* our deaths live. And are they all as beautiful as this lady?" The man's nostrils distended as he coughed up a short, plosive laugh. The young woman remained impassive.

"I'm told that there are other death-worlds," said the man, his grin lingering, though his eyes had darkened and become grave. "But for those who live lives outlandish and reprehensible, for those who dare to *love*, Venus is their resting place, the home that they can look forward to at the end of a long, bad day."

"So *you* wish, Mr. Twist," said the young woman.

"So I wish, too," I said. I swallowed hard, surprised by my own boldness.

"Lord forfend," hissed my mother; and then, ostensibly looking out the window at the chiaroscuro of the desert's expanse, her gaze concentrated itself upon the reflection of my father's face in what remained of the wound-down pane. "Lord forfend that you should wish for the same resting place as this man. He is an *outlaw*." She pursed her lips, the loose flesh about her jowls slopping back and forth, her dewlap tremulous as a neurotic turkey's. "It's just as I told you"—she continued, talking to the image of my father now—"we should never have come out here. The people are savages. We'll all be murdered in our beds." How provincial, I thought, how discourteous to refer to a man as an *outlaw*. But at the same time, how enviable to be accorded such an appellation.

"'That time I was hanged, that was due," said the vilified one, bowing his head slightly, in ironic deference, to indicate that he had picked up my mother's sibilant harangue, "to the vindictive sanctimony of my elders." He winked at me; sniffed at his boutonniere, a creamy blue-veined orchid plucked from the rain forests of California, or from maybe even beyond, where the lands of the frontier stretched out into the unknown. "Outlaw?" he continued, his gaze flitting between my progenitors in as kindly a manner as pique would allow. "Ma'am, I am a gentleman. A wastrel, some might say; some, even, a *gasbag*. But a gentleman, nevertheless. A *southern* gentleman. From deepest Louisiana." He touched a finger to the brim of his black Stetson and tilted his head. "A pure piece of swamp-bred scum."

The young woman opened and closed her mouth in what might have been either a yawn or a subdued groan of exasperation. "No, they don't all look like me," she said, as out of sync with the conversation as she appeared to be with reality. "Everybody's death is different. But it is always beautiful. My world is full of beauty."

Richard Calder

"Forgive the lady," said the tall man, "she's a long way from home. And the only way she'll be getting back—the only way her people will be *allowing* her back—is with me in tow. They're strict about these sorta things. But—" He raised his hands to within a few inches of his face, palms together, fingers entwining; and then the digits flexed, forming a steeple. "But I'm not going." He turned his head, allowing my parents a reprieve; stooped a little, inspecting the woman who played comatose at his side. He grinned—amused, it seemed, at his failure to tease her out of her cataplexy. Humoring her, he pulled down the black veil of her bonnet, as one who would cover a face that was due to see no more of this world, sad, fallen planet that it was. "No, I'm not going. Not for a long time yet, at least. Of that you may be *certain*."

"I can wait," she said, softly. "I can wait."

My mother looked out over the twilit desert, her brow creased with contempt. I regarded her, my stomach rumbling with loathing. A fat hen? No, no; not really. She, like the city, was spider-like; a fat, fat spider I would have liked to torture to death, to dismember piecemeal at my leisure, a morbidly obese, cannibalistic pig-spider engorged on the meat of its offspring.

"We'll be in Tombstone soon," said the tall man, with a simplicity that indicated that the orator in him was temporarily at rest, dreaming, perhaps, of matters eschatological. "It'll soon be night."

"Indeed, Mr. Twist. I can feel it coming," said the young woman, the comment drifting from between sensual, yet cold-blooded lips as if from the painted, undemonstrative mouth of a ventriloquist's dummy. "The night. Indeed. A sulphate night all speed, violence and sex. We are going to be busy." My mother lifted a hand to shield her eyes and ward off the jagged rays of the setting sun, even if her ears could not similarly filter out a conversation which, I knew, she would have considered

7

quite shameless. *That Venusian hussy,* I fancied her thinking, *that impertinent necrobabe has manifested herself on Earth merely to torment me.*

"'Busy'?" said the tall man. "Whenever you use that word I always have the feeling I'm soon gonna be ducking bullets." He sighed, and it was such a sigh that you knew the spirit of the theatre infused every corpuscle of his histrionic blood. "Still, I guess I can't keep you waiting for ever, darlin'. A man has to die *sometime.*"

"Keep me waiting? No, not for ever, Mr. Twist. You're quite right: Your day will come *sometime.* And then, when I have you in my arms, tight, so tight you'll never escape, we'll at last be able to go home."

"Your home, you mean."

"*Our* home, Mr. Twist."

My father cleared his throat. "You'll feel at *home* in Tombstone, sir," he said, vulgarly playing upon the death-angel's importunate, sibyl-like pronouncement, at pains now to oil the social machinery effectively spiked by his wife's series of coarse, feeble-minded snubs. He wanted, of course, to extinguish the spark of ire that had been rekindled in the stranger's eyes, to douse it with a dose of feigned bonhomie. "I'm *sure* you'll feel at home. Tombstone, they say, is the fastest growing town between St. Louis and San Francisco. There is a wealth of opportunity to be had. Alchemy. Hyperphysics. Psychogeography. Electrospiritualism. Each discipline peculiar to this unearthly neck of the woods flourishes, they say, and offers a good return for the investor. I myself am a horologist. There is a want of good horologists, I have heard, in the West. For no matter how alien the laws and denizens of this sciosophical land, all people crave an accurate knowledge of the time, no? What, sir, is your line of business?"

"We are entertainers. We sing, we recite, we declaim, we play—"

"The devil's music," said the young woman. "We play—"

"You play in saloons?" a voice interpolated from a pinched orifice that, to any reasonable person, was readily identifiable as a pig's anus, but which, in my mother, substituted for a mouth.

"We do," said the tall man. "Destiny has decreed that, for tonight and other nights—many may they be—we shall be appearing at the *Birdcage*. Perhaps you would like to come along?" He winked at my mother. "I can offer you tickets."

"We've really got a lot of settling in to do," said my father. "And the girl," he added, jerking his head toward me in a cursory acknowledgement of my existence, "I have to make sure she starts school. She's enrolled in Mademoiselle Moutarde's establishment. It's said to be the finest school in the West. Of its type, that is." His facial muscles tensed. "She has special needs."

"Why, bring the girl along," said the tall man, displaying his teeth and their gleaming veins of gold, as if to bribe my father with a promise of strange riches.

"We do not frequent saloons," said my mother. "Lord Alcohol will not make vassals of *us*." Her face shone, as if it had been summarily waxed and polished by invisible attendants to the gods of self-righteousness. "We have taken the pledge." The tall man seemed locked in an attempt to outvie my mother, his lips pulling back to reveal more of his gleaming teeth, her face upping the ante, shining like a callused pearl.

"The pledge?" he said at last. "But she's only a kid."

"We are all sinners, sir," said my mother.

"We certainly are," said the young woman. A thin smile animated her otherwise deadpan face. "In sin we trust." The tall man seemed to emit a low, guttural noise from deep in his throat, as if imitating the satisfied, postprandial moan of a mountain lion. Then, for the first time, he awarded me a look long and beneficent.

9

"How old are you, little lady?"

"Nine, sir," I said, smiling nervously, eager to win more of his attention.

"Nine. Why, I wasn't much older than you when—" He stopped himself and pulled at his shirt collar; swallowed, as if gulping down a pill that was powerless to ameliorate an old affliction, but reminded him he was still alive. "And what's your name?" He loosened a collar stud; rubbed his neck.

"Nicola E. Newton."

He reached out and offered me a hand.

"Pleased to make your acquaintance, Nicola E. Newton. My name's Twist. John Twist. And this lady"—he nodded toward the young woman whose head now rested, as if senseless, against the coachwork—"this dead-to-the-world dormouse, this amoral amoret, is my very own Miss Viva Venera." I put my hand in his; we shook; and then my father extended his own hand, doubtless about to offer up introductions on behalf of himself and his wife. However, a shriek from my mother had us screwing our necks about with such violence that we might have all shared the fate Mr. Twist had escaped when he had cheated the hangman. Even Miss Viva, disinterred from the twilight world of her drowsing consciousness, even she swung her head into an attitude that threatened dislocation, surprised into life by the appearance of the skinny, naked creature that ran alongside the stagecoach. The creature's great loping strides, its hectic pink hide suggestive of an epidermis that was about to overheat and peel off like the skin of a hundred-percent-burns victim, immediately identified it as a zany. My father shrank backwards in his seat, though whether from my mother's hysterical clawing and bellowing or from the sight of the creature that kept pace with us, I was unsure. I, who sat farthest from the window framing our pursuer, was crushed between my father's ribs and the ribwork of the coach's panelling. But though the breath had been momentarily squeezed from my lungs, bringing to my eyes tears so sharp that they might have been laced with chilli, I was still able to observe how Mr. Twist had risen in a crouch, a hand running down the right lapel of his frock coat to throw back the skirt and reveal the radiant, ebon-handled Colt that hung from his leather-clad thigh. Another zany—its skin like runny cheese, or pale, gummy plastic—had drawn level with the loping outrider who had originally startled us. Miss Viva put her head out of the window and looked back down the trail.

"Oh Lord, Mr. Twist, there're hundreds of them! Like starved children, they are, like bad fairies, like changelings from the wrong side of toy town. And they're catching up with us, catching up with us *fast*!"

I heard the driver lash his team and scream encouragement with such unlicensed fervor that he might have been whooping in the pit of one of those burlesque theatres such as they have in dear old downtown Boston. I used to dream of running away to such a place, as some kids dream of running away to the circus, or with gypsy folk.

"Hey driver," called Miss Viva. "You got someone up there with a *splattergun*?"

"They took him," returned the driver, throat raw with threats and entreaties recently directed, with a splattergun's rowdy lack of discrimination, at the entire equine race, "they took him for their damned mutant rottiseries and spits! Oh, poor Sam, poor Sam Zabriskie! Those zanies are gonna turn him into *spam*. Him with twelve children and his wife run off with some piece of saddle-trash from Phoenix, and him such a good man an' all and, and—"

"Enough!" called Miss Viva, pruning the driver's bathetic valedictory before it had had chance to flower. Mr. Twist took off his Stetson and tossed it on his seat, where it took up residence alongside Miss Viva's painted fan, similarly thrown aside when the press of events had first sent some brand of supercharged adrenaline coursing through every niche of our bodies.

"We're near to Tombstone," said Mr. Twist. "The town has a militia for this sort of thing. Why ain't the cavalry *here*?"

"Academic," said Miss Viva. "I suggest unilateral action."

"Agreed," said Mr. Twist. More zanies had joined the two who paced us. "Disgusting things," he muttered, in that feline drawl of his.

"Shall I give them the death kiss, Mr. Twist?"

"You're a regular little H-bomb, darlin', but—"

"I'm an E-bomb, Mr. Twist!"

"You're an electrospiritual wonder, for sure, but there's an interplanetary treaty that says—"

"That says I have to be prim and proper. Have it your own way, Mr. Twist. Wouldn't want to get my visa revoked. If I *had* a visa, that is."

"Uncle Sam's not gonna make you *persona non grata*. Too much to learn from your friends. How else we gonna stay ahead of the Reds if we don't have an E-bomb?"

"Uncle Sam might deport me if he found out I consorted with *you*."

"Maybe, darlin'. Maybe. Still, that's no excuse for unsupervised testing. Behave."

"Wouldn't want to upset the balance of power now, would I?"

"Move aside, Viva darlin'." The Colt jumped into his hand, its sweet argent lines blurring as it went all gaga at the touch of its liege. It reared up in his fist—finely- manicured nails, I noticed, and elegant, long pianistic digits characterising that scrunched bunch of ligaments and flesh—and fixed its evil eye on the zany nearest to us. The evil thing regarded us with a banal surmise before turning its attention upon its fellow creatures to communicate, with a squawked warning, that their attack had encountered an unfortunate contingency. The Colt answered the thing's squawk with its own hoarse shout, a brief hack, expectorative, contemptuous. The zany leapt to one side, running momentarily crabwise, its loping gait transformed into a skipping, hopping, confused agony of limbs, its bulging eyes turning from watery blue to a bluish purple that seemed to reflect the rays of the dying sun. Blood gushed and bubbled from a hole in the side of its head. And then, tripping, falling, it tied itself up with its own spindly legs, as if about to present itself as a starved, diseased offering of subhuman poultry for the ovens and barbecues of its peers.

"Whoo," cried Mr. Twist, with appalled self-congratulation. He cocked the pistol and loosed off another round; the bullet found its mark, likewise blowing the brains out of the zany whose name it bore. The short, scrawny creatures, with their skeletal faces, their muscle-wasted legs that yet hurtled their bodies across the desert at a speed that could equal our stagecoach's own, flapped their arms, rolled their eyes, ululated in their bastard-human tongue, and began to fall back. Mr. Twist, to send them on their way, fanned his pistol in the style of the classically trained shootist, metacarpus caressing the hammer as if the gun, no fast lady now, were a baby he was easing of colic. The truculent infant, appreciative, spat up its last nuggets of lead, each one of which drilled its target through, heart, liver, oesophagus and brainpan.

"Can I help?" I ventured, shifting beneath the sweaty side of beef that constituted my father's torso. Mr. Twist laughed.

"You want to learn to shoot, little lady?" And then, uninterested, it seemed, in my hastily nodded affirmative, he looked at Miss Viva. "Disappointed, darlin'?" *I* was disappointed he afforded me such little notice. "It'll take more than a crew of zanies to get me giving up the ghost."

"I've never supposed it wouldn't, Mr. Twist. I'm a patient woman, as I've hoped you've learnt to appreciate." He condescended to again let his gaze settle upon me.

"She's a cheated woman. That's what she is." He winked. "Hell hath no fury, Miss Nicola. Thank the Lord you're not a boy."

"I do, sir," I said. But dammit, I thought: boys have all the fun. And if any of the "little ladies" in Tombstone were like Miss Viva, I would be careful—most careful—to embrace perdition in the same way as, I suspected, had Mr. Twist.

Mr. Twist looked out the window, focusing his eyes to penetrate the dustcloud of our slipstream. "Zanies here, zanies there, goddamned zanies everywhere. Yeah, sure is a lot of them ugly wretches in these parts, but our friends seem to have lost the spirit for the chase. They're running around like headless chickens."

"Fried chickens," said Miss Viva. "And finger lickin' *bad*."

A bugle sounded in the distance. My father straightened himself, disburdening me of his weight, and both my parents began to dust themselves down, inspecting limbs and other mortal commodities to see whether they had sustained hurt.

"The cavalry, Mr. Twist, the cavalry's here!" Miss Viva took off her bonnet and waved it out the window, her eyes suddenly inflamed by an inner light that consumed the frigid landscape of her funereal visage, leaving her bleeding two tearful runnels of blue, melted ice. The bugle's clarion sounded nearer. She shivered, like one coming into the open air after a long hibernation; and her coiffure, lacquered into a frosty beehive, partly unravelled. A mass of corkscrewed, steely blue locks—the color matched her cold, jewel-like eyes, the streams of lachrymose mascara—spilled onto the jet-black cloth that shrouded her slim shoulders with ecclesiastical propriety.

"About time," said Mr. Twist. The Colt went gymnastic, twirling itself about his index and then middle finger in a silvery blur, as if his digits were isometric bars. And then that vain piece of ordnance was stashed firmly back into its holster, its master drawing the curtain-like skirt of his frock coat across its bedchamber as swiftly as he had some minutes before laid his servant bare.

The state troopers drew alongside, several of their number awarding each of us an impersonal appraisal from behind their Raybans. With a perfunctory tip of the hat from the captain to the ladies in our entourage, they proceeded to escort us toward our destination.

"Just look at them clowns," said Mr. Twist, "in their pretty little tailored suits. Just like they were fresh out of a pantomime." He cupped his hand to his mouth. "*Hey boys, what kind of a town is this when a man can get near assaulted by mutant reprobates just outside the city limits?*"

"It's the Town too Tough to Die, Mr. Twist," I said, helpfully. "At least, that's what some people call it." I glanced at my mother whose fingers were pushed through her blouse in an evident attempt to loosen her stays. Mr. Twist, I think, noticed the glyphs that must have been glinting in my eyes, as obvious and banal as the pulsating advertisement hoardings such as had come into view. They lit the skyline up as the sun dipped below the hills, bright throbs of electric color displayed all across the spires and ribbed vaults of Tombstone. Interpreting the signs I was flashing him he parted his lips in that fox-like grin of his. At that moment he knew, I'm sure, that my dearest wish was to see my mother dead; and dead, preferably, in the most horrible of circumstances.

"You have a fine daughter, ma'am," he said. "I predict that she will enjoy some…some *extraordinary* fate."

Tombstone grew big, yawning with a vulgar disregard for fate and futurity, so long had it pre-empted the future in all but a few of its forms. It revealed buildings like broken teeth, cavities of enigmatic darkness, slobbery chewed-up streets that seemed to be constituted of the same drool that our coach found itself trundling across, streams of effluent that flowed out of pipelines winding into the desert like great, desiccated worms. Spray shot up from the wheels, patterning the windows with a steaming green slime, some of the sullage finding its way into the coach's interior and onto my mother's lap. I choked back a laugh; and then, unable to restrain myself, indulged my propensity for *Schadenfreude*, letting out a bark of vicious joy; to my delight, Mr. Twist, not one—as I was to learn later—to maintain a show of false concern with equanimity, snorted, and then let forth a throaty, uproarious sally to complement my own. A vein stood out on my mother's forehead as she contemplated, first, her spoilt clothes, and then those who mocked her predicament.

"Really, Mr. Twist," said Miss Viva, taking up her fan and settling back into her seat, "these poor, educationally subnormal people have had enough to put up with."

"I'm sorry," he said, sides still quivering with amusement, "I truly am." He looked at me and put a finger to his mouth in an ironic signal for *hush*. My heart swelled. I knew I had made a friend. If this was what they called "making a friend", for I could find nothing in my short life with which to compare the experience.

We cleared the little inland sea of industrial waste and entered Tombstone's outskirts. The cabins, shacks, rundown clapperboard houses and mobile homes—a curious assemblage that recalled a fairytale world of dark forests and wicked witch's cottages while remaining rooted in the aesthetics of trailer-park sleaze—were soon obscured by the dust cloud that billowed from the stagecoach's rear wheels. And then we entered the city proper, a place of stone and soaring perspectives, the coach slowing now as it contended with pedestrians who darted to and fro across the streets.

The troopers who had provided us with their too-late-in-the-day convoy peeled off and disappeared into a courtyard above which flew the flag of Arizona, their beige dress-uniforms giving them the aspect of bronze soldiers about to be packed away in an infant Titan's model fort. I eased myself up off my seat and looked out the window adjacent to me. We seemed to be surrounded by another sort of escort now, an array of ribs and fans that ushered our entry into this fabled city, the upper, overarching storeys of the buildings that stretched to either side of us resembling the massed, raised sabres of a guard of honor.

"The visionary city of James Renwick," said my father. "At last I see it with my own eyes." I believe he continued to talk, enjoying the sound of his own soliloquy, his philistine disquisition on the city's prodigious architecture, but I could no longer hear him. All he seemed to be saying, as was often the case when his presence became intolerable to me, was *barf, barf, barf, barf, barf*.

I tucked my feet beneath my thighs and, raising myself up, leant on the window, craning my head to gaze upwards. Those rampant piles, grey and menacing, rising to a weightless Neo-Gothic sky—a stone canopy sabre-twilled, pinching at the purpling heavens with gravity-mocking vaults, spires and campaniles—all seemed to draw me out of my shoes. It was as if I had liquefied and, evaporating, were being summoned into that firmament of towers, tenements, turrets and tracery, to become one with that mist-like vision and float in its cumulus of granite and brick until the end of time.

We were in a defile. At ground level, a cloistered walkway ranged along, like idealised dwellings of artisans as conceived by a William Morris transplanted into the wild, warped West. The mullioned windows of shop fronts presented goods I was familiar with from back home, but also artifacts peculiar to the landscape in which I now found myself, an immigrant surely as gauche as any from some other time, some other country. Looking as intently as I might into a candy or liquor store, or into the pages of one of my favorite philosophers or poets—Nietzsche and Baudelaire had, of late, served me well in playground one-upmanship—I appraised the streets. Well-stocked with both candy *and* liquor, I was pleased to discover, and even, to my amazement, books; but it was an emporium that prominently displayed a large, resin model of some monstrous abortion of God that, in the end, I fell to taking particular notice of. Squat, horned and hatchet-tailed, the chimera had been copied from the wretched pages of the *Saturday Evening Post*, or else, perhaps, from one of those editions of *Dr Seuss* that I had disdained to read even when I had been a little girl, all of two or three years ago. It was supposed, I knew, to be a representation of a Venusian.

"Oh," I mumbled, unable to keep my thoughts to myself, "do they really look like *that*?" I glanced at Miss Viva, a blush searing my cheeks. I was about to offer an apology for my indiscretion, the promiscuity of my tongue, when Mr. Twist rescued me with a coolly observed aside.

"Just decorating the store, Miss Nicola," he said, "like a wooden Injun. But Venusians"—his throat tightened, as if he'd caught a sudden cold—"they're polymorphs, y'know?" He coughed; spat. "The model is just an impression, of course. Or rather a *supposition*. Nobody's seen a Venusian in primal state. Including me."

"No human could stand it," said Miss Viva. No; the beauty, I thought. The beauty would surely melt the retinae, confound the brain.

"There seems such a ragbag of things in the shops here," I said, pressing my nose to the window, as eager to divert the conversation into a channel where I was less likely to embarrass myself as I was to hide my burning face.

"Ever since the West got, how shall I put it, *distended*," said Mr. Twist, "it seems to have accommodated history in its own leisurely, eccentric way, adopting those things from the outside that suit it, discarding those that don't. It refuses

18

to think of itself as a hostage to necessity. But I guess you've noticed this on your way here from Boston."

"The country only really seemed to start to change," interrupted my father, sense suddenly emerging out of his unending drone of gibberish, "after we'd left Colorado."

"All those wrecks of airplanes," I said. "The desert was a real airplane graveyard."

"Of course," said Mr. Twist, "no plane can pass into the West."

"They know that *now*," I said, grinning.

"It was then," said my father, determined to make his point, even while grinding his teeth as he restrained himself from clipping my ear, "it was then, after leaving Colorado, that we got the first inklings of the immensity that lay before us."

"Immensity?" said Miss Viva, rearranging her creased skirts in preparation for our impending debarkation. "Some say that what's limitless can't be *immense*. Some say the West goes on forever."

"Or until it reaches the stars," I said. "They say that if you travel far enough west, you'll—"

"But *I* say fiddlesticks," said Miss Viva, ignoring my contribution. "You shouldn't believe such nonsense. Like all things, the West has an end. And it's called *Venus*."

"Nicola will be at school soon," said my father, looking down at me. "She can learn more of such things there."

"School. Yes. And not before time," said my mother, who seemed almost recovered from the funk occasioned by her first sight of zanies. I stared between my knees at the luggage that protruded from beneath my seat. "We're hoping that if *anything* good is to come out of our move West then it's to be a sound moral education for our daughter." She took a deep breath. "A moral and *penitential* education."

"That's what we have been promised," said my father, with an unctuous smile. "We hope Tombstone will be a new start for all of us." He patted me on the head, then took to arranging my plaits, so that one fell over my left shoulder, the other over my right. "Business," he added, with a feverish, tic-like need to convince himself that his prospects were bright, "is booming. Booming at least, I'm told, for those with the right skills." *And such an unlikely refuge*, I felt like saying, *so far from the eastern seaboard, is sure to put your creditors off your scent for some time, isn't it, Daddy? You calibrator of dead time, you charlatan, you mountebank, you snake-oil salesman, you?* I noticed that Mr. Twist was straining to focus on the *I Like Ike* button that decorated my father's lapel. I willed Mr. Twist's eyes to resolve the image so that, knowing it to be a symbol of that other, entirely worthless America that lay outside the lands of the West, he might also know my father for the man he really was.

"School's not so bad, Miss Nicola," said Mr. Twist, relinquishing his intense scrutiny of my father's tailoring. "You might get to learn about Beddoes. Nothing's so sweet a complement to a man's life as a grounding in Thomas Lovell Beddoes. "*Young soul, put off your flesh, and come/With me into the quiet tomb*." Oh yeah, he knew about the undiscovered country, all right. The skull beneath the skin. I've tried to put a few of his lyrics to music. But I mostly sing my own compositions, you'll understand. Work that offers some explanation, some meaning, to my curious life and"—he smiled at Miss Viva—"my Death."

"I think I understand, Mr. Twist," I said, still directing my gaze to the floor in an attempt to win more of his sympathy.

The chassis moaned and creaked with violent deceleration, our driver reining in his team as we approached the stage.

"Seems," said Mr. Twist, "that our present journey and our brief and happy association are at an end." The coach stopped; Mr. Twist leant over Miss Viva and opened the door.

My mother eased herself out, Mr. Twist's gallantry unthanked, her rump massaging the jambs. It was as if she had thought it necessary to lubricate them with an offering of human lard before she dared place a tiny, swollen foot upon the ground. Miss Viva followed, taking with her the valise that seemed the pair's only luggage. Mr. Twist put his hat back on and gestured to myself and my father, indicating that we should precede him. We complied, exiting the coach and swinging down onto the baked earth.

I stood by the roadside, rotating my neck to take in a circuit of my new home—shops and malls with lancet windows; gables set with lucarnes, each one of which was flanked by a miniature flying buttress; street corners graced by tall belfried towers and the flashing light shows of high capitalism. As I gaped at the stone panorama with the moon-faced fervor of a halfwit, about to ask the svelte gunslinger and his doxy of an occasion when I might meet with them again, I discovered, on bringing my sight once again to bear on the coach, that Mr. Twist had already stepped out onto the street, taken his companion's arm and, with a jangle of spurs, begun to squire her across the parched midden of the main drag. The hemline of Miss Viva's flounced black skirt swayed about her knees, her beautiful but sadly impractical high heels adding to the bombazine's agitation. Dust rose in their wake. *But,* I wanted to shout, *but you promised you would teach me how to shoot*! My reserve, uncompromised by drink, did not avail me an opportunity to remind Mr. Twist of his offer, however. The pair walked on, threading their way through the crowd.

No wonder, I thought, as I watched them depart, no wonder my parents had been so alarmed by their presence. The deeply lined face of the man, flesh rilled and pocked like the surface of the moon, the scar (just visible above the high collar) that circled his thin, saurian neck, his sheer *altitude*. And the young woman, with her bleached complexion, elliptical, sleep-starved, ice-blue eyes, and her aspect of a somnambulist lost in an Arctic wilderness of the mind—all these things were as romantic, as heart-crushingly, ball-breakingly romantic as the elegant, but terrific cliffs of the surrounding architecture. And now my two heroes were leaving before I had had chance to say goodbye. I was about to try to conjure up the requisite amount of will that would allow me to call after them when my father took me by the ear. He redirected me back into the coach with the recommendation that I should bring out our bags and trunk, and then assist the men who were unloading the rest of our luggage from the stagecoach's roof-rack.

Inside the coach I prepared to haul the heaviest bag out from under the seat and onto the road. It was then that I spotted the little beaded purse lying in a corner of the seat that Miss Viva had occupied. I snatched it up and sprang through the door.

"The lady!" I cried. "She's forgotten her purse! I must find her!"

It had been the excuse my shyness had needed.

"Wait," growled my father. But I was already eeling through the crowd, breaking into a sprint as soon as I had a clear run of ground. When I sensed I was safe from immediate persecution, I stopped, turned and delivered the speech that I had been rehearsing for days, relieving my body of the suppurating hatred that had swilled about like a blister of sulphuric acid, eating me from the inside out all through the interminable journey west.

"I know you. I know you *all*! Sitting behind your lace curtains, manifestly speaking English but in reality saying only *barf, barf, barf, barf, barf*! Ghost people, yeah. Unreal! There is ignorance, and there is wilful ignorance, hear? You *choose* to be ignorant. It isn't that you have low IQs or are disadvantaged in any meaningful way; you're stupid because you like being stupid, in the same way that pigs like rolling in their own shit. It suits you! It makes you feel good!" I held up my hand, expecting catcalls and brickbats; but none came. I calmed my voice, giving in to my weakness for pedantry. "Ignorance, for many, is a lifestyle choice. And ignorance, moreover, is aggressive, not passive. It seeks to convert. It is evangelical. You people: you want the world to be your sty. You want to sire piglets and fill the planet with one great, inhuman *Oink*! If knowledge is power, then ignorance is power, too, because ignorance is a form of knowledge; it is an interpretation of the world. A tool. A means of control. To live among you"—I was calm no more; my tub-thump had become a full-blown bout of hysteria—"in a place of dead ends and dead time, is to grow up without hope. And I tell you, if I live among you for much longer, then I shall either go mad or"—I pushed my fingers through my hair—"or I shall *kill* you all!"

I bent over, letting my body fold from the waist so that my near paralyzed arms swept the floor. Inhaling greedily, I corrected; assumed the posture of one nominally sane; hopped onto the boardwalk; ducked under an empty hammock; skipped over the outstretched legs of a tobacco-chewing idler and then leapt over a gutter overflowing with that by now familiar green industrial slime, to land among the crowd who jostled shoulders in main street. A few people gazed down, alternately shocked, infuriated, or with faces radiant with loathsome pity. For a moment I felt nauseous, light-headed, and I feared I was to have one of my periodic attacks of epilepsy. Soaring towers, their ribbed vaults sparkling against the damson sky; arches of stone, running diagonally, transversely, spinning, spinning; great avenues of stained glass—these looming perspectives were sucking me into a smashed prism whose shards lacerated my eyes.

I blinked; breathed deep; pulled back my shoulders, ignoring the curiosity of the mob. Nearby, in an alcove next to a hostelry, stood a statue of Our Lady, clothed in marmoreal robes. A small lizard ran over her chipped bosom. I crossed myself and ran on, looking quickly over my shoulder to check that I wasn't being followed. Hunched, weaving through the mass of humanity that hid me from view, I discovered myself drawn to the mouth of an alley situated between two shop fronts, and walking down the alley's length at last spied the shapes of a tall man in a black hat, a young woman in a doleful bonnet.

I raced along, brushing against the pedestrians who choked the passageway's skinny borders. Again, a carnival of faces peered down, angry, bemused; faces—both men's and women's—with rouged cheeks, lips tarred with black cosmetics, noses and brows studded with cheap metals and jewels. Breaking into the next street I involuntarily halted and staggered backwards as a bedlam of bodies rushed past. I turned left, right...everywhere, an obscuring wall of flesh met my gaze. Craning to orientate myself I saw that rising over me was the vault of a great cathedral, its buttresses a shade of burnt sienna, the hue of the desert before the Indian Wars had turned it pale with sickness and fear. The giddiness once more took hold of my brain, sluicing away all thoughts of further pursuit with an astringent douche of vertigo.

"Miss Viva," I cried, casting my plea beyond the wall of anonymous faces, "Miss Viva, you've forgotten your purse! And Mr. Twist, sir, I want to come with you. You said you'd teach me to shoot, didn't you? Won't you help me, sir? Won't you help me, please?"

My legs turned to gelatine and I found myself on my back staring up at the pinnacled heights of the magnificent elevation before me. The purse had fallen by my side, its clasp opening to reveal its contents: a few silver dollars, a palette of make-up and a derringer, its barrel as argent and as finely crafted as Mr. Twist's big, bad Colt. I reached out and took the miniature pistol in my hand; dragged it toward me, the tines of my fingers leaving hoe-like trails in the road's dust and filth; tucked it into my pinafore-dress's pocket. The gargoyles looked down, as had the crowds I had passed through: angry, yet also, it appeared, grinning, as if they were zanies contemplating a meal of epileptic child. Bats wheeled in the empurpled sky. Yes, I thought. It all *seemed* earthly, more or less, this Tombstone, this land called the West. But strange, too. Very strange. What was this corridor between worlds? And what life could I expect here? Might not, in fact, death be preferable to such a life? The kind of Death that Mr. Twist was in love with?

The stars had come out. But where was the evening star? Near to and beyond the horizon hung that star of death, tonight made the more inscrutable by the great curtains of quarried rock that lined the *très riches* canyons of Tombstone. And I suspected that even if I had had X-ray eyes, it would have been equally lost, either behind the urban haze, or the same clouds that obscured the Milky Way. Still, I allowed my mind to focus on its overshadowed albedo, brain-waves concentrated on the diamond-bright image of a world that I pictured my two heroes, my two glorious sinners, to be walking toward. Walking as they had done all their lives down the long, lonely trails of the West, walking across the frontier and on, on into night, love and redemption.

And later, when I had been returned to my parents, and put to bed in the room atop the house that my father had decided to rent, I slept with Miss Viva's little gun beneath my pillow. *Home*, I thought as I drifted away from the horror of that word into a land of gun-smoking dreams. *Take me away from this place called home, let me be a perpetual exile, a lone rider, lost in the absolute foreignness of the deserts and the plains.*

Chapter Two
Cabaret Mort

Above the zinc bar, between a kaleidoscopic array of mirrors, hung a full-size reproduction of Henry Fuseli's "Titania and Bottom". I stared at the figure of the coquette that dominated the right-hand side of the picture's foreground. She was a fairy woman, it seemed, and she returned my gaze, staring back at me lazily, with amused disdain. At her feet was a tiny old man. Collared, and secured to her wrist by way of a long, taut leash, the gnarled minikin looked about disconsolately, trapped forever in an abject servitude defined by the brushstrokes that had created him. Fuseli. He had had a hair fetish, I'd read. Like Baudelaire. And he had rendered, in the painting above, and, more fabulously, in his pornography, that class of being of whom the saloon girls who crowded the bar's length were the particular. The girls—beehives piled into fabulous coiffures, frosted meringues streaked with pink, blue, green and purple dyes—were houris of a fetishist's seventh heaven.

I eased my way through the throng of cowboys and ruffians who lurked about the gaming tables and found a segment of bar that was unoccupied. I climbed onto a stool; snapped my fingers at the bartender. The floozie sitting next to me turned and looked me up and down. The jukebox was playing "Milkshake Mademoiselle" by Jerry Lee Lewis. The cigar smoke that swirled above my head was busily twisting itself into impossible, self-referential geometries, the ceiling fans sucking the blue-grey haze into the saloon's upper atmosphere in imitation of the fireworks at Bikini.

"Whisky," I said, as the bartender sidled to where I sat. Lips pursed in effeminate disregard, he poured a measure of muddy liquid into a glass and shoved it toward me with his knuckles. With thumb and middle finger (pinky daintily extended) I lifted the glass to my lips, threw back my head and consigned the fiery stuff to the keeping of my bowels. "Leave the bottle," I added, knowing that this was the protocol, and also knowing that I would want more, much more.

"A little girl drinking whisky," tittered my neighbor, the floozie whose gaze had remained fixed upon me with wanton presumption. "How singular."

"I'm not a little girl," I said quickly, facing her. I drained what was left of the moonshine, inspecting the sarcasm artiste over the glass's dirty, thumb-printed rim. She had Apache blood. Her duotone beehive—black streaked with silver; severe; strict as hickory—was adorned with the tail feathers of exotic, desert birds. It was a beehive lustrous as the bodywork of a newly sprayed car, its heavily lacquered sheen full of nostalgia for the autos, kitchen appliances and gizmos I had left behind when my family had entered the West. Her face had been trowel-fed on a diet of rouge, mascara, eye shadow, lipstick and foundation. A diet that had sustained her, I felt, from infancy to adulthood, and led to a kind of sexual bulimia that had her bingeing on and then regurgitating the trappings of femininity. Her torso, slicked with the sick excess of those trappings, was encased in a steel-ribbed corselet patterned with waspish stripes, a peplum of tassels performing shivers and little fits of flirtatiousness about her upper thighs where the fishnet of her stockings terminated in a zone of smoky nylon.

All the girls who populated the bar area—a bevy of fantastic fowl perched on a long, zinc branch—were dressed similarly.

I poured myself another whisky.

"Whatever would your father say?" said the saloon girl.

"He's a horologist," I said, somewhat irrelevantly. But what did I care. Lord Alcohol was whispering his greasy, sweet nothings in my ear, urging me to once again join him in his happy holiday camp of oblivion.

"A whorologist, huh? So how come we haven't seen him around here?" I ignored her. "You want to buy a girl a drink?" she added.

"It's all mine," I said, placing my hand proprietorially on the bottle.

"Oh, we *are* thirsty tonight, aren't we?" She slapped her side; inspected the crushed insect that stained her palm, then leant toward me, opened her mouth and ran her tongue in an indolent circle about her monstrous, painted lips. "Go on, just a little one. Just a little drinkie. Just a little drinkie-poo." I gulped at the hooch, its aroma counterpointing the smell of cheap perfume wafting from the girl's dusty skin, potent as the sulphurous discharge of an active caldera. My teeth began to chatter. The alcohol had begun to bite.

"How old are you?" I said. For a moment, we were locked in ocular combat. And then she turned away. There was a rustle of agitated thighs, of nylon-sheathed legs rubbing together, fly-like, as she crossed and recrossed them, a fly-like susurration, to the power of two, three, four, as of a parliament of insects on a summer's night. It was as if memories of another life, a child's life, had, unsought, risen from beneath her skin, to annoy their host with a rash of morbid souvenirs.

"Seventeen. Why?"

"It's just that the girls in my school are older than me, too. And you seem to disturb me in the same way that they do."

"I disturb you?"

"You most certainly do." Miss Viva, I thought, Miss Viva might understand. I rolled a measure of whisky around my mouth, swallowed, coughed. My interlocutor was distracted by another insect, summarily despatched with a second slap of her hand. I nudged her with my knee. "Tell me: What do you think it must be like to have your soul eaten by a Venusian?" I poured myself yet another whisky, careless of the consequences.

"You're precocious, honey. *Precocious*. You must be a real teacher's pet."

"I'm a bluestocking," I said. "But I hate teachers. All teachers. And I hate school."

"You been playing hookey?"

"You might say," I said, "that I have a certain penchant for hookey." Again, I nudged her. But you haven't answered my question: What do you think it's like to be loved by a Venusian? Loved to death, that is?"

"What do *I* know about Venusians." And what did I know, I thought.

"They eat souls," I said. "But they don't kill. They're like jackals: they're scavengers. They only take the dead."

"Well, ain't they the considerate ones."

"And it was they," I said, pretty much exhausting my knowledge of Terran-Venusian history, "who intervened in the Indian Wars and transformed the West into a psychogeographical 'event.'"

"And what the hell is *that*?"

"It's—" At school, when I had asked that question, I had never received a satisfactory response. Neither had I found a book that could explain the mechanics of the American frontier's transformation, in the second half of the nineteenth century, from a continental expanse of plain, mountain and desert into a fantastically long corridor that bridged interplanetary space. The Cold War had meant that so much about

Venus remained classified. "It's something—it's something that has been *détourned*," I stuttered, hardly knowing what I said. "It's something that has undergone semantic displacement."

"You sure you ain't a Venusian yourself? You sure talk like one." Oh, if only it were true, I thought. I looked into the mirror behind the bar. My own face looked back at me as if to say *You'll always be a Plain Jane. You'll never be a necrobabe. You'll never be Nicola Venera!* My reflection became agitated, the head bouncing lazily from shoulder to shoulder and then lolling in acquiescence, the face painted on that little orb—its features achieving stasis in an expression of vapid fatalism—like one painted on eggshell, or on a ping-pong ball. Oh, that face. It was a face common to girls of my years, I suppose, as well as being suggestive of table tennis; but that did not make it any the less insufferable. I let the whisky tumbler slip from my fingers. It dropped to the floor, shattering with a crisp detonation. "I guess not," said the floozie. "Venusians: they can be one real mess of trouble. We've got one appearing in the cabaret here. They say *she's* trouble. Yeah. Most certainly. But generally speaking you don't see many aliens around these parts. Not these days, at least."

"I'll have you know I'm a *friend* of Miss Viva Venera." The jukebox had been turned off. My words were louder than I had intended. But the eyes of the saloon's clientele were directed toward the stage and I was ignored by everyone except my pick-up.

"You're a bumptious little brat, aren't you? Be quiet. I want to see the show." But my lips refused to be sealed.

"I said she's my *friend*!"

The girl's own lips puckered, as if she were a quality control tester in a pickle factory; and then her arm shot out, so swift it seemed that she might have been taking a correspondence course in gunslinging. Her palm connected with my left shoulder and knocked me backwards. My feet pointed briefly at the ceiling and then, as my ankles aligned with my ears—a briefer moment spent in space, tumbling, grappling hopelessly with the laws of gravity—I hit the beer-sloppy floor.

"Aw, get lost, you little creep."

Marvellously drunk, I dismissed her from my thoughts. A numb peace enveloped my sprawled body. Unwilling to move, my gaze focused on what the *Birdcage* offered this evening as entertainment.

The stage was set high, and the clear view provided by a gap in the milling crowd allowed me to fully appreciate the inverted vision of two dancers hoofing it across the boards, a tinkly piano accompanying them. The choreography brought to mind that spoof of Mickey Spillane's fiction, "The Girl Hunt" sequence from *The Band Wagon*. And I almost expected Fred Astaire and Cyd Charisse to emerge from the wings and join in, a troop of Busby Berkeley showgirls from another lot, another decade, perhaps following. But for the man and woman who tap-danced there was only the consolation of their own footsteps to suggest that they were in a celluloid wonderland, and not a louche den of faro, whisky, floozies and beer.

A passing cowboy, blind to my supine, inebriated body, almost crushed me beneath his boots. He, like so many other cowpokes and ruffians hereabouts, wore black lipstick and mascara, goth-gang make-up appropriate to the macabre 'graveyard look' that Tombstone had made its own.

I shook myself from my reverie and got to my feet. Walking to the bar, I punched a hand into my pocket, pulled out some of the dollars that I had filched from Miss Viva's purse and threw them across the zinc counter. I took my bottle, clutching it to my chest covetously, scowling at the whore who had perpetrated my assault, and then I threw some dollars at her, too.

"Don't need you," I said, "don't need any of you." And then I turned my back on her and the bar and walked across the saloon to a spot where I might be able to watch the cabaret undisturbed. As I walked through the crowd, the dancers finished their turn, made their bow and then, to a desultory few claps, withdrew backstage. I was heading toward a small recess beneath one of two staircases situated to either side of the stage's heavy curtains (The stairs curved and ascended to a second floor where, I presumed, the saloon girls did their business.). I ducked my head, moving into my chosen covert. The table therein, shrouded in obscurity, was bereft of patrons.

I sat down; looked across the deserted orchestra pit and surveyed a stage naked but for the upright piano that stood flush against the farthest proscenium arch. A placard supported on a rickety easel announced the next act, *The Amazing* JOHN TWIST *and His Death, the beautiful* MISS VIVA VENERA. The tables before the stage, like those marshalled in intersecting lines the length and breadth of the great oblong that constituted the saloon's floor space, were all occupied by sullen, brutal men drinking, playing cards or else fondling the demi-mondaines and the dollymops who sat on their laps and relieved them of their winnings.

The brilliance of the chandeliers, only partially veiled by a smokescreen of atomized tobacco, stabbed at my eyes. There was no escaping that splintering of light. Big, Versailles-like mirrors hurled white-hot daggers at me from every wall, as if a phantom knife-thrower lurked behind each limpid surface. I closed my eyes, apprehensive that the dazzle might precipitate a *petit mal*. But the brilliance was inescapable; it tore through my tightly clenched lids like the pure, angelic light of a nuclear blast. I sat, blind, my mouth pressed to the neck of my bottle, sucking furiously on it as if it were a teat. My throat seemed to ignite, as if that teat were facilitating the siphoning off of a Molotov cocktail. My brain combusted in sympathy, my skull transfused with some equally explosive mixture designed for the waging of a guerrilla campaign against rational thought.

The sounds of the saloon rustled inside my ears: iron filings inside a tombola. And then, as I felt the giddiness and nausea subside, the white noise separated into its constituents: imprecations, coarse laughter, insidious giggles and the endless shuffling of cards and concussion of poker chips, the endless bawdy slap of hands against female rumps.

I reopened my eyes, and I was confronted—my heart surprised into a flutter of excitation—by the appearance of my two untamed minstrels, Mr. Twist and Miss Viva, he in evening dress complete with top hat, she in a showgirl's outfit somewhat like Marilyn's in *Bus Stop* and somewhat like those worn by the floozies who lined the bar, though Miss Viva's corselet was spangled with black sequins and was cut even more daringly. She shook out her great mane of ashen, vulgarly streaked hair, styled, tonight, less strictly than it had been when I had seen her last, her beehive unloosening somewhat after the manner of Brigitte Bardot, or perhaps a less majestically coiffured Jayne Mansfield (Ah, But Miss Marilyn, Miss Brigitte, Miss Jayne, fair as you were, you all paled beside my Venusian.). A stagehand wheeled a large, tarpaulin-shrouded contraption center stage. It was some fifteen feet in height. The stagehand withdrew; Mr. Twist walked to one side of the mystery prop, Miss Viva to the other (she wiggling her rump so that the ostrich plume that adorned it swayed back and forth, a feathery metronome). They bowed, arms held out to present the grimly wrapped offering to the audience. And then Mr. Twist stepped up to the footlights, cleared his throat and held up a white-gloved hand in an unsuccessful attempt to win the saloon's attention.

"Ladies and gentlemen," he called out, phlegm at the back of what might have been a metal-plated throat gurgling like acid in the diaphragm of a bullhorn. The buzz that rose from the tables nearest the stage abated as the vibrations of that hoarse, industrially tuned voice caressed the ears of the gamers with the grating impact of fingernails drawn across slate. "I am here to tell you a tale stupendous and strange, a tale that will distress, discombobulate and dumbfound you. Listen. Marvel. And despair." He held out his arms in a pose suggestive of a huckster. "My name is John Twist. I was born in the swamps of Louisiana. As soon as I'd hopped out of my mother's womb I was bad. Stealing, fighting, breaking every commandment that the Lord ever made and committing sins so outlandish and heinous that not even the Lord himself, I guess, had had the foresight to catalogue them, much less to offer proscription. When I was eleven I ran away from home. By the time I was twelve I had killed my first man. Soon after—for justice, though contrary, is no laggard—I was arrested and sentenced to meet my maker. Or should I say, rather, the gentleman who reigns supreme"—he banged his heel against the floorboards—"*below*. My friends"—again, he spread his arms wide—"I was taken to a rendezvous with the hangman." He pirouetted; and as he did so Miss Viva tugged at the tarpaulin. The linen cloth fell to the floor, revealing the contraption hidden beneath to be a fully articulated gallows. A banner suspended from its crossbeam read *Sic Transit Gloria Mundi*.

The chandeliers seemed ready to explode, so intense was the sunburst of light that radiated from their crystal beads and spindles, photoelectric shrapnel set to slash at and shatter the stale air like a spray of ice-cold, razor-edged champagne uncorked to celebrate the Grim Reaper's nuptials. The jukebox, which had briefly enjoyed a loud, renewed life during the intermission, and which had been turned down, but not off, when my heroes had first appeared on stage (the reprised sounds of Jerry Lee competing with Mr. Twist to win the attention of the public) was now killed, its gaily-lit perspex swamped by darkness. At the same time, the hullabaloo that rose from the gaming tables dropped in volume, the curiosity of those customers who were still capable of focusing their alcohol-compromised vision on the unfolding drama pricked by the comparative silence.

A man in a black hood walked onto the stage. Mr. Twist lowered his head in resignation as the actor playing the hangman took his arms, wrenched them behind his back and secured them with cuffs, one pair about the wrists, another about the elbows. "And I, ladies and gentleman, and I only a child!" shouted Mr. Twist as the hangman led him up the steps that connected the stage with the scaffold.

On reaching the platform the hangman realigned his victim so that Mr. Twist was again facing the audience. A hood, like the hangman's own, but without eyeholes or a hole for the mouth, was pulled over Mr. Twist's head; and then the noose that dangled from the crossbeam was slipped over the head and tightened about the neck, the hangman manoeuvring the compliant body so that it was positioned over the trapdoor, a parcel ready to be mailed to the old man downstairs, do not return to sender. "And so it was, ladies and gentleman, that I, John Twist, went to my doom, fully expecting to meet my damnation." The hangman busied himself behind Mr. Twist's back. I guessed at once that we must have arrived at that point in the proceedings when the harness Mr. Twist would have been wearing under his shirt was to be attached to the invisible wire that would effect the illusion of death by strangulation.

The hangman stepped to one side, put his hand upon a lever and pulled. The trap opened, and, to the accompaniment of a diuretic rumble, Mr. Twist fell, the tails of his jacket flapping like the stunted, useless wings of a gigantic bird robbed of flight by evolution. Almost immediately the rope went taut with a wet *thwap*! that should have broken his neck. Mr. Twist hung, head to one side, legs pedalling in the air.

The house lights went down. Howls of complaint rose and circulated through a fog of blackness punctuated only by the red embers of cigar butts. Then a single spot bathed a section of the stage in an elliptical patch of milky luminescence; and at its center stood Miss Viva. Into the tunnel of light she walked, toward the audience, toward me. Her hips rolled with what might have been a patented come-on: a wiggle so camp, so immoderate, it was almost naive, that outré pelvis a perpetual motion machine dedicated to incessant flirtation. As she reached the stage's perimeter she pushed out her bottom lip and blew a column of air upwards to disrupt the blinding overhang of her fringe. In later days, in my Viva-haunted dreams, there was always that fringe, a fringe whose pointed ends fell, mixed and tangled with black, sticky, thickly painted lashes; a fringe that seemed designed for self-flagellation of the eyeballs, that left her, surely, with a vision of life seen through a pained, steel-blue haze. In the disk of the light cone, she prepared to address us. Hands akimbo, long legs held wide apart, tremblingly, like filigree *arc-boutants* supporting a superstructure that was weathering a minor earthquake, she looked down into the obscurity of the saloon, the jet scales of her corselet twinkling like a constellation populated with countless black stars.

"I am Viva Venera, from the Planet Venus. The spacebridge that you call the West permeates every aspect of my world. It touches each and every one of the energy forms that constitute my people. When John Twist began to expire, choking to death from a botched hanging, it was as if a string connecting him and me had been tweaked, suddenly tightened, just as the rope from which he hung was tightening and squeezing out his life; a string, a connection that stretched across the interplanetary void."

A pot-bellied ruffian with the meticulous gait of the hopelessly drunk staggered past me, half-falling into the alcove, his thigh brushing against my table. Righting himself, he walked on toward the stage. Drawn to the light cone like a crippled moth to a moonbeam, he whirled an arm above his head, plying an imaginary lariat, as if to solicit Miss Viva's attention by indicating that he meant to capture her.

"Hey, you, necrobabe! Gimme some of that ol' Venusian lovin', girl!"

"Yeah," followed a voice from the shadows, "I dig you deeply too! Be *my* necrobabe, sweetheart! Give me chaos and Eternal Night!" The drunk who had by now reached the pit suddenly stumbled and fell. I think he was unconscious before he hit the floor; and the one who had seconded his swinish proposal fell concomitantly quiet.

"I scented a soul crying out," said Miss Viva, unfazed by the hecklers, "not a soul such as *you* dumb cowboys possess"—there was laughter from the audience—"but a noble soul, a soul to be kidnapped, consumed. I followed the thread that connected me with the one who called out in pain and terror, followed it across space, across time, my essence shifting into an image of Death that conformed to an archetype that slept deep, deep in his unconscious. I was his anima. I was the beauty of the abyss, the siren of his decease. I was, I thought, irresistible. I appeared to him, my energy form entering the thoughts that racked his oxygen-starved brain. I appeared to him as a little girl, the darling of his dreams." Mr. Twist emerged from the shadows. His assistant, who had played the role of the hangman, must have taken opportunity of the darkness to free him from his harness and cuffs. And Mr. Twist now joined Miss Viva at the front of the stage. "You are dying, Mr. Twist," said Miss Viva, turning to him, her face transfixed with longing. "Come with me. Let me take you to paradise." Her wan-faced companion stood looking out at the audience with wide, vacant eyes.

"Where am I?" he said, his voice brittle.

"You have left your body, my love. And soon you will be leaving this sad, sad world. Forever. Come with me. Rest your head upon my breast. Come, come with me. Come away.

Lie with me here, by this quiet, babbling river. This stream of time and space. Do you hear it? It flows through towns and cities that no longer concern you. Through the turmoil of places that can no longer do you harm. Sit with me here by its shores. There is nothing to worry you now. No cares. No sorrows. Come with me, let me take you into myself. Let us become as one."

"Yes," croaked Mr. Twist, "yes, yes." His voice was even more brittle than formerly. Cracking, disintegrating, the iron larynx gave way to metal fatigue, his affirmation compromised as if by a wind, suddenly gusting, that had torn away his words. He moved toward her, tears running down his cheeks. "Take me away from here. Oh please, take me away. I've been waiting for you so long…" But then his body jerked; he put a hand to his heart, as if startled out of a sleep. And when he spoke again, he spoke clearly. "No; something is dragging at my legs, pulling me backwards, I can't, I can't, I—" Miss Viva's brow darkened; she put out a hand as if to grab him. The spotlight which illuminated both players was extinguished and a cry of frustration emanated from the afterimage of Miss Viva's gaping, enamel-bright mouth, a circle of red and pearl left imprinted in the blackness that filled the proscenium arch.

Several seconds passed, and then the whole stage was lit—I screwed my eyes into crescents, such was the violence of that refulgent display—the scaffold dominating center stage, as before, but with its erstwhile victim now seated behind the piano that stood by the wings, his left hand pumping the keys, vamping a boogie-woogie bass line. Miss Viva leant against the piano's side, gazing down at Mr. Twist with the hot, embittered eyes of one who had been jilted.

"After an hour, they cut him down, ladies and gentleman." Her feet tapped at the floorboards in keeping with the rhythm Mr. Twist was pounding out of the piano. "That's right, ladies and gentleman, an *hour*." Her pelvis began to sway. "The undertaker took him to the mortuary. Left him lying on a long, cold slab. But—" Mr. Twist's right hand ran up and down the keyboard in glissandos that gave notice of his intention to break into song.

> "*It takes more than a length of rope and a noose*
> *To put the Twist in Death's calaboose...*"

And no one could have much regretted, then, that the jukebox had been killed; for here was another Killer, another Jerry Lee. "Ladies and gentlemen," said Miss Viva, as her partner, refraining, for the moment, from treating his audience to a second couplet, contented himself with humming a counterpoint to the insistent, grumbling riff, "ladies and gentlemen, John Twist was still alive! He jumped off that old mortuary slab, brained the mortician who was about to fill him with embalming fluid and was set to run off into the hills. What could I do? What could I do but follow him? I had been cheated. Cheated of a soul!"

> "*But there ain't no way, till his dying day*
> *That that pretty little alien will cut him loose*"

"I shifted myself into the world of matter!" cried Miss Viva, over the raucous, manic piano playing of Mr. Twist. "I made a human girl-child's body for myself! No, no, there ain't no way—"

> "*There ain't no way—*"

"There ain't no way I'm *ever* gonna cut that man loose!"

> "*Until that is—*"

"Until judgment day!" Miss Viva had begun to jive; and, as

the house lights came up, I saw that much of the saloon had followed her example. The floozies who lined the bar, in particular, had taken to kicking up their heels with fanatical abandon, the tassels of their peplums swishing about their hips, surely murdering whatever micro-life—flies, ticks, mosquitoes, jiggers—had dared to encroach upon their space.

> *"Yeah, it takes more than that to send me Venus-side*
> *(Pretty lady don't let it be via hom-i-cide)*
> *Judgment day will someday send me her way*
> *('Scuse me if I don't rush to make you my bride)"*

Another man brushed past my table, though in a manner even more insensitive, more oafish, than the drunk who had previously shouldered his way to heckling distance of the stage. Now that the house lights were up again I could see, however, that this latest incursion came from no inebriated buffoon. This man, whose gross shadow had fallen across my covert and who had now stationed himself immediately beneath where Mr. Twist and Miss Viva performed their rock 'n' roll duet, this man looked as sober as he looked mean. As tall as Mr. Twist, but without his becomingly rangy physique, he displayed, with a certain vainglorious insouciance, the burly frame of one who habitually wrestled with grizzly bears. He wore chaps and a poncho, a barrel chest erupting through a rip in the poncho's grubby burlap. It glistened, slicked with oil. A long, matted beard extended to his waist; and his hands—worn-down fingers sandpapering each other—hovered above the butts of the two revolvers that hung from either fulsome ham.

"Wait no more, pretty lady," yelled the intruder. The music, which had died a little as both Mr. Twist and Miss Viva had noticed the one standing beneath them, now met with its *coup de grâce*. So abrupt was the stillness that descended that it was as if a speeding train, a rock 'n' roll express, had crashed into a gargantuan baffler imbued with the power to confer a total and uncanny silence. "Judgment day," he added, "is here." The big man's voice, unimpeded by the sonic pollution that had just a moment before saturated the saloon, boomed across the tables, the bar, the stage, like a bell tolling across still waters warning of a coming storm.

Mr. Twist rose, went into his crouch, a hand flinging back a tail of his coat and groping for his Colt. As his fingers clawed impotently at the air he looked down at his hip and, with vast disappointment, realised that he was unarmed. The man had walked to the edge of the pit; his pistols were unholstered and he was pointing both guns at the soft target that had presented itself to him. Mr. Twist's hand continued to grope and claw, a pathetic five-fingered beast possessed by an *idée fixe*.

"No!" screamed Miss Viva, putting herself in the line of fire. "Don't you *dare* shoot him! He's mine! Mine!"

I gripped the sides of my chair, my stomach ascending into my mouth and then, slamming into reverse, plummeting through the bottom of my abdomen, bifurcating to shoot down my legs and explode, like a dynamited haggis, at my feet.

Pushing Mr. Twist to one side, Miss Viva—demonstrating extraordinary athletic prowess—jumped up onto the top of the piano and stared defiantly down at the assassin. Opening her mouth, she screamed. A bolt of lightning tore out of the little pink cavern of her throat and then jagged across the space that separated her from the despicable, hated man who threatened to snatch the soul she had coveted for nearly thirty-five years. The bolt passed into the assassin's own mouth—opened wide in shocked-stunned welcome—and blasted an egress through the chamois leather of his chaps at the latitude of his out-sized thighs. "Wheeeee!" cried the errant young woman, "I am beyond good and evil. Beyond, *beyond*…" As the charred, smoking body fell limp to the floor, a terrible stench of roasted meat filling the saloon, the grinning murderess from another world hopped down from the piano and put a hand reassuringly on the shoulder of her companion. "Present threat duly negated, Mr. Twist."

A small crowd of the fascinated and the appalled had flowed toward the stinking body. The crowd congregated in a semicircle, sniffing at the electrostatic scent that permeated the air. The carrion-sweet smell, if offensive to human sensibilities, was, if the ever-widening grin on Miss Viva's face was reliable testimony, an olfactory rollercoaster, an addictive thrill for those amorphous, shape-shifting jackals who sometimes assumed human form.

I got up and walked over to the curious gathering; found a chink in the wall of whores, gamblers and drunks, and peered through it.

The assassin had been reduced to an overdone steak, the oil that had lathered his chest so thick that a patina of it remained, like a residue of fat in a frying pan. I looked up. Miss Viva was urging Mr. Twist to sit down on the piano stool, where his assistant, minus his hangman's mask, awaited with a glass of *aqua vitae.* I was startled to discover that her eyes had found my own, their sapphire flames, like cold acetylene, scorching my optic nerves. Despite the chaos that was rapidly taking hold of the saloon, those eyes, those brilliant, alien eyes did not flinch from their one-on-one engagement. I fell into their depths as if transported out of my shoes and socks into a great stained window of Chartres blue. Her beauty was so much more raw, so much more dangerous, than that of the girls who flocked about the combusted body; so much more wonderful, so much more terrible, than that of the girls at my school.

"It was self-defense," she said, addressing the crowd in a level voice while casually blowing a stray, aquamarine-streaked lock out of her line of sight. "You saw that maniac draw first. We were left with no other option."

"It's all right, Miss Viva," said one of the bartenders. "I saw everything."

"I should think you did." She pointed, looking down her arm and appraising me through the sights of her splayed fingernails. "You," she said, with an imperious nod. "Come up here and give me a hand with Mr. Twist."

I ran to the right hand side of the orchestra pit to where a stepladder provided access to the stage. Clambering up it, I stepped onto the boards, turning to confront that vision of death, her morgue-happy face shining with a cold, indifferent light. And then I turned to look at Mr. Twist. He seemed possessed, like someone else, not the person I had met on the stagecoach; no, no, not the same person at all. He was still the chiselled, deeply sun-tanned image of a leading man, the owner of a face with the half-lidded, snake-like eyes of a practised seducer. But now the face seemed to be simmering, each pock and pore of his ominously handsome countenance bleeding with corrosive, self-destructive energy. Beneath, rising, like a dead face to the dark, gaseous surface of a swamp, was another self, one that belonged to a little boy, a confused, frightened little boy who had just cheated death.

"I don't understand. I thought you might *want* him to die, Miss Viva." I sank incisors into lip flesh in a vampirically savage fit of embarrassment; again, I thought, me and my promiscuous mouth. I tasted the salty lick of boorishness on my chastised lips, and felt my cheeks roar with flame.

"What are you *doing* here?" she said.

"Mr. Twist—he said he'd teach me to shoot."

"Teach you to shoot? What are you talking about? Shouldn't you be in school? At home? Shouldn't you be anywhere except in a late-night saloon half out of your mind on *liquor*?" I suppose I must have been slurring, or unsteady on my feet. I turned my head away, unable to bear the scrutiny of those stainless-steel slivers that were her eyes.

44

"I don't live at home," I said. "I'm a boarder. But I don't like school. I hate it. I ran away."

"Are they *apprised* of your truancy?"

"I won't be missed," I said. "And I plan to be back by morning." Miss Viva shook her head and sighed. "Who *was* that man?" I said, looking down at the roasted carcass dressed in charred but still identifiable poncho and chaps. The throng that had gathered about the body had begun to disperse. Soon, the little party that occupied the stage—Mr. Twist, Miss Viva, their assistant and me—were his only and reluctant mourners. Like students in an operating theatre, we looked down dispassionately at the body, remains of a new procedure that had gone fantastically wrong.

"A bounty hunter," said Miss Viva, softly, pushing out her bottom lip. "But don't tell. Mr. Twist sometimes likes to be thought of as a respectable individual. A scholar. A gentleman. Not a man wanted in a half-dozen territories." She shrugged. "All outlaws seem to have a secret hankering for respectability. Though you'd never catch him *admitting* to being concerned about other folk's opinions."

"Opinions about whether one is *respectable* or not? Oh no, no, you wouldn't catch *me* admitting it either," I said. "I don't give a hoot for other folk's opinions."

"Well, now that you're here." Miss Viva took the glass from Mr. Twist's hand, took a sip of *aqua* for herself, put the glass on the floor, and then stooped to ease an arm under his arm, grasping him about the ribs. Mr. Twist's assistant copied, grabbing the nerve-frazzled gunslinger under his other armpit. Together, they hoisted him up from the stool. "Now that you're here…you can help. Take his legs." It was strange, I thought. Mr. Twist seemed fully conscious, but a paralysis seemed to have overcome him, as if he were a rabbit whose autonomic nervous system had had glue poured into its works, freezing it to the tarmac in the face of a speeding, oncoming hearse.

"He's sometimes like this," said Miss Viva, perceiving the question mark wiggling behind my face's attempt at impassivity, "not always. But when annihilation seems so close—well, then it's as well he has me."

"Childhood trauma?" Miss Viva seemed irritated at my follow-up, more clearly articulated query, flashing me a look that I took to be a criticism of my presumptuousness. But then she laughed.

"You're a *precocious* little girl, aren't you?"

"Precocious? Everybody says that," I said, bristling a little. "I suppose it's true." Miss Viva raised an eyebrow, but otherwise seemed to give me no more thought. I had taken Mr. Twist by the feet and was ready to proceed with our mercy mission and evacuate him to a place of sanctuary and rest.

Mr. Twist had begun to mumble:

> *"Young soul, put off your flesh, and come*
> *With me into the quiet tomb,*
> *Our bed is lovely, dark, and sweet;*
> *The Earth will swing us, as she goes,*
> *Beneath our coverlid of snows*
>   *And the warm leaded sheet.*
> *Dear and dear is their poisoned note,*
> *The little snakes of silver throat,*
> *In mossy skulls that nest and lie,*
> *Ever singing 'die, oh! die.'"*

"Ready?" said Miss Viva. She and the assistant lifted the forward section of Mr. Twist and, with me hefting the tail section, we backed out, past the piano, past the dusty, magenta curtain and toward the wings and the area backstage, a grotto cluttered with trunks, baskets, wires, pulleys, costumes and masks.

And, gradually, we negotiated our way upstairs, where Mr.

Twist and Miss Viva had their room, there to put the pooped gunslinger to bed.

*

"There's another he has to face," said Miss Viva, "one more clever, more dangerous. His name's Charles Cockaigne, an Englishman who's made his rep as a bounty hunter working the Canadian border. He's newly arrived in the West. But he's good. Very good. And very, very *fast*. Faster, even, than Mr. Twist. Certainly nothing like that fool I terminated downstairs. We've run into him before. In New Mexico. That time, we barely escaped." I stood by the window looking down at a street cobbled with grey, polished stones that glistened with the images of reflected street lamps. Just above me, it seemed, a weathervane creaked in the dry, cool wind blowing in from the desert. "We've heard rumors that Cockaigne is arriving tomorrow, on the stage coach."

"I still don't understand," I said. "Why are you protecting Mr. Twist when you so long to eat his soul? I mean, don't get me wrong. I'm glad you protect him. I don't want him to die. I want him, *both* of you, to stay on Earth forever." My wish for Mr. Twist's longevity was somewhat self-serving. Mademoiselle Moutarde's egregious establishment promised days, months, years of death-in-life. How wonderful, then, to be able to set out and ride into the frontier, those lands dividing the rational from the irrational, out of which none had ever returned. Frantically—I had felt as if a pair of thumbs were pressing against my windpipe, a constriction that sometimes presaged a fit—frantically, desperately looking about the room, I knew, knew, *knew* I would have to escape. Escape the school, my parents, Tombstone, the West; escape life itself. But crossing into the frontier would remain a dream unless I had someone to guide me across the millions of miles that separated me from my objective. Someone like Mr. Twist. And Miss Viva. "I don't think you can begin to guess just how important it is to me for the both of you to remain incarnate."

I studied Miss Viva's ghostly image in the dirty window-pane. She stood leaning against the brass bedstead. Behind her, stretched out on the mattress, lay Mr. Twist, drugged with what had been a great, eagerly gulped draught of laudanum. She gazed at his sleeping body as if he were a child in a crib, and she an anxious young mother.

"I don't want to ravish him," she said quietly. "When we become as one, when I take him back home to Venus, his home too, then—it will be like a wedding. The wedding of Mr. and Mrs. Twist! Can you understand that? My people say there is one, one very special soul that we meet in each of our long, lonely lives. I dine on mankind only every hundred years, and even so, I have sometimes gone hungry thinking of that soul waiting for me, that special soul who will make me complete. Consummation, when it comes, has to be perfect. I won't have some deranged fool bounty hunter butting in and spoiling my special day."

"I don't see how you will ever *have* a special day if Mr. Twist remains in the land of the living. As I trust he will."

"A day will come," she said, her voice steady with resolve. "My body does not age as your body ages, nor does my spirit grow so easily weary. The passing of time has little meaning for me. Not at least when I am with Mr. Twist. Still, I grow impatient sometimes. If only he'd died that first time we met. If only I hadn't grown so attached to what is *vital* in him." Her voice faltered, betraying a slight catch. Blushing, I looked out into the night.

The dust storm had abated and the stars stood out like diamonds in a black velvet display case; but the Earth needed to perform a greater roll of its nocturnal round before Venus would be visible, close to the horizon in the early morning sky. I imagined, then, as I gazed through the transparent lines of

Miss Viva's reflection, gazed through the scratched, fly-specked pane and into the neon-splashed sky, I imagined a hundred, a thousand, a million or more Vivas. Mistresses of death flying above the rooftops of Tombstone, above, indeed, all the rooftops of all the cities of the world, flying, dipping, wheeling and diving into the bedrooms of men, women and children to relieve them of the burdens and sorrows of this life. Taking them to their bosoms, that flock of Deaths would lift them high into the ice-bejewelled clouds, up to where there was no longer air to breathe and onward to that bright star, only constant in this transient universe, only hope of lost travellers like myself. And perhaps, I thought, as I studied Miss Viva in the casement's tainted looking glass, perhaps it was the only hope for her too; the only hope for all her kind.

"You need us, don't you, Miss Viva? All your race needs us. Without our souls, you couldn't bear to live. You'd die of loneliness." Below, on the sidewalk, in a pool of light cast by a lamppost, a man had appeared. He was an Indian, it seemed. Athletic, powerful, his burnished skin—even at this distance I could see that it glowed with energy—was like soft leather cured by a prairie breeze. He was dressed in a black business suit and wore impenetrable shades; his shoes were Italian winkle-pickers, polished to a vitreous shine. Indeed, the only item of garb that gave hint of his ethnicity was the single eagle's feather that protruded from the headband disciplining his long, sheeny black locks. I knew, at once, that he was of the Chiricahua Apache. And I also knew at once that, though his eyes were hidden, he was staring up at me. Galvanized by a thrill of disquiet, I turned about. Miss Viva had straightened herself, and had taken command, it seemed, of her emotions.

"Won't they punish you—at your school, I mean?" She had walked to the dresser and, like a rag-picker, was sorting through the accumulated junk that littered its surface. "Perhaps some money will help. Bribery is a universal solvent for getting yourself out of sticky jams such as the *hugely* infelicitous one in which you now surely find yourself." She opened a drawer, rooted around and slammed it shut. Then she opened another drawer, her brow suddenly creasing. "My purse," she muttered, "where have I put my purse?"

"It doesn't matter. I'll be back in my room before midnight. No one will know I've been in town."

"You don't understand. I didn't only have money in that purse. I—" She put a hand to her *décolletage* and shook her head. "My powers are limited, especially here on Earth, encased in matter as I am, and so far away from the frontier. They give me an edge, but sometimes it's reassuring to have some backup." She began to throw clothes onto the floor; then stood back, hands on her hips, and clicked her tongue. "I guess it's not worth fretting over. I'll just have to find me a good gunsmith when it gets light."

"I should be going," I said, feeling the weight of the derringer pulling at the big pocket in my frock. "The new school—it's very strict." And, I thought, very hateful. I remembered the time, just a week ago, when I had stood outside its gates, a new girl come to enrol. Above two high imposing arches of reticulated metal a semicircle of rusted filigree had proclaimed *Academy for Wayward Girls*. The school was the realisation of a vision induced in some hapless protégé of Jimmy Renwick by penny dreadfuls, tertiary syphilis and midnight suppers of raw liver washed down with fermented epidermis of toad. A grim pile of granite and slate, it had been visible only by the jags of lightning that seared the louring clouds, bursts of a divine flashgun each one of which seemed to take a bleak pleasure in illuminating the mad fantasia of turrets, rafters and eaves. I had felt I was about to walk through the gates of Hell.

"And you won't run away again?"

"I always run away," I said. "It doesn't matter. They can't teach me anything. None of them can. It's like the other schools I've been sent to. I run away from them all." I studied my shoes. "It's all been a plot, a long-term plan to turn me into the worst type of prom queen." I turned to again look out the window. The Indian had gone. And something told me I would be wise to leave before he should put in another appearance.

I walked to the door. But as I put a hand on the doorknob, I found myself unable to turn it. I gazed over at the unconscious form of Mr. Twist, his long, wiry body anticipating the peace of the grave.

Miss Viva picked up a petticoat that had spilled from the rifled dresser. She studied it, as if reminding herself to upbraid the laundry woman whenever they next should meet, then let the silken underthing drop to the floor. "I suppose they tell you tales, don't they?" she said. "The teachers at your school, I mean. Silly, ignorant tales about Venus?"

"They say—" I looked her in the eye; whether I offended or not, I had to know the truth. "Why didn't you conquer the Earth, Miss Viva? Why did your people come here at all? And why did you scourge the West?"

She stared back at me, meeting my boldness with frigid calm, eyebrows raised, like a teacher confronted by a gifted but annoyingly pertinacious student. It was a look which, in others, I was quick to censure, but in her I was happy, more than happy, to endure. "We didn't come here to conquer you," she said, slowly, so that I might comprehend. "We came here because..." Her brows knitted and she averted her face. "You've been coming to *us* for so long, for so many thousands of years, your souls drifting westwards to follow the setting sun beyond the confines of this world, to come home, home to the planet of the blessed. Why, after all this time, should it be so unusual for us to want to visit *you*? You have sustained us. You have made our lives whole. We wanted to be with you, at last, in the flesh. We wanted to touch you, feel you, even as you feel each other."

"You came to us like—lovers?"

"Like hungry lovers. Like those starving for the physical life that you had enabled us to glimpse far away on a world populated only by beings without flesh, energy forms who, familiar with your dreams, had begun to covet your bodies."

"But the Indian Wars—"

"It would have been the same wherever we had chosen to manifest ourselves. You begged for our help. You all did. You said it would bring peace. You seduced us with your yearnings and your agony. And so we gave you what you asked for: medicine to ease the pain. Medicine that you called *weapons*. We gave to Indian and White Man alike. Was it our fault you used our gifts so profligately, so savagely? We had no wish to harm you. We loved you. But we had such little experience of life on this Earth. Even today, when you ask for our help, the technology to make ever more destructive weapons, still we help you. We have even, of late, helped your scientists in the West begin work on an E-bomb! We are careful, now, of course, to help only one side, in case the mad, wicked destruction we witnessed a hundred years ago is repeated. But this Cold War of yours is getting out of hand. How can we any longer have such faith in your instincts for self-preservation? How can we believe that U.S. military superiority will not tempt some crazy fool in the White House to launch a first strike? How can we continue to have such unqualified faith in *America*? Ah, but how can we *preach* to you? We ourselves are fools. Fools for love. And our love, I sometimes think, will kill you all."

"But why should you care? If we die, it will just mean more souls for you and your people."

Miss Viva compressed her lips, transforming her mouth into a pale cicatrice. It seemed she was trying to prevent her icy demean from melting as her frustration with me threatened to bring her to the boil. "Why should we care, Miss Nicola?" Her voice was infused with a studied, almost sarcastic degree of respect. Eager to demonstrate scholarly grace under pressure, she relaxed her ramrod stance, leant back against the dresser, the small of her back supported by the notched edge of its topmost plane. Her right hand toyed with the lamp that stood beside her, spinning its shade and wafting a cloud of dust into space. She continued her lesson. "Because you're right: without you we, whom you know as Death, would ourselves die. There has always been a *dérive* between our planets. Once, it was the spiritual corridor by which your souls travelled to their consummation. But, until we learnt how to convert that corridor into matter, until we ourselves learnt how to assume material form—oh yes, we haven't *always* been shape-shifters—such journeys were always one-way, like the passage from life to death itself. It was such a moment of joy, for us, when we arrived on your world and were, at last, able to share and enjoy your flesh. When we understood what harm we were doing to your planet we left. And if some of us return, it is only because we cannot help ourselves. Once tasted, the life we had known on Earth—a sweet life in which we loved you as physical creatures as well as your Deaths—was hard to renounce. Now, when they negotiate the *dérive,* my people are carried to this world by the sound of the penultimate heartbeats of those of you with whom we have become inextricably linked; those of you who become our favorites; those of you whose doom it is to most inspire our love." Though her sentences had been measured, I could see she was upset. Indeed, her cool superstratum masked an inner life beset by all manner of anxieties. "That, my dear," she said, "is why we *care*." Any further conversation between us would, I knew, only exacerbate her discomfort. I decided to leave her to rest—whether peacefully, or in a state of angst—with Mr. Twist.

"I think I should be going, Miss Viva."

"Yes, I suppose you really *should* be going." Once again, pulling out the drawers of her dresser, she fell to burrowing among linen, starched blouses, ribbons and bows in search of her errant purse. I glanced once more at the supine gunslinger, his heavy, bruised eyelids revealing sclera that were like the nail clippings of a little alabaster god. Then I opened the door.

"Perhaps I'll see you again," I said. "Mr. Twist said—" But Miss Viva, I could see, was in no mood to reply. I walked into the hallway with only the prospect of retracing my steps through the dark, winding streets of Tombstone and reinstating myself in my room in Mademoiselle Moutarde's establishment. With no prospect whatsoever of having Mr. Twist teach me how to shoot, or of sharing a life that seemed to offer me a fierce redemption.

Chapter Three
The Manitou

I had not gone back to school. That night I had wandered the streets. *Nobody loves me*, I had thought. That much was clear. Ma and Pa: I expected their disapprobation. But to be rejected by Miss Viva: that was too bad. To hell with it. I would make her love me. I would do something to win her over, both her *and* Mr. Twist.

I walked aimlessly. By morning I had come to Boot Hill.

Though situated on the edge of town, the precinct of Boot Hill is Tombstone's heart, the Gothic cityscape *par excellence*. Its outlying tenements are interspersed with churches, temples, and—markers of locale that signal the spirit of place more than anything else—cemeteries, great tangled expanses of tombs and mausolea that are like scale models of the enclave itself, for Boot Hill affects the appearance of a vast necropolis. Even those residential high-rises that provide an introduction to its freakish piles and follies are like giant cliff-faces riddled with catacombs. Each morning the restive inhabitants may be seen, emerging to look blearily out onto the resurrected world; they, it and even the bugs that crawl across their unswept floors incontinent with reluctant life. Further in, the architecture becomes as imposing as any commemorating notables interred in some Brobdingnagian Père Lachaise. Here, Boot Hill transforms itself into a place of dead giants, interred for long centuries in a massive Golgotha, a petrified jungle of cistic prominences, a towering boneyard. And these bones have been carbonised, fused into struts, beams, architraves, girders, lintels; all is shrouded in black, a pall that honors the town's contemporary population, the unknown souls who hide behind shuttered windows and barred doors, and those who wander restless, in the black, refracted light of the funereal day. This place of busy, incongruous life grows in sullen majesty and elevation in the long defile that constitutes the approach to the reservoir. As the traveller proceeds there is an intimation that the morbid promise awarded by the sights that had rushed by when he or she had first entered Tombstone is about to be fulfilled. For at its apotheosis—where it hugs the line of the town's water supply—the enclave is built almost entirely of black marble and confirms the long-held suspicion that one is entering upon a gigantic nineteenth-century urban burial place, its houses like family vaults, its offices and malls like great tombs celebrating latter-day pharaohs whose riches have been hoarded against the encroaching night. The high, anonymous walls sometimes contribute to bouts of what might be called an *appreciative dyspepsia*—the town's ubiquitous tomb-like dwellings, its ambience of the grave, being such a rich but unrelenting visual feast. It is as if the onlooker had been invited to sit down for a forthcoming wake only to be served endless courses of black chocolate, black cakes, black meringue and black nougat. The streets are oddly mute, as though the enclave's phantasmal denizens consider it necessary to comply with the spirit of place and talk in undertakers' whispers as they go about their business. Sometimes a hansom cab will pass by, each hansom black as the surrounding bricolage of buildings, its horses sporting plumes—like horses that one might expect to lead a funeral cortège—their hides as sooty and as sleek as the varnished panelling of the carriages to which they are harnessed. But then the lively clatter of wheels will disappear into the distance and all will be as quiet as formerly.

Hemmed in by Gothic vistas that were homages to death and decay, feeling that I had undergone a premature burial and had just awoken to a full understanding of my fate, I found a doorway and slept rough; and, on waking, had played the misty-eyed street urchin, begging a little change from passing couples. By evening, denied a hot meal and a proper bed, I was already contemplating a return to school.

Walking by the reservoir, thinking upon the punishment that would be waiting for me at Mademoiselle Moutarde's, I discovered, after several nervous glances over my shoulder, that I was being followed, and my thoughts turned from the grimly nostalgic to survival.

The sun was setting, splintering the sky with its familiar neon glow. Across the stillness of the big reservoir stretched the desert and the violet hills. I had not been able to clearly identify the man who followed me. Mercurial as the bats that flitted above the rooftops, he slipped, imperceptibly, from one doorway to the next, blending in with the shadows cast by the deserted restaurants and bars. The esplanade was usually filled with promenaders at this hour, but a violent wind had emptied restaurant, bar and esplanade alike; and I decided I too should should relocate, less to avoid the pummelling of the coming dust-storm than to find a place where the press of humanity would dissuade my stalker from committing himself to an assault.

There were no thoroughfares that led back into town in my vicinity, but, spotting a slim passageway that ran between two hotels, its entrance criss-crossed with planks of wood nailed perfunctorily to the walls, I tossed aside the half-eaten hamburger I had rescued from a litter bin, and walked over to it, trying not to hurry and thus betray my fear.

It took little effort to remove the few boards barring the ingress. Lifting the barbed wire that remained, I eased my way through, one of my socks notching up yet another tear as the cotton caught on a barb. I noticed, then, the abundance of graffiti. One slogan read: WE ARE CLOSER TO THINGS INVISIBLE THAN TO THINGS VISIBLE. Another: LIVE WITHOUT DEAD TIME. Another: HOW DO YOU KNOW YOU'RE NOT DEAD ALREADY—THE WORLD ENDED YESTERDAY. But all these slogans had been struck through with splashes of black paint, making them almost illegible; and about the brickwork that had served as a bulletin board a rival claim on the passer-by's attention displayed itself in the form of a series of crudely daubed swastikas.

I stumbled over broken glass, tin cans, mangled bicycle wheels and an old pram, until I came to the alley's end, a slim rectangle that gave onto an unknown square. I repeated my earlier performance with barbed wire and boards. Stepping forward, I paused to check that the strands of rusted barbs were well clear of my clothes, and then extricated myself from the alley.

I ventured into the open. About me the square—a lunar landscape covered with rubble—was overshadowed by burnt-out tenements. Rubbish dumps and shacks punctuated its center. This, it seemed, was a piece of Boot Hill's unconsecrated ground that had been left to the mercies of entropy.

As I had emerged into the square—so like a bomb-site—two boys appeared from the dark heart of an adjacent building. I watched, stomach churning, as they stumbled across the piled masonry and rubble and toward me, their mouths set in horrid grins. Obscured by the deepening twilight, their faces seemed like portraits whose canvases had been drenched with thinner, or like Plasticine busts broiling under an ultraviolet lamp. I had dreamt of zanies ever since the incident in the desert, and sometimes those nightmare images of mutant flesh invaded my waking hours, superimposing themselves on the faces of people I randomly encountered. The weight of the small item of ordnance that I had latterly removed from my frock pocket and secreted inside my underwear now chaffed against my skin as if to urge me to take it from its dank confines and have it fulfil its purpose. And then the burden of dream lifted. I refocused my eyes. No; those boys were not as those who so often haunted my thoughts. But though I could now clearly see that they were human, their visages still chilled me in the way the sight of a snake, a rat or a spider chills, summoning up irrational fears that cannot be easily explained or dispelled. And the chill had numbed my resolve.

Their faces were elongated: high foreheads topped with sprigs of cropped, spiky grey-white hair; high cheek-bones, thin, tapered chins; and flesh that was pale grey, like their eyes, giving them the aspect of metal men, or of insect people whose chitin was reinforced with steel. Like so many of Tombstone's inhabitants, they wore black lipstick and eye shadow. Elongated, thin—like their skulls—their bodies yet communicated a sinewy power, but also a certain pathos, embodying, as they did, a coldness, a seeming impotence of feeling, as if they constituted my own century's failure of af-fect. Their clothes were like something out of a biker movie: jackboots, tight black leather pants, and tin helmets such as were worn by German troops in the Second World War.

My stomach continued to churn. If only, I thought, if only I could be a necrobabe; if only I could be cool as ice! The inner rumblings that had besieged me all day finally gave way to a full-blooded vulcanism, spattering the ground with a clear, white vomitus of whisky dregs, bile and pure heartache. I closed my eyes; leant against the wall next to the passageway, my face turned into an exposed girder, my lips so close to the iron that my taste buds perked with a vicious tang of ferrous oxide.

When I opened my eyes I saw that one of the boys had propped himself against the wall, his face turned toward me, his eyes staring into my own. He had made a homunculus of a hand and walked it across the wall's pitted surface, his long, painted fingernails creating a sound effect that recalled the staccati of high-heeled shoes on tiles. It was an aural constant—like that of adolescent babble, the swish of hair against silk, the fricative music of nylon against nylon—that had followed me from school to school. My head spun; the sensible axis about which the rest of the world revolved, albeit imperfectly, or sometimes not at all, was in this desperate, ruined wasteland non-existent, without currency.

"Just like a little doll," said the boy, in a raw-throated, rich and wholly incongruous *basso profundo* (for he was no more than a few years older than myself). "It will give me great satisfaction to add her to the Mistress's collection. She will look sweet in armor, don't you think? I will teach her to do…tricks."

He sprang away from the wall and landed in a crouch atop a small mound of rubble. His companion joined him, slinking to his side with a kind of peasant grace, an insidious, balletic magnetism. In a handful of years it would translate into the kind of icky-sticky charm that, I believe, some moronic females find alluring. Their gaze never left me. Ruskin noted that the first requirement of Gothic architecture is that it shall "appeal to the admiration of the rudest as well as the most refined minds." But my surroundings—the blasted, if still haughty, dissecting planes of turrets, façades covered with fretwork, the accumulation of ornament that is most characteristic of the Gothic style—seemed, this night, in this place, to invite only the appreciation of violent minds, minds bred in the wilderness. There was no sanctuary, here, for refinement.

"The girl's plump, is she not?" said the boy who had initiated contact. "And her face, it's...it's nondescript."

"Nondescript is the kindest thing that may be said of it," said his companion.

"I'm not nondescript," I said, gainsaying the multitudinous glint of my reflection in the shards of glass and steel scattered about my feet, shards that resembled the scintillant droppings of an artificial, clockwork-entrailed rat. "I'm not some piece of chattel, either." I stared at them, one by one, challengingly. "I'm a necrobabe!"

"A necrobabe? Ha. I don't think so, precious."

"Wouldn't matter if she were. We're not afraid of Venusians."

"Right. Venus sucks. We don't need her charity."

"Damn right. We don't need no E-bomb to see off the Reds. We got ourselves something better."

The two boys rose to their feet. "Don't be so concerned," said the one who seemed to be the senior. "You're lucky. You're going to get to see the light. So many evil things have polluted this nation since we decided to pussyfoot around with the Rooskies. Only a *Führer* can save us now. And we're gonna take you to meet her."

"Perhaps you have not heard of our Mistress?" said the other boy. "She is Death. The Queen of Death. The greatest such mistress in the universe. And soon *everyone* will be serving her, just as we do."

"Yeah, all them stupid cowboys, they're gonna either be her lunch, or her slaves!"

"We're as good as any damned cowboy."

"Indeed we are. Not that folks around these parts are *real* cowboys. How could they be when there ain't no goddamn *cows* any more?" It was true: "Cowboy" had long been a misnomer, a mere euphemism for "white trash". But I was not about to engage in a discussion on how the language and trappings of the Old West still permeated the alien West of the mid-twentieth century.

The sky seemed to be descending; I felt crushed, driven into the rubbish-strewn ground. And it was hot, so hot. The clamour of the boys' words infested my ears, turning them into insectarium that were like twin insane asylums filled with psychopathic bees.

Boy senior walked over to me; took a firm hold of my arm and pulled me to his side. The sensation of his thick, strong fingers digging into my skinny arm as if he meant to impress his fingerprints into the bone prompted, unfortunately, a degree of disgust so powerful as to evacuate my mind of all thoughts of coolly biding my time. The right moment to dispose of him and make my attempt at freedom was, I had known earlier, not now; but the horror of his touch precipitated me into action.

Blood surging to my head, I rammed the heel of one of my Mary Janes into his instep, and, as he made an involuntary bow, as if to congratulate me on my spunkiness, brought the wedge of the shoe's patent-leather toe into his groin, a kick that, high-stepping as it was, almost put me on my back. The boy's cheeks imploded, he suddenly aged fifty, sixty years into that condition of post-menopausal toothlessness shared by several of the schoolmistresses of my abandoned school. The other boy jumped into the air like a jack-in-the-box, his face also aged into that of an old woman who had had a hatpin thrust deep into her backside.

Taking advantage of the arresting of time occasioned by my toe punt, I ran toward the door, my frock belling, rocking from side to side. Without looking backwards, despite the imprecations that boxed my ears, I had lifted the barbed wire and re-entered the passageway before I believe the first thought of pursuit had stirred my persecutors from the spot where I had left them, rooted by incredulity.

I ran straight into the arms of a tall, powerfully built Indian.

"Easy," he said, as I fought to free myself from his embrace. "Easy, easy." I went limp, knowing the struggle to be unequal. Looking up into the man's face I realized that my stalker had been the Apache I had first seen standing below Miss Viva's window the previous night. He did not return my stare; instead, he directed his attention toward the boys who, by now, had recovered sufficiently to sprint to the mouth of the passageway. They stood there, teeth bared, hands raised, frozen in poses of pubescent fury. "Tell your Mistress that this little one is mine," said the Indian. "And tell her that I shall be calling upon her. Soon." The boys hissed and spat like tomcats; and then they took to their heels, scampering back to where they had appeared out of the shadows, to lose themselves in a maze of ghost-habitations, dark, denuded superstructures with graffiti-scarred walls.

The Indian looked down at me. He was older than I had supposed, but otherwise conformed to the image I had formed of him: sharp-suited, with Italian shoes that shone like glass, and with a single eagle's feather protruding from a bandanna that disciplined a great mane of sheeny locks.

"Yes," he said, a smile gradually creasing his wind-cured, burnished cheeks, "yes, you have the smell of a Death on you, the smell of a Venusian." He eased his grip. A few seconds before and I would have again tried to break free and run, but I no longer feared him. Whether my brief acquaintance with Miss Viva had conferred on me a sympathy for alienness, or whether my desire to be brought into the honorary sistership of the necrobabe had reached the ears of a fairy-godmother, I don't know; but I knew, then, just what he was.

"You're a Death too, aren't you?" I said. His smile widened.

"I am Cochise," he said. "I am a manitou." I slipped from his arms, stepped back and held out my hand.

"How do you do, Mr. Cochise." We shook. "My name is—"

"I know who you are," he said. "Come." He turned and walked down the passageway toward the esplanade. "We must talk."

*

I squinted along the line of his arm. "On Earth, you call that star Vega," said Mr. Cochise. "The fourth planet in its system is my home. A death-world it is, like Venus."

We sat on a bench overlooking the reservoir. Massive pylons encircled the artificial lake, its great expanse of dark water saved from evaporation by the unearthly sciences practised in the West. Sometimes the pylons would crackle with hyperphysical activity; otherwise, the silence was absolute. He let his arm fall, but I kept my eye on the star.

"For many aeons," he said, "we were like the Venusians. Souls would travel to our world and nourish us, but we could not ourselves travel. When we did learn to navigate between worlds, it was not by psychogeography, but by building vessels that were able to transport the organic bodies we made for ourselves across the great stellar voids." He nodded toward the reservoir. "My ship is, in fact, quite near by. I sometimes wonder if it's still in working order."

"You're an energy form too, just like Miss Viva?"

"For many centuries I fed on the souls of those who lived on this land mass," he said, sawing his arm through the air so as to encompass the desert, the hills and the lands beyond. "I became one of their spirit-gods. That is how I came to adopt the semblance you see now." He plucked the feather from his hair; studied it, frowning. "I tire of this body sometimes. But I still have a sentimental regard for the people who once worshipped me." He flicked the feather onto the ground. "They called themselves *Nde*, 'The People.' The Spaniards called them by the Zuni word *Apachu*, meaning enemy. According to Cortez, who wrote about this matter in 1799, the Spaniards included as *Apachu* the Tonto, the Chiricahuas, Gilenos, Mimbrenos, Taracones, Mescaleros, Llaneros, Lipanes and the Navajos. We now, of course, call all of these myriad peoples the Apache." He kicked at the feather with the side of his shoe, sending it flying over the stones. "My people have changed. Perhaps changed too much. With cattle and farmland dead it has been they, more than any, who have excelled in those arts that make the West rich." He focused his eyes on me. "Chiricahua Apache dominate the economies of the towns and mining camps in Arizona Territory. They have practically cornered the market in the transmutation of base metals. And they sideline in some very revolutionary drugs. Dopamine and mescaline look pretty tame compared to some of the aphrodisiacs the Apache have cooked up. And then there's the work they've done on tryptamine hallucinogens, too. But I still remember how things used to be. Ah yes, I still remember what it was like when I first arrived."

"When was that?"

"In the late 1860s, just after the civil war. That was a bittersweet time, when the Apache still had some kind of life of their own, but were nevertheless being slowly exterminated. I savored their souls, but I grieved their passing. When the Venusians arrived—"

"You *saw* them arrive?"

"They arrived out of the East. A great tunnel of light opened up in the sky. And down they came to interfere in the ways of men. Yes, when the Venusians arrived, nothing was ever the same. I cannot bring myself to criticize their actions. Without their help, the Apache would have disappeared from history. But those times were murderous. Once the Indian and the White Man had got their hands on weapons of electrical mass destruction—the lightning-bolt howitzers and directed-energy machines that reduced so much of the West to a burnt wasteland, that created the mutations that even now haunt the desert night—then the stage was set for the creation of the West as we know it today."

"But what is it?" I said. "What exactly *is* the West? Miss Viva said that once upon a time it was the spiritual corridor by which human souls went to heaven. She said it became the way it is today because her people turned it into matter."

"A Death, unless it modifies itself, is bound to the energy-field of its planet of origin. To travel to Earth, the Venusians *had* to turn both themselves and the psychogeographical corridor connecting Earth and Venus—the type of phenomenon they call a *dérive*—into matter. What *is* the West? you ask. The West is a bridge; it is physical, but it is also transdimensional. Entering its corridor one passes into a parallel universe that, after a distance of some millions of miles, emerges on the other side of the interplanetary divide that separates the two planets."

"I think my family and I entered the West at Colorado."

"Well, as you must know, the corridor doesn't really have an entrance or exit as such, humans simply enter an area of longitude in the continental United States where reality becomes warped, smudged. It is because that area of longitude corresponds with the old Wild West that the corridor is *known* as the West. But to continue—"

"Oh yes, please do go on."

Mr. Cochise smiled and resumed his historical précis. "The Venusians immediately regretted the slaughter they had precipitated. So they sealed off the killing zone, consolidated it. The corridor connecting the worlds became a place where human beings could enter and live, but one governed by physical laws which would restrict, if not completely prevent, the wreaking of mutual destruction." He looked down at his feet and shook his head. "Humans in the West, of course, have learnt how to exploit the physical conditions existing here in order to construct radical technologies. And though the laws on which those technologies are based have no currency *outside* the West, the West has been able to sell the *products* of those technologies to a world willing to invest its money and talent in an inhospitable, nigh limitless land. It has been a very profitable arrangement for the U.S. government. They allow the West to go its own, wild way so long as the rest of America remains sole beneficiary of its strange science." He looked out across the reservoir, his eyelids heavy, as if he were going into a trance. "It's getting out of hand. The Venusians have already agreed to allow the West to begin work on the manufacture of an E-bomb, and lately there have been even more alarming developments. Very alarming developments indeed."

He licked his lips, relishing, it seemed, the silence that, absolute as it was, seemed to have impossibly deepened, to the point where the lake was a reservoir not merely of water, but of the universe's sum total of quietude. "There are many death-worlds," he said, "and not all of them are beneficent. There are, perhaps, as many as conform to your archetypes of heaven as there are those that conform to your notions of hell. I tell you: there is a being here, in Tombstone, who is from such a hell. She is entering into a bargain with certain people in Washington, a bargain that will give your government terrible power." He came out of his trance-like state of reflection, turned and looked down at the small girl seated by his side, whose face was by now doubtless a wide-eyed, open-mouthed caricature of Little Miss Muffet. "I must stop this creature, but, alone, I do not have the power. That is why I need your Miss Viva to help me. Will you bring her to me, Miss Nicola?" He reached into the breast pocket of his jacket and produced a gold-bordered business card. "Will you ask her to assist me in this matter?"

"I can't ask her. She wouldn't take any notice of me. Neither would Mr. Twist. They think I'm just a silly little girl."

"Then you must prove to them you're not."

"I know," I said, "I want to, but—" I swung my legs, the tips of my shoes scuffing against the pavement. "Why can't *you* ask her."

"I have wished to contact her myself, but I am followed, followed almost constantly. Those two boys who tried to press-gang you not so long ago serve the one I seek to destroy. And there are others who trail me, others who are more dangerous. I do not wish them to know that, here in Tombstone, there is another Death with whom it may be possible for me to forge an alliance. I would not give the enemy that advantage. Will you tell your Miss Viva then? Will you bring her to my house?" I inspected the address on the card and then looked up at Mr. Cochise. "I have, I must admit, been somewhat nervous about approaching her," he continued. "She has, how shall I put it, a *reputation*. I had felt it was probable that she would reject my petition out of hand."

"Miss Viva has problems. With Mr. Twist."

"The one whose soul she covets. Yes, I know of him."

"Mr. Twist is being hunted by a bounty hunter called Cockaigne. I think all of Miss Viva's thoughts are on Mr. Twist's mortality."

"I understand. She wishes him dead."

"No, no," I said, "at least not yet. She feels the time isn't right."

"Then you must try to make sure that Mr. Twist does not do us all the inconvenience of dying just yet awhile." He got up. "I must leave before the enemy's agents spot us here. And you must leave too. You have been seen with me and it is no longer safe for you in this part of town. Go. Go now. Go find the Venusian."

And then he strode off into the dark.

*

I ran through Boot Hill. I ran through Tombstone. I ran for nearly an hour, my side racked by an abominable stitch. I was lost to Gothic defiles, to dust-whipped, neon-splashed avenues lined with transplanted, woebegone cottonwoods, lurid passageways above which hung flashing signs advertising Marlboro and Pepsi. And then I heard the thunder. The wind—stronger than that which usually blew in from the desert at night—increased in strength. And then, to my astonishment, it began to rain.

I held a hand to my forehead, creating an improvised sunshield to protect my eyes from the shimmering, neon-glazed cobbles, spangled with the shattered images of the streetlamps. The patina of the sidewalk bled into the surrounding buildings, and, as the clouds rid themselves of their load, soaking me, I saw everything through lash-blurred aureoles of prismatic color. The cobbles, walls, hoardings and windows became radiant as if with strange, incongruous rainbows that only condescended to appear at night. But despite this superficial romanticism, this was not the kind of deserted cityscape that might inspire the lonely pedestrian to whistle a Chopin *nocturne*. Rather, its bricks and mortar exuded the atmospherics cited by people who have visited the Colosseum, the ambience of a fell architecture whispering tales of ghouls, devils and wraiths; ancient stones ingrained with old cruelties and death.

I pressed on, my feet skittering down wet, black, tessellated avenues, down, down between row after row of streetlamps, ferrous trees whose tops roared with light as if great fireflies roosted there. Between row after row of more natural scenery, the sickly cottonwoods that attempted to gainsay the arid wastes that lay just outside the city limits, down into downtown where I might be lost in the crowds and again seek out the *Birdcage*.

*

I looked deep into the cold, blue cabochons of her eyes, that gemstone regard seemingly unmoved by my account of recent events. And then the lids, heavy with black paint, weighted with the long, mascara-thick spikes of her lashes, fell, half-occluding those precious, radiantly pure stones. Then they were raised again, with an almost audible *ching*! as if they were cash registers ringing up a sale in a jeweller's shop. In the heartbeat of time represented by that batting of an eyelid I realized that the news I had brought her—of my near abduction, rescue and subsequent conversation with Mr. Cochise—had been dismissed, a bagatelle hardly worthy of further debate. It was as I suspected. Miss Viva was, this evening, racked on the exigencies of the next few hours, not of the past, or even the present.

"He said he'd meet him for a showdown in the cathedral," said Miss Viva. "Wouldn't hear of me coming along. Wants to prove himself. Wants to show he can still work his old magic, with or without a Venusian by his side. Fool." I knew the present crisis would have to be resolved before Miss Viva would deign to attend to what had transpired at the reservoir, and I fell to meditating upon what I should do to bring about such a resolution. But my thoughts were as chaotic as the hotel room, its smashed enamel ewer and broken looking-glass testifying to the recent spasm of violence it had been subjected to prior to my arrival.

Miss Viva lay on the bed, a peignoir negligently draped over her shoulders and thrown half across her white, nude body. She smoked a cheroot. "Cockaigne's fast. He's good. We should have left town. We really should have left here long ago. But Mr. Twist has his pride. Dammit. And pride's going to get him killed." She stretched out an arm and twiddled the reception knob on the big, mahogany radio that stood atop the night table by her side. Ignoring the stations, she tuned the dial so that the receiver could pick up only static and indecipherable background noise.

"I sometimes get spirit voices," she said, "transmissions from across the frontier, sometimes transmissions all the way from Venus." She laughed, her laughter mirthless, hollow. "Times like this, I find I like to listen to the music of the dead. It reminds me of home. Now Mr. Twist, he never had much of a home. Never had much of a family. Consequently, Mr. Twist has always found talking and dealing with human beings somewhat difficult. You understand? Maybe that's why we've always got along. We're sort of alike, Mr. Twist and I. We're both exiles. He from the human race, me from my own people. Maybe that's why we deserve each other."

The radio hissed, Miss Viva running a hand over its Bakelite *relievo* as if to soothe it. Within those airwaves alive with contained, sibilant threat I seemed to hear the chittering sounds of a jungle, the clicking of chelicerae magnified a million times, as if the little beasts of that jungle's steaming, primeval floor had been subjected to a mad scientist's experiments such as I had witnessed in the B-movies I had watched back East, movies I had enjoyed even more than MGM musicals.

"Have you been drinking?" I said. "I mean, don't think me *censorious*. I like a drink myself." Miss Viva pulled a bottle out from under her pillow and tossed it across the space that separated us. I caught it; smiled back my thanks. "Miss Viva, would you think I was silly if I said I'd like to be like you?"

"Be like me? Why?"

"Because you have this life with Mr. Twist. This life of passion and adventure. You're going to be with Mr. Twist always, aren't you?"

"You're a necrophile?" she asked, quickly.

"I don't know."

71

"Think."

"Well, I guess I like things better than people."

"Oh, that's not it at all."

"Mostly things, at least. But I *really* like Mr. Twist."

"I wonder," she said airily, "should I be jealous then?" A roguish grin animated the dead flesh of her mouth.

"I don't know what I am," I said. "I just know I want to be like you."

"You have no idea, little girl, what you're talking about. Not really. If you did, you would—" She curled her lip becomingly, just like Elvis. "You would scream with fright." I took the cap off the bottle, raised the bottle's neck to my lips and swigged. "You know," she continued, "I've thought about what you said yesterday. Remember? About it being logical for me to want Mr. Twist dead? I've thought about it a lot. Indeed I have. So don't think I count your opinion for nothing. And I've come to the conclusion: why *shouldn't* I let that piece of swamp trash die? I mean, he goes off, with a skip in his step, without so much as a by your leave, just to shore up his stupid macho pride. He treats me like, like *dirt*."

"I don't want him to get shot, Miss Viva. I want both of you to stay here on Earth. How else can I be your friend?"

"There, you see, you *ain't* no necrophile. You can't bear to let go of this world. You humans, you're all the same. You all want to go to Desdichado, but you want to do it on your own terms." Desdichado. The name had set my teeth on edge, as if I had tasted a sharp but delicious fruit, something like a mango spiked with vinegar. Desdichado. It was the town, they said, that lay at the end of the line. The town that lay at the limits of the frontier. The last town. But I had no inclination, then, to question Miss Viva on what she knew of that mysterious place. My concerns, like hers, were of the here and now.

"Please, *I just want to be your friend*."

"Nice. But let me tell you something about Mr. Twist."

"It's all right, Miss Viva. I know about his nervous disability. I sympathize. I understand. Anyone would get the heebie-jeebies after the kind of trauma *he* suffered as a child."

"You understand nothing. Mr. Twist doesn't suffer from an attack of *nerves* when he looks down the barrel of a gun; it's the excitement he finds debilitating. The excitement of being so close to oblivion."

"I'm sorry," I said. "I didn't realize. I didn't mean to imply—"

"Forget it," said Miss Viva, "you're forgiven." I sucked on the bottle; tipped back my head. "I suppose, callow girl, you might genuinely find it difficult to comprehend how Mr. Twist feels. But get this straight: he's no coward. It's just that he's grown too used to fucking Death. 'Yeah, I fuck Death,' he tells his friends. 'I fuck her in bed, under the table, against the wall, out in the street. I pussy-fuck her, ass-fuck her, fuck her in the mouth, fuck her in the ear.'" I shifted from one foot to the other, uneasy at hearing Miss Viva talk so; that anxious inner life of hers that I had had an intimation of the previous night had burst to the surface, shattering her glacial exterior. "After we've made love, you know what he says when he's dragging on a little post-coital weed? He says '*Death where is thy victory, where is thy goddamned sting?*' Guy thinks he's the fucking lord of darkness. Which I tell you—" I took another hit of whisky—"he ain't." I walked over to her and placed the bottle back in her hand. I decided it might be better for us if we got drunk together. "When he comes face to face with another gunman, it's like he's on the threshold of the ultimate orgasm. You know what I mean? Fucking Death for so long, that is, *me*, he's picked up all these unfortunate associational reflexes."

"Yes, I think I know what you mean," I said, still a little intimidated by the violence of her outburst.

"It paralyzes him. Nothing to do with fear, you see. But

everything to do with being in a nigh apoplectic state of anticipation…of union, the perfect high."

"Is that what he feels when he makes love to you?"

"He feels a shadow of it, sweetie. If he'd ever felt the real thing he'd never have survived. The final pleasure, the best happiness, is in the loss of the self, its extinction."

"I like the sound of that," I said, a little abstractedly. "I think all I've ever really wanted to do is disappear." Then, seeing that Miss Viva was in danger of being carried off by the gentle confusion of her own thoughts, I brought myself and, I hoped, her back onto more empirical ground.

"We should help him," I said. "We should try to give him the edge he needs."

"I told you before: he doesn't *want* help."

"But without it—"

"Without it he's gonna find out about death's sting pretty damned quick I can tell you. Pretty…damn…quick." She drank a little whisky; set the bottle down on the nearby table, though with a hand still greedily holding it tight. Then, yielding to Lord Alcohol's blandishments, she picked the bottle back up and brought the neck once more to her lips, demonstrating that she, like me, was a devoted servant of milord and all his line. She swallowed again and again, rejoicing at the glug-glugging that, for our kind, had so many times proved the overture to operatic flights of inebriation. I let her have her fill; I myself needed no more. Soon, I knew—the whisky I had drunk already rampaging through my skull—I would be as immortal as her.

I could tell that, despite all she had said, Miss Viva still dreamed of a perfect wedding. She did not want Mr. Twist to die this night. And I could tell, by her present bitterness, that, if he should die, I would lose not only him, but her also. With Mr. Twist gone, my Venusian would surely not tarry on Earth. And I would be alone once more.

I turned to the window, and, as on the previous night, Miss Viva's reflected image was superimposed upon the cityscape outside, the cracked glass a photographic transparency that was a montage of beautiful spectre and night streets scored with oblique scratches of slicing rain. A jag of lightning split open the sky, long fingers of crinkly light momentarily fluttering about the spire of the cathedral beneath which Mr. Twist would be awaiting his destiny.

"If you won't help him, Miss Viva, then I must. I can't let him get killed when I've only just made his acquaintance. I'm sorry, but you're not to have him...leastways, not just yet. I want him to stay right where he is: on Earth. I want you both to stay on Earth. I don't want to lose either of you." No, I thought; I want to be with both you and the man whose soul you long to feed upon. I want to be your confederate, and you to be my friends. I have nothing else; I have no one else; and I want no one and nothing more. Of all the people I had met after leaving Boston and entering the West, they were the ones who most easily fitted into the chunk cut out of my heart so long ago. The ones who, if not able to cauterize that cruel, foul, suppurating wound, would pack it with the right obsessional gel until a proper transplant could be arranged. "Goodbye, Miss Viva."

Despite being almost as drunk as her, I snatched the bottle from her hands and took one last hit, then I slammed the bottle down on the table. A trickle of liquor tickled my chin, dripping onto the escutcheon that decorated the breast pocket of my school blouse, the one with the Sacred Heart of Jesus bisected by a bolt of lightning. It seemed to ally me now, not with Mademoiselle Moutarde, but with the storm outside, the heavenly conflagration that descended upon Tombstone with a ferocity that could not have been more intense if the city had been secretly renamed Gomorrah.

Miss Viva closed her eyes; her breathing grew shallow.

Perhaps it was the alcohol, or perhaps fatalism, but she had loosened her grip on this world as easily as she had loosened her hold on the whisky bottle, and now, behind those kohl-daubed eyelids, had set sail for the planes and dimensions most familiar to her, memories of the lands that lay in the far West, now only tangible in dreams. Her supine body was motionless; no sign of life disturbed its delicate lines, its sensual curves; not a twitch or a flicker indicated that the alien being that inhabited this semblance of a human form had not discorporated and returned to its home. It didn't really disturb me; I had, during the handful of days since I had first met her, come to accept that Venusians often seemed dead when most alive. Miss Viva, I knew, laid out as she was on that big, pale-sheeted bed just like a corpse, contained within herself a life-force so powerful that, should it be unconsciously released, would surely destroy most of Arizona. On tiptoe, in stockinged feet, I slunk out of the room. Then, re-shoeing myself, I went down onto the streets to hurry through the sheeted rain toward my murderous objective, the cathedral.

I must be like her, I thought, if I am to survive, if I am to bring both her and Mr. Twist within the purview of my own will. I must be accounted among storm maidens, ice maidens, death maidens and other queens of the night.

I must be a necrobabe.

Chapter Four
Odi Et Ammo

With visibility compromised—heavy rain screened off the surrounding buildings—I seemed to stand alone, as if under a gigantic bell jar of smoked glass streaming with condensation. Only the cathedral, clearly defined, lay within that bleary compass, its exalted stones my sole company. The square was deserted, and all sound of carriages or conversation was drowned out by the perturbation of rain against rooftops and cobbled streets.

I scurried across the square's bleak expanse and entered the cathedral by its western façade, its grey parallelogram surmounted by twin towers that the lightning had still not done with. The forked fingers of electric current fluttered above heaven-pointed vanes like the hands of a prestidigitator, a God who had tired of men's worship and had determined to reveal himself as a charlatan, a pugnacious fraud. Passing through the median of the triple portals, beneath the great rose window—the dimly illumined blues and reds of its radiating wheel depicting the Virgin and Child—I paused briefly to gaze at the statues in the embrasures on either side of the doors, apprehensive that their eyes were following me, that they were something more than carved rock. I walked on, and entered the interior.

The center aisle was signposted with candlesticks; to either side of it lay darkness and shadows. Reaching the threshold of the center aisle, I halted. The storm was directly overhead and the lightning-glare streaming through the stained-glass windows and the comparative dimness of the great space before me was pinking at my eyes like some torture involving fire and ice. The glass stretching along the nave exhibited angels, as if between color-splashed specimen slides, as well as prophets, evangelists, the lives of the saints, Christ and the Last Judgment. It also advertised the crafts of alchemy, psychogeography and electrospiritualism, sciences that, offering some nexus between the human and the alien, the West had made its own. The window celebrating alchemy was particularly beautiful, the personification of the alchemic muse, resplendent in golden robes, pointed, with one hand, to the Gothic script that circled her, *A* black, *E* white, *I* red, *O* blue, *U* green, the transmuted vowels symbolising the alchemy of the word. With her other, more mercenary hand, she pointed to a diagram of carbon atoms that had been rearranged to build the diamond fibre that the West sold to the outside world and that Boeing had recently begun to incorporate into its airframes.

I blinked and kneaded my eyes with my knuckles. Recovering, I shook, as far as I was able, my sodden plaits free of water, and then smoothed my hands over my blouse, the cheap, wet rayon sticking to my skin, a puddle collecting about me on the slabs of the floor. I lifted the hem of my big, flounced frock and fumbled for the derringer that still lay concealed in the folds of my underwear. Finding it, I brought it to my side, letting its barrel point downwards at the end of my right arm, trying to think of it, as I knew I should, as an extension of my body, my will. I pulled my shoulders back, breathed deeply, my left arm patting my skirt back into place.

I walked down the aisle and toward the transept, my progress made the more tentative by the monstrous noise made each time one of my Mary Janes descended upon a flagstone. The fanfare reverberated throughout the cathedral, announcing my sorry-looking arrival. But I was greeted only by stillness and shadows. I began to think that Miss Viva had been mistaken, or had even maliciously deceived me, for the cathedral seemed deserted, with no one at prayer—not even a priest to be seen—and certainly with no bad men on view.

The flickering play of the tapers fell across my path. I walked on, interrupted only by the lightning, its intensity such that, momentarily blinded, I would sometimes be brought to a standstill.

I reached the transept; looked north, then south. The south window, I noticed, delineated a group of Venusians as they had appeared when they first arrived on Earth a hundred years ago. These particular Venusians—life models, perhaps, or copied from an early photograph—had, like the being who was Miss Viva Venera, chosen to clothe themselves in female flesh. They gazed out from their two-dimensional arbor into the cathedral's shadowy depths, past me and past the inconsequential concerns of this world called Earth. They weren't exactly clones of each other, but they shared the same design characteristics, the same alien femininity: the sleepy, elliptical, somewhat oriental eyes that the artist had evoked by quoting Giotto; the small, button, china-doll noses; the paradoxically plump, yet virginal lips; the milky skin; the further paradox of the high, austere, yet puppy-fat plastered cheekbones. Along with their small-boned yet radically curvaceous bodies, this standardisation of effect seemed a cross-fertilisation of the Madonna by a strain of ultramundane whore, a *look* that must, though its true import was lost, have presented, to them, a deep cultural, technological and spiritual significance. Yes, I thought, as I allowed my gaze to settle upon each of the window's cast, how similar they all appear. Not sisters, exactly, but creatures sharing the traits of a particular phylum. Their hair, for instance, displayed a variety of hues, even styles, one coiffure a shaggy mane of ringlets and curls; one perfectly straight, as if each lank had spent many hours beneath the crush of a hundred-pound steam iron; and one a spiky, idio-syncratic little explosion of contrariness. But all obeyed a com-mon denominator: unvaryingly dishevelled, each bedraggled crimp, *cut en brosse* and perm suggested that its owner had recently emerged from a night-long session of feverish sexual gymnastics. And that common denominator extended to all other areas of individual cosmography, informing the features, limbs and bearing of each girl pictured in the colored panes of glass, uniting them as sisters, if not in fact, then in kind.

I frowned, disentangling myself from my reverie, a dream of fair women of whose number I would belong, by an impu-dent act of will if by nothing else.

I heard a rustling in the direction of the choir, like rats over discarded newspapers.

"Mr. Twist?" I whispered.

I ventured onwards, moving out of the illuminated aisle and into an ill-lit shadowland, the choir's banked stalls ris-ing on either side. The thud of my Mary Janes recalled me to my brief time in Mademoiselle Moutarde's establishment, when the dissimilar, but equally alarming sound of a pair of perambulatory stilettos such as were worn by the older girls could at once chill and thrill me. But though my stomach was being tossed and churned by what seemed microgravitational forces, my heart beat with gladness, expecting, as it did, to at any moment find haven in Mr. Twist's welcoming arms.

A hand closed over my mouth. Like the stupid, wretched little girl I really was, I dropped the derringer, but, despite the compression of time occasioned by my panic, I man-aged—pulled backwards, my unseen assailant bundling me into a dark recess—to reserve a moment to congratulate myself that I had had the forethought to kick the miniature gun under a stall.

"Don't scream," said a thin, but masculine voice, "you dig? You scream, I'm going to have to do unspeakable things to your personhood." My head yo-yoed an affirmation.

My assailant's hand tasted of nicotine and metal and liquor, the skull-and-crossbones rings on his fingers having that smoky, lead-like, alcohol-rich bouquet of strong beer. I gagged and, as he removed his hand, spat onto the floor. Gripping me by the shoulders, he turned me around to face him. I noticed that we were behind the choirscreen; that my back was to a thick, fluted column that seemed to sway like rubber as, striving to bring the man's face into focus, I lifted my chin and my brain succumbed to a giddy drainage of blood. I noticed that two statues of obscure saints flanked me, stern with pious dread. I noticed, more than anything—even as spots of light disported themselves behind my eyes—that my position afforded no easy escape.

"I'd thought me and the Twist had frightened everybody away," he said. "What're you still doing here? You the kind of sick individual who gets a kick out of watching a man die?"

"I'm Mr. Twist's friend," I said, "you're not to hurt me."

"Oh, oh, oh, a friend, eh? The Twist has friends apart from that Venusian cunt he hangs around with? Well, what do you know." He narrowed his eyes with calculation.

"You're Charles Cockaigne, aren't you?" The downturned mouth wrinkled his stubbly chin into a cleft. I wondered if all Englishmen looked the same as Mr. Cockaigne. His hair was black, greasy and quiffed, styled in the manner I believe is called a *ducktail*. And he had long sideburns. A spectacular zit decorated his left cheek. But it was in his manner of dress that he was most striking. A drape jacket with velvet collar (fish hooks sewed into its lapels) and a shoelace tie was combined with drainpipe pants. Looking down at the floor to avoid those mean, rodent eyes (there really *had* been a rat crawling around back here) I saw that his ensemble was completed by thick, crêpe-soled shoes, like Elvis or Gene Vincent sometimes wore. He was, I thought on consideration, not typical of the English race, but one of those teenage hoodlums that, in old Londontown, ran in gangs and were called "Edwardians". "You're Charles Cockaigne, from England?" I reiterated, eager to hear him assert his *bona fides*.

"I'm from the Elephant and Castle," he said, in a nasty growl. "All right?"

"Of course. I didn't mean—"

"You don't ask who Charlie Cockaigne is. You say Charlie Cockaigne? You think Charlie Feathers. You think Carl Perkins. Charlie Cockaigne? Charlie Cockaigne? You think Hank Mizell, Warren Smith, Billy Lee Riley, George Jones, Carl Mann, Hayden Thomson, Sleepy Labeef. Get the picture? I'm *famous*, you stupid little tart."

"Of course, Charlie. I know you are." His grip on my shoulders tightened, squeezing the puffy sleeves of my blouse so hard that rainwater squirted from between his fingers.

"You know, eh?" He swept aside his drape jacket so that I might see the iron slung at his right thigh, a Colt whose gunmetal was as dully black as Mr. Twist's was a bedazzlement of silver. "Well, you know Charlie Cockaigne, you got to know *rockabilly*. You got to—" He began to gyrate his hips, not frenetically, like The Pelvis, but slow, with a kind of greasy voluptuousness, in the manner of a lap dancer, down-and-dirty, giving more than you would expect for a nickel a ride. "You got to know *rationing*. You got to know that, when I was a boy, the word 'teenager' didn't exist. You got to know *national service*. You got to know about, about"—his face buckled; I thought he was about to retch with disgust—"*Rosemary Clooney*." His pelvic exhibitionism arrested itself in mid-circumvolution and he looked upward, transfixing the giddy vault with his ratty stare. My gaze followed his, a vertigo immediately infecting my brain, so that my legs became as spongy as the sleeves of my blouse, though streaming with perspiration rather than rainwater. "He's up there, the Twist is. Hiding from me. I fire a few rounds over his bleeding head, and he goes and legs it. Like a woman. Always said the Twist weren't quite the legend he's been made out to be." And then he looked down once again, squeezing my upper arms with such fervor that I was lifted off my feet. "What's your name?"

"Nicola E. Newton."

"Louder!"

"Nicola E. Newton!" I yelped, feeling the tips of his fingers bury themselves in my flesh.

"Hear that, Twist?" cried Mr. Cockaigne, throwing back his head and letting his thin, rasping voice rise up into the fan vaulting, like a blasphemer intent on having some part of himself, his best, worst, most lupine part, enjoy intimacy with God. "*Nicola…E…Newton!* Says she's a friend of yours. I got her right here. Why don't you come down from wherever it is you're hiding and I'll let her walk free so that she can go home and play with her dolls and act like a little girl should." He looked at me askance, and said more quietly, but more unpleasantly, "And not act in a way truly incompatible with all civilized notions of childhood and innocence."

"Childhood is a state of anarchy and rebellion as much as it's a state of grace," I blurted. Despite the imminent threat to my life, I felt defiant and ready to reassert my unseasoned but radical intelligence. "I said childhood is—" My words were drowned out by a reprise of Mr. Cockaigne's challenge.

"Don't hide behind a little girl's skirts, Twist," he howled. "Come out where I can see you!"

"Up here, Cockaigne," came the reply. I looked to where the voice had emanated and discovered, peering over the stone balustrade of a gallery high above our heads, the thin, rangy, black-clad figure of Mr. Twist. "Let Miss Newton go."

"Not until I've got you in my sights, Twist. You're a slippery bastard, you are. Don't move. Okay? I'm coming to…have a little *talk* with you."

I was propelled forward, Mr. Cockaigne keeping a firm grip on me as he ran from the choir and into the transept. About us, the flagstones, anointed by the lightning-crazed windows, were lit with fitful splashes of brilliance. Charlie Cockaigne herded me through an arch leading to a spiral staircase.

With one arm held behind my back, I was shoved up the stone helix of the transeptal tower, my shins banging against the timeworn steps, skin breaking, blood trickling through my torn socks, shoes slipping off and tumbling down the stairs in a little two-part harmony of patent leather and steel-reinforced heels. No words were spoken; pusher and pushed were consumed with the task of rising up the endless screw that promised to deliver them to the spot from which Mr. Twist had addressed them. Panting, legs on fire as if they had been chastised with stinging nettles, lungs aching, I concentrated on each upcoming swerve of the ascent, hoping that the blind corner that lay ahead would give onto a horizontal. And then the torture ended; I found myself in a narrow aisle, another torture—trial by gunfire—about to commence.

Mr. Cockaigne released me, his attention all upon the man who stood several yards distant, the man whom the world seemed to refer to simply as "The Twist." Legs splayed, my hero flung back the skirt of his coat in a way that brought to mind the occasion when he had shot up the zanies who had attacked our stagecoach, picking them off like tin ducks at a fair. I hunkered at the foot of the balustrade; looked fleetingly down at the floor of the cathedral far below, and then, resisting a sudden mad, sickening inclination to hurl myself over the balustrade's lip and be sucked into the nothingness that informed the dimensions of the cathedral's walls, I looked up and refocused on the aisle. In the shadows, the two men seemed as if set in a block of dirty ice, frozen in the cold intensity of their confrontation.

"So," said Mr. Cockaigne, "you ready to renounce further discussion and consider, in a real and practical sense, the *meaning* of life? You ready to enter into a more-than-intellectual enquiry regarding the *great beyond*?"

"You ready to concede," replied Mr. Twist, "that you are a man given wholly to materialism, one who would destroy the life of a fellow human creature solely for the sake of the pitiful bounty on his head?"

Mr. Cockaigne shrugged, exasperated. "Certainly I concede. I *am* a bounty hunter. Doing very well, I'd have you know. Getting on. Paying my way. You've got to go that extra mile if you want to succeed, if you want *nice things*. And the bounty on your head's not so *pitiful*, Twist. Don't do your reputation a disservice by saying so."

"I'm sure I'm willing to go that extra mile too, Charlie. But not for things. Not for money. You want to know what makes life truly *meaningful* for me? The knowledge that someday I'm gonna walk down that same highway of celestial light that I first put foot on when I was a boy. I'm not frightened of taking a bullet. In fact, *my* problem is I'm sometimes a little *too* eager."

"Meaning for you lies in death?"

"Meaning for me lies on the other side of life."

"You *want* to die?"

The paralysis that Miss Viva talked of—the excitement of being so near to crossing the bar—seemed to infuse Mr. Twist's nervous system; but then, with a shiver that expelled the surplus energy that threatened to short circuit him, he regained his dead-eyed pep.

"No, not yet, at least," he said. "And not by your hand. I guess you could call me pernickety. But I see my end in a sloughing off of this world, not in an embrace of it."

"So then, you're disputing me?"

"Eschatologically speaking, I am, Charlie."

"Then let us debate last and final matters in the way we know best. Care to draw?"

"After you, Charlie."

"Oh no, no, no, after *you*."

It was as he spoke that *you* that Mr. Cockaigne, hoping, I think, to sucker his opponent by having his draw coincide with a gracious, if somewhat inappropriately effete concession to courtesy, fired. The fiery tongue of the gun's discharge bore a tunnel through the shadows, a tunnel that caved in—the shadows had immediately closed—even as the whip crack of detonation snaked at my ears and stung my tympanic membrane.

Mr. Twist did not fall. He did not return fire. Mr. Twist, with an spasm of speed equal to his enemy's draw, had disappeared. For a moment the Englishman stood as still as the stones that were piled about him, a latter-day knight errant a basilisk had worked its magic on. He seemed transformed into the same stuff as the cathedral, a statue in honor of the town's predilection for guns, gunmen and violent death. And then, with a flash of lightning revealing the archway that, it became obvious now, Mr. Twist had sidestepped through, he shook himself and raced after his prey. I pulled myself upright and followed, less swiftly but with a determination to somehow aid Mr. Twist in whatever extremity he found himself.

Mr. Cockaigne vanished under the arch. When I too had reached that same point I stumbled to a halt, arms extended, hands against the sides in the manner of one crucified, bracing myself as I took in the sight that met me.

The portal gave way onto the outside, a battlement that

ran about the base of the spire. Rain swept across its stonework, the angry, white pyrotechnics of the storm lighting up the figures of the gunslingers whose feud seemed to be provoking the wrath of the one whose house they profaned. Mr. Twist stood against an embrasure, insouciant, his feet placed either side of a machicolation, as if he were preparing to drop himself, as others had once dropped boiling lead upon approaching foes; or rather, as if Mr. Cockaigne, who stood with his back to me, pistol levelled at his adversary's chest, were preparing to drop him.

Neither option resulted. Mr. Twist, snapping his legs together, fell but three or four feet into the space between the corbels, the structure doubtless modified to prevent unwary tourists from plunging to their deaths. At the same moment as he fell, the bounty hunter's gun spat out a plume of flame, a bullet flying over Mr. Twist's head and ricocheting (there was an accompanying shower of flint) off the stones behind him. Mr. Twist had drawn, and I understood now that cunning, for a shootist, is a more valuable attribute than merely being fast.

Struggling to find his balance, and thus denied a shot which would have put a hole through the Englishman's heart, Mr. Twist managed, nevertheless, to score high on the left shoulder, spinning his man around and backwards. I had to jump clear of the archway to prevent myself being knocked over by Mr. Cockaigne's flailing arms and jerking legs as he stumbled into the cathedral's interior. However, I didn't jump smartly as to prevent the wounded man's good arm from encircling my throat. Squeaking like a piglet, I was carried along by his spastic trajectory into the shadows and, tipping over the balustrade, into space.

We fell together, I locking into his embrace with the desperate notion that I could somehow reascend to some eminence of safety by using his body as a ladder. The topsy-turvy vision I had had of the cathedral—glass and stone tracery in inverted lancets, ribbed vaulting that had usurped the ground—righted itself as my pilot performed an attitudinal correction, turning one-hundred-and-eighty degrees through the air so that he fell feet first. In a second or two, this plunge would drive his knees into his jaw, concertina his vertebrae and likewise despatch me to whatever torments awaited in that circle of Hell reserved for runaways and truants.

As I pedalled, legs engaged in a hopeless attempt to find purchase in the air, there was a loud purr. Looking down, I saw that the felid buzz emanated, not from another living creature, but from Mr. Cockaigne's spurs which had snagged in the long, velvet curtain that hung from the ambulatory to the floor. As the spurs cut more deeply into the fabric, the velvet seemed to come alive, rolling itself about his feet and calves, as if, indeed, the curtain had revealed its true nature, metamorphosing itself into a cat whose elastic limbs were playfully waylaying its master. A savage jerk, and the conceit dissolved. The curtain, checking our momentum, had acted like a bungee cord, tipping us so that our heads again pointed to *terra firma* before, bouncing us twice in the air, it was ripped from its fittings. With merciful gentleness, we found ourselves deposited upon the floor, our velvet caul gradually yielding as we attempted to claw our way free of its smothering attentions. At last we tumbled out, rolling across the cold, stone slabs.

I recovered from the shock of our descent far more quickly than Mr. Cockaigne; and I used that edge provided by my youth's vitality to immediately crawl under the choirstalls. Through a gap between a misericord and the floor I saw Mr. Cockaigne rise, his unsteady feet taking him first one way, and then the other. "Twist!" he shouted. "You've really done it now, Twist. I mean, I got to climb all those steps again just to make sure that you don't escape me a *second* time? I *hate* it when someone plays tricks on me. And just look at my threads! My drape, my strides! Do you realize how much a jacket like this *costs*?" Dust pricked at my nostrils as I slithered on my belly into the dark depths of my hideaway. I had spotted a glint of silver and, hoping that it was not merely small change that had escaped the gown of a chorister, I crept toward it, one finger under my nose in an attempt to forestall a sneeze. After several yards of such endeavor, and several minutes of having to endure Mr. Cockaigne's increasingly shrill peroration on the subject of his tailor and Mr. Twist's unsportsmanlike conduct, I stretched out a hand and felt under my palm the familiar contours of the little handgun I had purloined, so many days, so many years ago it seemed, now, from Miss Viva's purse. Clutching it tightly in my grimy fist, I began to wriggle my way toward the candlelight that poured through the slivers and cracks of what promised to be an exit. A loose panel, easily pulled free of its surround, allowed me to pass from the congested darkness of my sanctum into the meager but welcome light of the sacristy.

As I got to my feet, feeling like a chimney-sweep's assistant, a water baby badly in need of her elemental home, I saw Mr. Cockaigne turn into the transept, a hand on his bloodied shoulder. Impatient for his man to descend and be killed, the wounded hunter was ready to once more climb up into the middle air there again to do battle in the lightning-licked central tower.

"Charlie," I said. He turned about, the skirts of his long jacket describing a wide, swinging arc, his crêpe-soled shoes squeaking like tortured rodents as he pirouetted on his Edwardian axis. "I can't let you hurt Mr. Twist, Charlie." He studied me with bemusement. I held the derringer behind my back, and he must have wondered at my brazen importunity, so much so that it had the effect of defanging him, for he did not raise the good arm that still held fast to his pistol. "Mr. Twist and Miss Viva are going to help me, you see. They're going to help me get out of Tombstone. They're going to help me get to the frontier. I can't let you spoil that." His eyes were thunderous, his brow like corrugated iron, but his mouth turned up at one corner in a concession to amusement, as if to take a little chit like me at her word might somehow unman him. "If I'd have met *you* on that stagecoach that brought me here, maybe things might have been different. You live outside the law too, don't you? You have appalling manners, Charlie, but perhaps, despite of everything, we could have been friends instead of enemies. It's too late, of course, to think upon that. All I know is I have to stop you before you ruin any hopes I have of the future. Sorry, Charlie, but that's the way it has to be. If it's any consolation: I hate you for what you're trying to do, but I love you for what you are. You have genuine roughhouse *style*."

I lifted a hand, revealing the derringer gleaming in my fist. Too late, Mr. Cockaigne recognized my intent, raising his arm to countermand the order I was even then giving the small, hard, vicious relative of his own weapon, one that was in no mood for family reconciliation. The derringer barked. Mr. Cockaigne grunted, a red stain similar to that which surrounded the hole in his left shoulder now complementing the hole that had suddenly opened up in his right. His arm fell; his hand went into spasms, and his pistol clattered onto the stones.

"Oh *Jesusssss*!"

In slo-mo, Mr. Cockaigne fell backwards, hitting the floor spreadeagled with the sound of a balloon filled with sheep's guts, bursting.

I moved toward the body, unsure whether I approached a corpse or a still living and still dangerous man, the derringer all the while giving off a smell that, though one I was familiar with, seemed, at that moment, particularly fragrant. I knew from now on cordite would always be my perfume of choice.

The body twitched. I came to a halt, the derringer a dead weight in my hand by virtue of its single round, spent and irreplaceable by one who had been unable to find or steal further cartridges. "Charlie? Have you expired yet?" I enquired, seeing that the body had become quiescent.

"Stay away from him, Miss Nicola," said a voice. I looked to my left. Mr. Twist stood leaning against the curving pillars that served as a gateway to the staircase leading up into the tower.

"Did I do well, Mr. Twist?"

"You sure did."

"You said you would teach me how to shoot. Remember?"

"You might need a little coaching. But that shot did the trick, that's for sure, even if it was a teeny-weeny bit off center. Lord, if the round *I'd* loosed off had been better aimed I might have saved you some work. We are but human, Miss Nicola." Mr. Twist's eyelids drooped as he assumed his characteristic snake-like look of pitiless introspection, his gaze running across the fallen bounty hunter's body, toe to head, head to toe. "Now wait a minute," he murmured, as if to himself, "just wait a minute here." He walked toward me, gesturing that I should step to one side, his pistol raised to cover any eventuality.

Without warning, Mr. Cockaigne sprang into a sitting position, his teeth gritted as, with one, huge pained effort, his right arm, gainsaying the mashed gristle and bone that should have left him immobilized, reached inside his drape and pulled out what I recognized to be a machine pistol, the kind of thing the Israelis like to engineer during long, lonely nights in the kibbutzim. Mr. Twist, however, did not fire; nor did he try to escape, as he had done when pressed into a shoot-out in the gallery above.

"Haven't you learnt anything about the West, Charlie?" he said.

Mr. Cockaigne squeezed the trigger of his weapon. There was no response.

And then Mr. Twist *did* fire. It was a shot that opened up a crater in the bridge of the Englishman's nose. Mr. Cockaigne slumped back onto the stones, a real wax mannequin now, for sure, no confusing *that* tailor's dummy with the living.

"Mmm. Nice symmetry," said Mr. Twist. "A bullet through each shoulder and now"—he whistled through his teeth—"let's just say I've always been a pushover for a good ol' triangulation." He strode over to the fresh corpse and stood astride it. "Newcomers like him never learn, Miss Nicola. Things that work in the outside world don't always have currency here. Particularly things like *weapons*. We're inside a psychogeographic event. The West has its own laws, its own ways of doing things, a *modus vivendi* that's been established over long years, in the knowledge of terrible war and devastation. You just can't import something like a *machine pistol* in here and expect it to function as it normally would. The collective alien intelligence that created the West just won't have it. You might as well try to import a Cadillac, an airplane, a telephone or a TV."

He gave the corpse a playful kick. "The West, Charlie," he said, addressing the newly departed, "is a land that has been warped and modified by a people that *love* us. The West will allow us to exercise free will, it will allow us to live, cheat, fornicate and murder—oh yes, it will most *particularly* let us murder—but it will not allow us to indulge ourselves in autogenocide. No modern, potentially *mass-destructive* tech gets in here, that's the rule. Ol' Charlie Cockaigne, you really should have accepted the parameters of the new universe you so blithely walked into. If you'd gone to an *alchemist*, for instance, you might have been able to pull something that would have truly given me cause to fret."

He took his hat off and held it over his heart. "Death is the ultimate transformation," he said, by way of an impromptu elegy, "the final sea-change. After all the masks have been ripped off, this last disillusionment is the only gateway we can look forward to as offering us the possibility of turning our backs on this wretched world so that we may be…somewhere else." He replaced the hat on his head. "Men like us, Charlie, we have a core, at which lies the problem of becoming who one already is, of being authentic. And then, at one onion-peel remove, there's the Punch-and-Judy layer, the riff involving the narrator and his amoral moll, or muse, the girl who is beyond Good and Evil. Did you ever have a girl like that, I wonder, Charlie? And then we have the outer skin, the shifting patterns of the real, that is, the world, mirroring the uncertainty of our self-hood; the world and all its correspondences of sex and violence. Ah, Charlie, damn you and farewell, and rest in peace beyond this vale of sadness, this place of onion-peel masks."

A howl rose from beneath the rose window. Something was approaching us, loping down the nave from the direction of the western façade. Goose-pimples rose on my arms and I felt the desert's night-time chill in my bones. I began walking backwards, my gaze fixed upon the pale form that approached, swift yet steady, lit by the avenue of candlesticks that stretched down the center aisle. It's a zany, I thought. They've breached the city's defences; they'll kill us all, take us back to their cliff-top lairs and marinate us for a midnight feast. But then as the white shade grew closer and its appearance became more distinct—the candlelight lambent upon its hoary coat, so that the creature seemed bioluminescent—the thing that I had taken for a zany was revealed as a wolf, a white wolf with bright, ice-blue eyes.

"Mr. Twist—" I shouted, the tremulousness of my voice, I hoped, providing enough semantic content to inspire him to put a slug in the beast, even if words had failed to communicate the full extent of my terror. The wolf continued its run. Near, now, so near that I could hear its breath, almost feel, upon my skin, the cold spray of spittle that lathered its jowls; and then, as it reached the end of the aisle, it seemed to become elongated and at the same time to rear up on its hind legs. Its snout disappeared, its fur seemed to rush toward its head, and a dress materialized just as the torso, clouded by what might have been an aura of ectoplasm, firmed into the contours of a small-boned but well-rounded young woman.

Gliding out of that backdrop of candlelight and shadows, so smoothly, so quietly, she seemed almost to be floating an inch or so above the floor, the Venusian known as Viva Venera drew up to my side and took my hand in her own.

"Mr. Twist," she said, "you were right, and I was wrong. You *did* manage to handle things by yourself." She slurred a little, and her cheeks were flushed, but her recent alcoholic binge had seemed to have left her otherwise unaffected.

"Not quite, darlin'," he said, smiling at me, as if Miss Viva's polymorphic show-stopper had been nothing unusual. "Cockaigne was fast. I had to get tricksy…and rely on a little fortuitous help." He winked. "The cosh boy," he concluded, with a nonchalant shrug and a nod toward the outstretched body, "is dead."

I cleared my throat, ostentatiously. "You're late, Miss Viva."

"It's Mr. Twist who's late, Nicky," she said in an undertone, her familiarity new and hugely pleasant. "Or should be. The late Mr. Twist. Isn't that right?" She smiled at the one whose soul was hers.

"Yo."

"I wasn't going to intervene unless I really had to. It's time Mr. Twist got some of his confidence back. But he should know I can't wait forever."

"Over the years your patience has done you credit," said Mr. Twist. "You can wait a little longer, darlin'. I *know* you can."

"He did seem," I said to Miss Viva, pleasure at her warmth translating itself into prattle, "well, how can I put it…*careful*? I

think you might be kept waiting a good many years yet. Yes, I
was surprised, indeed I was, that he exercised such care, such
restraint, Mr. Twist being such a good shot and all. I mean, just
look at how he took out those zanies!"

"As I've explained, shooting zanies and shooting an armed
man are not quite the same thing for Mr. Twist," said Miss Viva.
"You looking for a hero? Don't be. Not if you want to be like me,
my sweet. Heroes do not appeal. Not even the tragic variety. I
go"—she lowered her eyes in an ironic display of passion—"for
little boys lost. But maybe you'll come to understand all this
in the coming days."

"I'm to accompany you then?" I said, summoning up my
best smile.

"Isn't that what you want?" Miss Viva sighed. "Isn't that
what you've *always* wanted? Why should we deny the inevitable? You saved Mr. Twist's life." I looked down at the derringer,
turning it in my hands.

"Do you resent me for that?"

"For saving Mr. Twist's life? No, I think I can allow you
that. But"—her gaze followed my own—"I really *ought* to
resent your purloining of my handgun." I blushed and she
laughed. And then she took my hands in hers and folded
my fingers about the gun's warm metal. "A present. From me
to you. Thank you, Nicky. You were with Mr. Twist when he
once again escaped death. You're part of our journey now." She
released her grip; and then I felt long nails digging into my
cheeks as, angling my head, forcing me to stand on tiptoe, she
leant over, brought her own head down and placed her lips
on my mouth.

The sensation that followed resembled something that
might have been communicated by a tarantula crawling along
the roof of my mouth and disappearing into my gullet. My
teeth tingled, and then seemed to vibrate, each nugget of cal-
cium like a struck tuning fork, high-pitched notes combining

in a chorale of demented children's voices, a monotonous *Om* chanted by hysterical cherubs that shook my skull, my jaw, my spine. The noise—it was painful now, an ache that was becoming a searing riot of flame—tore down my vertebrae and into my legs to be finally conducted into the stone floor through the splayed toes of my stockinged feet. The cathedral seemed filled with star-bursts.

Miss Viva withdrew her lips with a big *smack*! and, corresponding to the firework display that had erupted along my optic nerves—so much more violent, more marvellous, than the storm outside—a tiny blue flash emanated from the corners of her wet, thickly-painted mouth, as if she were a fire-eater who had still a little paraffin left over from her act. She drew back and looked at me with a certain fastidious, pretty beetling of her forehead.

"Yes, Nicola, you're a big girl now, and part of our journey. Our long, long journey to the edge of things. And beyond." She put a hand to her mouth, as if checking that her lips were free of the residua of our recent intimacy. "The price on Mr. Twist's head keeps pushing us farther and farther West. Toward the frontier. But are you sure, absolutely sure that's where you want to go?"

I nodded vigorously. "I have to run away," I said. "And the farther I get from *here* the better. Here is so cruel," I swallowed hard, "and so boring."

"Then it's the train we need," said Miss Viva. "The railroad that begins west of Tombstone. If we ride out now we can catch the morning express. But the train will have to pass through Utah and Nevada before we can think about reaching California. Space-time becomes quite radically bent after you leave Arizona Territory. And it gets wilder the nearer you approach the frontier. After California, it's pure madness."

"Will it take long?" I said. "We must travel millions of miles!"

"The journey will be long, yes. The train is fast. We will cover, perhaps, as much as thirty thousand miles in a day. But it will be some time before we reach our objective."

Mr. Twist had grabbed the bounty hunter by his boots and pulled him into an alcove. He joined us now, putting his arms about his two women.

"And beyond the madness, ladies, beyond the crazed insanity of the corridor that connects the worlds, that's where we'll find our home."

"So," I said, "we're going all the way to Desdichado?"

Mr. Twist waved a hand toward the giddy vault like the ham actor he was. "Desdichado! City of Night! Indeed, Miss Nicola, indeed, indeed, we are heading out to the farthest limits of the West. Desdichado! Yes! There the West is beaucoup Wild! There the sun sets…and there it rises!" He held his arms aloft, as if he meant, through grace bestowed by some kind of anti-gravity, to dive into the cathedral's loft; and then he began to rotate. "Ah, ladies, ladies—the moral conviction of Gothic architecture!"

My own mood, as well as that of my companions, was so ebullient that, though I felt duty bound to remind Miss Viva of the message I had earlier brought her—that is, from her fellow Death, Mr. Cochise—I was fearful that by doing so my prospect of happiness, fragile as it was, might be fatally compromised. I was about to commit duty to my mental trash can when it occurred to me that a commitment to what might turn out to be even grander adventure could only cement the link that had grown between us, underwriting her affection and making it permanent. I had, in the last few days, engineered a friendship that promised to free me from my bondage to family and home. If that friendship should blossom into love, what services might she and Mr. Twist not do for me?

I pulled out the manitou's business card. "You remember

what I said to you back in the hotel, Miss Viva? About the man who wanted to see you?"

"Oh," she said, her expression suddenly, but not atypically, drained of all life. "Yes, I suppose I do remember. What of it?"

"Should we go to see him, do you think? Before we head out for the frontier, that is? He seemed a *nice* man." Miss Viva blew out her cheeks and then allowed the air to escape in a piqued spasm of violent decompression.

"What's all this about, Viva?" said Mr. Twist, his afflatus punctured, and suddenly brought down to Earth.

"Oh, it seems there's another Death in town. A Death from another world. Wants me to go see him."

"I think it's important, Miss Viva," I said.

Miss Viva raised an eyebrow. "It always is, Nicky," she said. "It always is."

"We shouldn't linger in this town, darlin'," said Mr. Twist. "Not after tonight. The law's gonna be out looking for us."

"We'll clear this little matter up with"—and she reluctantly studied the gold-bordered card—"with this *Cochise*, and then we'll be on our way." She looked down at me, forcing her lips into a placatory smile. "Don't worry, Nicky, you *will* go to Desdichado. You will. Really you will."

Mr. Twist again held his arms aloft and began to rotate. Not, this time, so much the celebrant of the dark urgings of his blood, as a man submitting to an ungovernable fate. And, coming to rest, holding us tight, he led us out of the cathedral and into the rain-lashed streets of the Town Too Tough To Die.

Chapter Five

Nicola's Adventures Underwelt

I pulled my boater over my eyes; rainwater spilled from the brim, a little water finding its way between my cuff and wrist, coursing down my arm like an icy, subterranean rivulet. Putting my mouth to the intercom, I announced myself. "Nicola E. Newton. You remember me, Mr. Cochise? I've brought Miss Viva here. And Mr. Twist, too."

The rain, since we left the cathedral, had been unceasing. And the air had grown chill. We had stopped briefly at the *Birdcage* for Miss Viva to change her clothes and for Mr. Twist to restock with ammunition (The hat I had borrowed from Miss Viva was far too big for me but served the purpose of keeping my head dry.). After taking a hansom into Boot Hill, we now stood outside the dwelling—tall, turreted and as funereal as the other habitations in this precinct, if standing in its own grounds—that the card I had been given identified as belonging to the manitou.

"Please. It's very wet out here. Won't somebody let us in?" I heard muffled, distorted voices and then a click as the intercom was shut off. I looked up. The door of the gatehouse had been thrown open and a man in uniform walked toward me, his form picked out by the stutter of the electrical storm. Hunched, he drew up to the gates, eyes dull beneath the black overhang of his peaked cap. Through the bars, I offered him the card that Mr. Cochise had given me. His gaze flitted between the card and my face, as if he were looking for some kind of correspondence between the scrawled, and by now hopelessly smudged, characters and whatever briefing he had received concerning my unfamiliar phiz. Evidently satisfied, he took a key from the recesses of a greatcoat that had been hurriedly slipped over his shoulders and fumbled with the big padlock looped between the ribs of the ornamental iron gates. The padlock came loose. The gates swung back, allowing a narrow ingress. I walked through, followed by my friends, head tucked into the folds of my upturned lapels, gravel crunching beneath my feet.

As we matched the guard's steps, I kept my gaze on the house. The windows along the lower floors were lit with a sallow, lugubrious light. Ahead, in the barren courtyard beneath the house's façade, were a few buggies. A horse, slung with a travois, was tethered nearby. A row of totem poles formed a portico.

I strode on, my torso bent at a forty-five degree angle to the oncoming squall, the light from the house resolving into little rainbows by way of the rain that clung to my eyelashes. Some ten yards before we reached the porch, the door opened. An elderly Apache woman stepped back into the hallway and allowed us to make a hurried entrance.

She was thin, her cheeks incurved from toothlessness, their state of collapse accentuated by the rigor with which her hair had been pulled back from her face and secured in a cannonball of a bun.

I removed my boater. Miss Viva turned, about to offer the guard thanks; but he was already scurrying back along the path. I passed a hand over my face, the thin woman's attention demure but unsparing. Her long fingers smoothed down the folds of her riding-habit. "I am Mr. Cochise's housekeeper," she said, licking her lips, long witch's tongue gliding lovingly over what looked like scar tissue, that mouth having been cracked and frayed, perhaps, by the dryness of her life's affective Sahara or, more probably, as a result of having in its time kissed a fist or two or three. "This way," she said, curtly.

We walked steadily down the hall, its walnut-panelled walls hung with bows, arrows, tomahawks, peace pipes and other Indian antiquities and bric-à-brac. Dusty vitrines displayed shards of pottery, tribal fetishes and other pieces of native art. Mounted along the hall's cornice the petrified skins of several stuffed animals struck poses of panic and terror: stoats, weasels, foxes, otters. All looked down as if to warn that what had befallen them might easily befall me. Lowering my shoulders, as if fighting against the wind that I could still hear blowing outside, I clove to the old woman's shadow. Soon, we stood before a heavy oak door that suggested the entrance to the cell of a monk, or of a madman, a real-life Man in the Iron Mask, perhaps, interred in marginally more civilized conditions than his fictive counterpart.

The housekeeper spun about; looked down at me. I thought she might be about to snatch me up and carry me off to her gingerbread cottage, so witch-like did she appear. But instead, she knelt, so that her face was level with my own; smiled, and took from her pocket a bag of rock candy, proffering it so as to encourage me to sample her wares. "To help you sleep, little one," she whispered, conspiratorially, "and to give you beautiful dreams." I dipped my hand into the bag and pulled out a black sugarplum. I popped it into my mouth, and then, thinking better of it, retrieved it with my fingers and deposited it in my frock pocket, my eyelashes batting furiously in an effort to convey both my thanks and my intention to eat it later. The woman stood up, her smile still in place, faced the door and knocked.

There was a dry-as-dust *"Come."* Our escort opened the door, stepped aside, and then held out an arm to indicate that we should enter. I obeyed dumbly, continuing to lead, like a regimental mascot elected to go on point. Miss Viva and Mr. Twist followed, Miss Viva's hands resting on my shoulders, as if to reassure me. The door closed, the snap of its latch echoing off the bare walls and high ceiling.

I essayed a few steps forward, freeing myself of Miss Viva's constraint, edging toward the big desk that dominated the room's spartan surround, staring up at the manitou who sat behind it.

"I am glad that you could fulfil my errand, Nicola," said Mr. Cochise. He eased himself back into the encompassing wings of his chair. He looked away from me and concentrated his attention on Miss Viva. "Good evening to you, Death."

"Good evening to *you*, Death," said Miss Viva.

Fumbling with, and then flipping open the lid of a little silver casket, Mr. Cochise extracted a cigarillo; put the cigarillo between his full, red lips and lit up with a heavy, marble-inlaid lighter. Behind his desk hung a map of the United States. It was an old map, perhaps one he had acquired when he had first arrived in the West. Though faint, the outlines of California were still clearly visible. In the atlases I had studied at school, a portion of the state was missing, replaced by an area of black, such as had filled in the area of central Africa in nineteenth-century maps. That swathe of black cut through America's west in all modern cartographies; not because such land was *terra incognita*, but because of the demands of national security. For a few seconds, I forgot everything else and stared at the cracked, faded representation of the old West, wondering at the fact that I stood at a point of its latitude and longitude that no longer existed. Or rather, had been transformed in such a way that it constituted part of "darkest America", a parallel universe, a bridge that, though only known to the outside world as a blanked-out strip of land between the Rockies and the Pacific, formed a million-mile physical link with Venus.

Someone coughed, reminding me where I was. I tore my gaze from the map, took off my hat, and sat opposite the desk in one of the chairs provided, the boater crouched on my lap like a miserable, rain-soaked marsupial. Miss Viva and Mr. Twist sat down to either side of me.

I was near to being overcome by weariness, the sallow illumination that pervaded the room, indeed, the entire house, along with the monotonous sound of rain dashing against the windowpanes, insidiously soporific.

"I will come straight to the point," said Mr. Cochise, his gaze never leaving Miss Viva. "There is another Death in Tombstone, beside we two; a Death from the world of Niflheim."

"Hmm," said Miss Viva. "Niflheim. Yes. I've visited it, many years ago." She glanced at the mortal whose soul she longed to devour. "Long before I met *you*, Mr. Twist." And then she redirected her gaze back at Mr. Cochise. "But how is this possible? Only a handful of death-worlds have the technology to allow their Deaths to journey to other worlds, and Niflheim isn't one of them."

"It seems you are out of touch. They do have the technology. And now we have one of their number on Earth, in the West, attempting to sell Washington all kinds of weapons. Infernal stuff. Weapons that make H-bombs, or E-bombs, look like toys."

"I thought the E-bomb was a kind of *ne plus ultra* of big bangs," said Mr. Twist.

"The E-bomb, if it were ever deployed on Earth, would represent the quintessence of Venusian power," said Miss Viva. "In many respects, a Venusian *is* an E-bomb, that is, a construct of electrospiritual energy. The release of such power is devastating. But I believe Mr. Cochise is talking about another order of magnitude entirely. I believe Mr. Cochise," she said, addressing him with a proud inclination of her head toward the ceiling, "is talking about a Q-bomb."

"Are you a scientist, Miss Viva? On your home world, I mean?" I said, fighting against the sandman who was singing his lullaby inside my skull, the sandman who threatened to cover me in a mantle of sweet exhaustion and send me sailing into dreamland.

"I'm many things, munchkin. Suffice to say I know enough about the Q-bomb to know that it musn't be developed. By anyone. It's monstrous."

"Q-bomb?" drawled Mr. Twist. "Over the years I've had enough trouble getting my mind about this E-bomb business. Now what the hell is a Q-bomb?"

"Supersymmetric particles clump to form an object called a Q-ball," said Miss Viva, talking very quickly. "Superbomb possibilities arise because the laws of physics inside a Q-ball are not the same as those in the outside universe. Inside a Q-ball, those alien laws should permit a proton to disintegrate into its constituent quarks, something forbidden in the everyday world. And that would unleash the energy that binds the quarks together. It is possible to assemble a Q-ball from supersymmetric particles, such as squarks. And once you actually have a Q-ball all you have to do is fire a beam of protons at it. Once inside the Q-ball, the protons will break apart, liberating their binding energy."

"Ka-boom?" asked Mr. Twist.

"Ka-boom indeed," said Miss Viva. "A bomb that releases *electrospiritual* energy is something to inspire terror. But a Q-bomb—"

"What would it do, Miss Viva?" I said, unaccountably aroused.

"Do? It would unseam space-time, Nicky. It would mean

the end of the world. The end of all life on this planet. It is a doomsday weapon."

"The bomb would be customized, of course," said Mr. Cochise.

"Of course," said Miss Viva, "they always are. Customized so that the souls of the billions it killed were reserved for the delectation of the Death that made the weapon."

"So," said Mr. Cochise, "would you wish to see a rogue Death from Niflheim use such a weapon to eat the Earth?"

Miss Viva swallowed. "No, I wouldn't. I have done many bad things during my recent tenure on Earth. Un-Venusian things. I have even killed without love. But I cannot bear to think of humanity being eaten by an energy-form from Hell."

"Then you will help me?"

"Mr. Twist and I, and our new friend, Miss Nicola, had hoped to leave town. We feel we may have overstayed our welcome. But if what you say is true I must help you. What do you require of me?"

"I need to gain entrance to our enemy's lair. And for that, I need the assistance of one versed in psychogeography. The enemy's house is in Boot Hill, nearby, in fact. But her real dwelling-place lies deep below the house, in a great under-ground chamber that she has engineered, so big it is something of a town itself, another town beneath the town of Tombstone. It is fortified, and she has many guards. To attack? That would be suicide. To burglarize, and to steal the Q-device that she has recently assembled: that is my objective. To steal it before the bomb is acquired by the U.S. Government."

"You need *one versed in psychogeography*? But you have such skills yourself," said Miss Viva.

"You forget, sweet lady, that I am far from my home world. My powers are diminished by distance, as are yours. But I am farther, much farther from home than are you. Miss Viva, I need the help of a Venusian."

"There are humans in Tombstone," I said, "who are experts in psychogeography."

Miss Viva laughed. "They know next to nothing. Humans have *sometimes* come near to grasping its elements. Debord, for instance."

"Well," I said, "he defined psychogeography as 'the study of the precise laws and specific effects of the geographical environment, consciously organised or not, on the emotions and behavior of individuals'."

"Yes. Your book-learning does you credit, as always. But before Debord, another human, Ivan Chtcheglov, more pertinently declared that psychogeography 'must be sought in the magical locales of fairy tales and surrealist writings: castles, endless walls, little forgotten bars, mammoth caverns, casino mirrors'."

"Fear mirrors," said Mr. Twist, absently, "for there are those that say that thereby Death enters this world."

"It is but one of many ways, Mr. Twist."

"Castles, endless walls, little forgotten bars, mirrors—is that the route we have to take," I said, "if we're to find this other Death and, and—"

"Neutralize her," said Mr. Twist, helpfully.

"The route we will have to take," said Mr. Cochise, "will be through a backdoor in the world beneath our feet which I have already discovered to be a hot spot, one ripe for a psychogeographical incursion. Yes, that will be our personal *dérive*. Miss Viva, let me explain..."

I yawned; my eyelids had grown leaden. I could no longer concentrate on what was being said. Oh Nicola, you've had a busy day. For a moment, I fought to prevent my eyes from clamping shut, but then I conceded to their imperative.

Wrapped in darkness, I strained to catch a distant cry. In

the bleached wastes beyond the city's edge I had detected the whistle of a train. Did it emanate from the railroad that had been built out of Desdichado? When it was complete—and that would not be for some time yet—that hyperphysical link, they said, would allow travellers from the East Coast, such as myself, to pass into the frontier in under ten years. But the railroad, surely, was too far away for me to have heard the whistle of one of its trains. Had that noise, then, been the howl of a coyote? *You mustn't succumb*, I told myself, in an attempt to discipline my instincts, *you mustn't succumb to unconsciousness. Tomorrow, you may be running far, far from here, running toward the borderlands of this world and the next, soon to be immersed in the world of dreams forever.*

But I had the body of a child; and, knowing nothing from that moment but a buzz of unintelligible conversation that lulled me into deeper and deeper vales of perfect rest, I snuggled into the chair's damp, cloying folds. Its back, arms and wings seemed to wind about me, like a bank of moss, and I an enchanted traveller destined to fall into a hundred-years sleep and wake in fairyland.

*

I slept deep, but not, it transpired, for a hundred years. And when I awoke I was greeted not by cold dew, but by the deliciousness of silk sheets next to my skin. It was morning and the curtains of my room had been pulled back, a shaft of warm sunlight bathing the huge, canopied bed on which I lay, like a beggar-girl who had recently served a King's pleasure. The smell of freshly made coffee filled the air.

"I've brought you breakfast," said the girl at the foot of the bed. She moved to one side, a silver tray burdened with hot, buttered toast and coffee pot held before her. I sat up, pulling a creamy sheet up to my neck to effect a show of modesty. I leant against the headboard, and the girl deposited the tray in my lap. Head throbbing, I picked up the china cup, already thoughtfully filled, and, hand trembling, sipped at the hot black coffee.

I put the cup down, smacked my lips and looked up at the girl through my eyelashes. "I'm the housekeeper's daughter," she said, answering my unspoken enquiry.

"Well, hello, Pocahontas," I said, my gaze unwavering. The little Indian maid was about my own age. And she was pretty. Very pretty.

"Don't call me that," she said. "That's not my name. I mean, would you like it if I called you Figgy?"

"Figgy?"

"Figgy Newton," she said, a look of sad triumph on her face. She passed the back of her hand across her forehead in a theatrical gesture of enervation, an almost-Venusian gesture, it seemed. "That's what *I* think I'll call *you*." She turned about and walked across the room, swinging her skirt, it seemed, with a studied, perambulatory come-hither, a locomotive affectation such as I had often seen older girls adopt (Just before we had left Boston to travel into the West, at about the same time we had all heard about the launch of Sputnik, the bobbysoxers had worn skirts with an even bouncier, more generous cut than that of Pocahontas's.). The sway and swish of the material exerted an irresistible force that tugged at me, and I had to dig my nails into the mattress to prevent myself from being involuntarily dragged out of bed, as if I had just had a ring inserted through my nose; *naughty girl, bad girl*, you almost expected Pocahontas to say. She stopped before a door and took a key from the waistband of her skirt.

"You're new to the West, aren't you?"

"Does it show?"

"A little. It's just that not so many people come West these days. There's such a strict vetting procedure."

"Well, Senator McCarthy saw to that."

"Your parents must be real solid types."

"Mmm," I said, with disgust. "Real WASPS."

She placed the key in the lock, her long red nails scraping against the butterfly clasp as the key slipped and grated inside the ward's rusted vitals. "This is your bathroom," she said.

"Evidently the bathroom hasn't been used for some time," I said. "Pocahontas."

"I said you're not to—"

"If you're going to call me Figgy, I'm going to carry on calling you Pocahontas. Until you tell me your real name, that is." She snorted, her back still turned to me, her gaze fixed upon her task.

"Haven't had a guest here for *ages*." She brushed aside a thick wad of hair that had fallen over one eye and glanced at me askance, playful, contemptuous. "Haven't *ever* had a girl from Boston." I ignored her glance and its cheap, semantic content; I ignored the blatant character assassination implicit in her words.

The lock's tumblers surrendered and the door creaked open. A sliver of scum-encrusted walls and cobwebby ceiling greeted my curious gaze. Pocahontas disappeared into the bathroom, and I threatened my tongue with terrors should it revolt against better judgment and talk of love and friendship and big, wet, soppy kisses beneath the cool, crisp sheets.

Soon, my little Indian maid returned. She stared at me, boldly; hooked a thumb in the waistband of her skirt. "You need clean towels," she said. "I'll go get some." But she did not move.

I pushed aside the tray and, taking care to wrap myself in a sheet, swung my legs over the edge of the mattress, so that my feet dangled a few inches above the floor. I looked about the room, inhaling the musty air while glancing cursorily at the majestic yet melancholy fittings: the great four-poster with its black velvet canopy, the worn rug, the damp walls and the warped surface of the escritoire upon which—unsettled by the concussion of my feet upon the floorboards as I slithered off the bed—a lonely anglepoise teetered. Abandoning my inspection of these symbols of domestic entropy, I refastened my gaze upon Pocahontas.

She chewed her lip; stroked the pleats of her skirt, her bold stare relentless. I averted my eyes, hunched my shoulders, almost flinching. That pretty sphinx was laughing at me on the marge of my vision; and I felt my cheeks glowing like boilerplate that strove to contain imminent self-combustion.

"Your friends are waiting for you," she said. "You'd better get ready. Don't want to be late for the party, do you?" I heard the bedroom door close; and when I looked up, I discovered she had left.

I stood; let the sheet fall to the floor; staggered the ten paces that separated me from the bathroom.

The steel washbasin seemed clean, at least. I turned on a tap and bent over to splash my face with ice-cold water. I straightened, hands clasped to my cheeks, water percolating through the gaps between my fingers, a lovely sensation of icy oblivion salving my burnt, stinging flesh. I spread my hands; held them up to my face; peeped through the fanned digits at my reflection in the cracked, fly-specked mirror; and then I walked back into the bedroom and went over to the window.

Below was the prospect of a courtyard that seemed to lie at the back of Mr. Cochise's house. He and Mr. Twist were struggling to lift a manhole cover while Miss Viva looked on, her usually sleepy eyes slitted into uncharacteristic emblems of fiery vitality.

*

We were in the underground system of aqueducts that supplied Tombstone with fresh water. A half-hour earlier, we had descended beneath the courtyard of Mr. Cochise's house and had found ourselves in an octagonal structure with four tunnelled openings that gave onto a central chamber. This,

I knew, was a conduit-head, the structure in which water from the reservoir was gathered near the source, before it passed into the main distribution system. Proceeding into the darkness, we had entered the central chamber. It was an intestinal stone maze. Above, about us and below, a vast and intricate array of elevated canals wound through the town's cavernous depths. We walked in single file along a narrow footbridge that ran parallel to one of the uppermost waterways. Mr. Cochise led, a flaming torch held aloft; I walked directly behind him, Miss Viva and Mr. Twist in the rear.

To one side of me lay a channel scooped out of what seemed a single block of granite. It stretched back some hundreds of yards to disappear into the shadows. On the other side, over the slender handrail, was a panorama of other such channels, each one supported by a series of brick arches which, in turn, rested upon other arches, until the torchlight which dully illuminated them could no longer compete with the darkness of the great chamber's nethermost depths, and the fantastical architecture was lost to view.

Sometimes, when we passed beneath the arch of a bisecting aqueduct, a chaos of bats would suddenly materialize out of the nothingness, circling us, their shrill, dissonant song rising above the ceaseless noise of rushing water. And then, after we cleared the arch, those clichés of the night would regroup, depart and again rest undisturbed, hanging from the mould-caked bricks of the arch's underside.

Mr. Cochise stopped; we copied. And then he turned to face us, pointed to indicate that, here, the footbridge bifurcated and that we should take the path that forked away. He went ahead and we followed. The slim, iron latticework of the footbridge extended over a black void, no lines or planes of stone to orientate us above, below, or to either side. When we had progressed a stone's throw along its length we were circumscribed by darkness, the flickering tongue of the flambeau the center of our universe, a point of light we clove to like children around a miserly camp fire in the deep, deep heart of a midnight glade. The only other illumination to penetrate the void were pinpoints of red that dotted the fathomless depths beneath us. Little rashes of rubiate brilliance, they were grouped in patterns of five, six, seven and eight, and seemed to move, albeit almost imperceptibly, against the pall of unresolvable pitch-black. Feeling giddy, I looked up and, for the first time since descending into the town's god-like plumbing, I espied a limit to this underworld. A wall appeared. At first it seemed a wall of smoke; and then, as my eyes strained to resolve the apparition, the smoke coalesced and I saw that this was a wall of stone. A rock face that, like the prodigious engineering that threaded the town's vast subterranean expanses, had, in its extent, seemingly no beginning and no end, though it was, I soon found, as near as it was real.

The footbridge terminated at a modest-sized door, such as might front a house, if such a house were to be found halfway up a sheer mountainside, set flush against its smooth, glossy stone. All other indicia of human habitation—windows, lintels, gables, roof—were missing. Only that door, alone in a wilderness of sheer verticality, and made the more strange by its commonplace brass doorknob, punctuated the *tabula rasa* that confronted us. As we approached it, Mr. Cochise stepped to one side and allowed Miss Viva to draw close to what I earnestly hoped was to be our exit from the huge, oppressive chamber.

"It gives way onto a service area off which various generators are maintained," said Mr. Cochise. "But my investigations have given me cause to believe that it is at this point that psychogeographic entry into the heart of our enemy's fastness will become possible."

"Yes," said Miss Viva, running her hand over the door's oak panels, "it is an ordinary enough door. But it *does* show signs of semantic displacement. The message it's giving out conflicts with its appearance." She put both hands on the door, pushing, here and there, as if she was trying to force her fingers through the wood. "A psychogeographic event," she continued, "Intertwines with this world. To enter it, one must do so by a *mundane* passageway." Eager to rid myself of the cloying shadows, the dark immensity that crowded in from every side, I ground my teeth with a sudden inveterate hatred of things psychogeographical, their psychomoronic waste of time, thought and life. But then Miss Viva stepped back, opened the door and passed through. Though my horror of the void was at once relieved—I had pushed past Mr. Cochise in order to disassociate myself from the shadows as soon as possible—I yet involuntarily paused before crossing the door's threshold. Peering down the narrow corridor, more in wonder at its ordinariness than at the prospect it threatened to open up, I steeled myself and walked between the jambs. Soon, I was hurrying across concrete tiles, Miss Viva's progress determined and fearless, her swaying hips, the flick of skirt one way, and then the other, a goad urging me onwards.

Another door greeted us; Miss Viva crashed through it. As I myself passed through, Mr. Cochise and Mr. Twist trotting behind me with fatalistic accommodation, I saw (thought that I saw, then was sure that I saw) that my surroundings wore different colors, lines, forms, that everything, everything had begun to change. The smooth, sure texture of the tiled floor had begun to assume the tactile dimensions of cobblestones. When I looked down to establish that the sensations communicated by my feet had not been engendered by hysteria, I did indeed discover that the corridor was cobbled with grey, wet stones that glistened with the images of reflected streetlamps. I lifted my head to see Miss Viva shoulder aside another door. I struggled to keep up, a mist issuing from walls that seemed to be diminishing into a fugitive perspective, ferroconcrete transformed into white, swirling vapor. Lurching through this third portal I discovered that we were in a deserted street, its macadam slick with night dew and rime, boarded-up tenement buildings rising on each side of us.

I looked up at the night sky. There seemed to be no cloud cover, but neither did there seem to be stars or moon. And then I realized that we were still underground.

"Are we beneath the enemy's house?" I said, looking up into what I guessed was a stone vault so high as to be completely obscure.

"We are," said Mr. Cochise. He inclined his head toward Miss Viva. "You are to be congratulated, Death. You have brought us into our enemy's lair."

Miss Viva frowned and nervously toyed with a stray elflock; attempted, somewhat clumsily, to assume an attitude nonchalant and cavalier.

"This is some basement," I said.

Mr. Cochise looked about him with satisfaction. "Though the corridor we recently passed through was of modest length, we have in reality shifted some half-a-mile," he said. "Yes, we are indeed in the cellar, the vast basement, if you will, beneath the enemy's house. One which we would have found impossible to access, if it had not been for Viva Venera. Normally the only route to this place is through the house itself."

I panned the desolate landscape. Here, beneath the streets of Tombstone, was the mirror-image of the Gothic town above, but a ruined one. It was a cracked, perverted image, a scale-model that seemed to have been comprehensively subjected to accelerated decay, the wrecking-ball, general neglect and a liberal use of high explosive.

"But this is not a place that has been destroyed, Nicola," said Mr. Cochise, who, subtle Indian that he was, must have been able to track meaning in a face that had doubtless grown wild with speculation. "These are not ruins that you see. No;

they are building here. They are building another West. One that they hope will one day, and one day soon, replace *our* West. One that will, perhaps, replace the Western World."

"Then why does everything *look* destroyed? Or rather," I said, "as if it's rotting away?"

"Because," said Mr. Cochise, "the Death who is Mistress here is not a Death such as your Miss Viva. She is not a Death like me. Death here does not offer transformation, nor does it offer a way into the light. In this place, despair reigns. And cynicism. And smallness of heart." It sounded like the world I had tried to run away from. Fifties America—its games shows, its suburbs, its easy prejudices—had been infused with a similar agenda, its own death-in-life distilled into a potion offering a false dawn.

With a rehearsed flick of the wrist, Miss Viva swept her fringe out of her eyes, tilted back her head so that her small nose pointed to the star-less heavens, and began to walk down the street, mock-confidence accentuating the swish and sway of her hemline.

"Come," she said, "we have work to do, Mr. Cochise. The sooner we can rid the Earth of this intrusion from Niflheim the sooner I, Mr. Twist and our young friend can leave Tombstone and head toward the frontier." Mr. Twist strode after her.

"Spoken like the woman I yearn to die for, Miss Viva," he said.

"Like the woman you *will* die for, Mr. Twist."

It was then, I think, that I first began to regret having reminded Miss Viva about Mr. Cochise's request for assistance. What use would I find for her unconditional love if I should not survive this expedition? I longed to put Tombstone behind me.

Mr. Cochise, with a half-dozen skips and hops, again took the lead, and I quickly sought Miss Viva's shadow, scampering along in our party's rear, fearful of being lost in the anonymous ghost-town streets that wound through the construction work that littered Tombstone's cellar.

Her shadow was no comfort blanket. It could not protect me from the prospect of dread that rose on each side. Hanging gutters and broken vanes pointed down like the long, cruel fingernails of witches; the suggestion of human and less-than human forms lurked in the obscurity of doorways; swirls of mist circulated about the roots of streetlamps, rose from drains and invaded the cracks and fissures of black marble walls, a thin, white mist that shone with an inner light. Occasionally, through a gap in the buildings, or above a rooftop, I spied the battlements of a castle rising from a distant prominence, looming over the city with an intent as awful as it was romantic. I had been transported to the illustrated pages of a book of folktales; the half-formed, empty, underground city was imbued with the same picturesque sense of undefined threat.

We walked in silence, the scaffolding-clad engineering grotesqueries that lined our route, with their genuflections to the Neo-Gothic muse and their expositions on the theme of the tomb and the mausoleum, conspiring to confer their blessings on our nervous recalcitrance with their evocations of a silence final and supreme. And then drifting through the silence came a single word. I looked at my companions, unsure whether I was hallucinating. Their puzzled expressions assured me that I was not. *Ve-nus, Oh Ve-nus*, repeated a mocking, singsong, little girl's voice, over and over again.

Two boys appeared from the doorway of a nearby building, the same boys I had met that day in Boot Hill when trying to elude Mr. Cochise; the same boys, yes, I thought—double-checking their biker apparel and their German military helmets—and the same melodramatic entrance. "*Achtung!*" one of them cried, so much reminding me of some character in a boys' war comic that I expected him to add "*Gott in Himmel!*",

"*Donner und Blitzen!*" or "*Der verrückt Amerikaners sind hier!*".
It was not, of course, the boys who had been teasing us with
that recitation of *Ve-nus, Oh Ve-nus*.

From the same building from which they had emerged
stepped a young girl, and despite the fact that she was dressed
in a radically different manner from the way in which I had
seen her only that morning, I knew immediately that it was the
little Indian maid. Her torso was clad in a corselet of gleaming
plate armor, so that she resembled a medieval knight, if such
knights had been given to dressing in a manner similar to the
cut-high-on-the-thigh floozies of the *Birdcage*. The steel-tas-
seled peplum contrived to reveal a tiny isosceles triangle of
lace that signalled the apex of her thighs. She stood barring
our path, legs apart, hands on hips, the boys adopting slouched,
tough-guy attitudes to either side of her. Her fingers played
with the guard of the short sword that hung from her hip, or
else fidgeted with the ruins of her stockings, caressing a bronze
thigh that peeked through its incongruously erotic strategy of
shreds. My chest tightened in an agonizing tourniquet, blood
backing up until my face flushed. From the riot of fire that
consumed my cheeks, I felt that I displayed the apoplectic
countenance of an Old Testament prophet who was about to
turn his back on the God of his fathers to embrace the burnished idol of a strange new faith. Our party halted, and each
of its members surveyed the other, seeking an initiative.

"*Ve-nus, Oh Ven-us*," sang the transformed squaw, regaining our attention. "Those notes, Figgy," she continued, now in
a speaking voice, "those four notes of divine music represent
the opening bars of one of Frankie Avalon's greatest record-
ings." The boy to her right held a porcelain doll to his breast,
rocking it in his arms with only the faintest hint of irony;
and then, bored, he let it fall to the ground, its bisque skull
shattering against the cobblestones. A thousand baby spiders
poured out from the smashed china, scuttling across the black,

gleaming stones. "It reached number one in the pop parade," added Pocahontas.

"But Venus sucks," said the boy who had recently committed infanticide. "Radio-electric measurements indicate that our sister planet has a surface temperature of seven hundred degrees Fahrenheit or more. And the planet's atmosphere, ninety-six percent carbon dioxide, three percent nitrogen, point one percent water vapor? What kind of place do you call that?"

Mr. Cochise took a step forward. His mouth opened, and he seemed ready to articulate something of importance. But a paralysis of confusion overcame him. Defeated, he let his mouth snap shut, his lips smacking against each other like the blubbery lips of a fish.

"Surprised to see me, Cochise?" said Pocahontas. "There're lots of things about me that will surprise you, I guess. You think I'm beholden to you for taking in my mother? Well, I'm not. I'm no slave, Cochise. And you're *not* my manitou. Queen Musidora is."

"Is that what the Death who lives here chooses to call herself?" said Miss Viva.

"Musidora is a real Death," said the girl. "She's going to be Mistress of all the West."

"She's going to be Mistress," said the boy who still studied the doll's shattered remains, "of all the world." His flesh gleamed with the sebum-refracted neon of the streetlamps and his own inner, wholly sanctimonious light.

"No more slavery for us," said Pocahontas. "We're going to have our own slaves. That's something *you* could never give us, Cochise."

Mr. Twist walked to Mr. Cochise's side. "They're just kids," he said. "What are we waiting for?" Pocahontas made us all a gift of an "I-know-something-you-don't" smirk.

"Look around you," she said.

From the lancet windows that decorated the half-built tenements a hundred pairs of eyes stared down at us.

"Is your Mistress then," I said, looking now at Pocahontas and raising an eyebrow, "so taken by the oleaginous charm of a turncoat?" She seemed unwithered by my sniffy remark.

"How can you betray me like this?" chipped in Mr. Cochise. But Pocahontas would not be baited.

I composed my features into what I hoped would pass as an equally annoying expression of "I-know-something-you-don't" and decided to try again. "Indeed, how can you place your faith in someone like this *Musidora*, someone who has so corrupted you?"

"How can I—" she said, her voice tight. And then, walking up to me, she shouted, a sudden unstoppering of emotion loosening her larynx, a wet, gale-force wind of articulation hitting me in the face with such force that I felt lucky to retain the skin on my cheekbones. "How *can* I? No, no—how can *you*. How can you *dare*. Musidora is the only person who's ever shown me kindness!" Regaining control of herself, she slinked across the few feet that separated us and pressed herself insolently against my body. "Didn't have to come down a silly *manhole* to get here. Oh no, the Mistress lets me in by the front door. Listen: I'm not a spy for ideological reasons, Nicola. I spy for love. I spy because I am so promiscuously affianced to a Death."

"She really does make a wonderful assassin," said the boy who still stared at the ground, mourning his dead doll. "Simply wonderful."

"It's so easy to kill a man or woman once you have seduced them," she said. "And nothing is so seductive as innocence. A little child can lead a tiger by the nose and do anything to it that it pleases."

"An assassin? Aren't you a trifle young to be thus self-styled?" said Miss Viva.

"Young?" exclaimed Pocahontas, with contempt. She made exotic, undulating movements with her arms, as if she were entertaining one conscripted to the pleasures of a louche nightclub. "Just imagine: The former SS brothel, revived by a post-*Götterdämmerung* entrepreneur with a conveniently erased past, is softly lit with candles. A harmonium, played by a grotesquely scarred boy who had been among the *Hitlerjugend* that had fought in the city's last, desperate stand against the Russians, fills the smoky air with a hypnotic drone as the parched voice of the chanteuse sings *Lili Marlene*. American, British, French and Soviet flags hang from the shattered remains of chandeliers. Ooh look, here comes Salome, dancing for the GIs and batting her long, black lashes." Her arms rose and fell, transcribing sinuous arcs, until the perturbed air seemed fit to eddy with whorls of incense. She froze in mid-dance; her upper lip curled; and then she let her arms drop to her side. She began to giggle. "Young? But we're not so young, are we, Nicola?"

She walked backwards, keeping her eyes on us, until she reached the two boys who seemed to be her personal guard. And then raising a hand above her head, she clicked her fingers. "Cosimo, Irma, Blanche, Lola-Lola, Tallulah, Marie-Thérèse!" I expected, then, to die; expected the figures who stared down from the lancet windows to stone us, shoot us, commit us to oblivion. There was a silence that seemed to crackle with anticipation, an iron stillness that propagated a clanging, industrial music in my ears, the white noise that precedes a swoon. I remained conscious, even if, instinctively, I had shut my eyes in preparation for the Big Faint that would quell my thoughts forever.

It was the rumble of wheels, a sharp, razor-edged rumble of iron wheels against macadam that, slashing at the bindings that secured lid to lid, forced my eyes to reopen and take in the sight of the carriage-and-four that careered along the street,

manned by six young girls. The sound of its heavy wheels resounded off the invisible ceiling of this netherworld, so high
above. The carriage came to a halt, awaiting us. Behind it a
big, armoured coach rolled up which, I was certain, was to
transport the soldiery whose purpose would be to deny us the
possibility of escape. Behind that came what I presumed was
Pocahontas's own carriage, an ornate, gilded affair that might
have been conjured up for a Cinderella, and then hijacked by
her ugly sorority.

Miss Viva, Mr. Twist and myself were ordered into the
front vehicle, the two boys taking up position on the carriage's
roof. The wet macadam; its vitrescent surface; the halos of the
street lamps immersed in its cold, yet hedonistic veneer; the
dazzle of the rhinestones on Mr. Twist's lapels—all these things
dazzled me, so that I again felt the symptoms of a fit swimming
through my brain. The sodium glare of the road surface had
become like grit behind my eyes, a snowstorm of powdered
glass. The contours of the walls on either side of us, distorting,
buckling, melting with my every step, were also feeding my
eyeballs to the grater. At last, I clambered in.

Seating ourselves, I saw, looking out the window, that the
buildings had disgorged their temporary occupants and that
we were surrounded by over a hundred well-armed soldiers.

And all of them were children, too.

Chapter Six
Mädchen in Uniform

The castle rose above us, its battlements crested with feathery mist. The mist, that had dissipated somewhat during our journey, was now beginning to regroup, thicken, descending from the black, starless heavens at the same time as it rose about our feet, a pincer movement that seemed designed to smother us in its wispy, white, wet plumage. We stood on a mount—earthworks that constituted part of this citadel's fortifications—a road snaking out behind us, twisting out of sight. High as we were above the underground city's rooftops, the barrel vault of the great basement had become clearly visible. Pipes, girders and the roots of trees protruded through its lofty concrete expanse. And connecting the vault to the castle's battlements were a series of flues and vents and elevators.

Our transport stood to one side, the horses exhaling clouds of steam. The small army of children had disappeared, left behind by the carriage's speedy negotiation of the streets.

The castle's iron gates, some fifty feet high, began to open. I looked down one last time at the dark, morphic dissonance of the city's chaotic architecture, empty of all but the urchins who had given their allegiance to the alien form that had promised them a new life in the service of Death. The periphery road that lay in the long shadow of the basement's outer wall—visible from this prominence—was a bright ribbon of neon and rime. Within its circuit the construction projects and engineering works that, paradoxically, suggested the aftermath of recent warfare, brought to mind pictures I had seen of Berlin—a Berlin as it had been immediately after the Second World War. And if not Berlin, then still a city immediately recognisable as the hub of an evil Teutonic empire, a vision in granite, marble and stained glass that owed a debt, not merely to the Gothic muse, but also, perhaps, to Albert Speer and Werner March. I spied a work-gang clambering over a tall, precarious assemblage of scaffolding, and the beginnings of a shop or a house, or perhaps, an office block or tenement, rising toward the bleak illusion of the sky. The scene glowed red, as if from behind a curtain of blood, as arc-welders cut away girders and iron latticework. Furnaces roared too, sending red-and-white sparks and embers into the air as other gangs of laborers prepared to realize countless more stone homages to *ruin*.

The gates rumbled, low, the infernal groan overlaid with a whine, like that of a cat, or of a baby puling. My little Indian maid passed beneath the arch, flanked by her two bodyguards. The girls who had ridden the carriage-and-four—all of them attired identically to Pocahontas—urged, first, Miss Viva and Mr. Twist, and then Mr. Cochise and I forward. They seemed eager not to be lost in the resurgent carpet of mist that had by now risen from the knees to the waists of the adults, though it was rapidly approaching the chins of us girls. Above, high above, through a grating set in the arch's masonry, I seemed to glimpse a multitude of red eyes staring down at us. Before I could verify my sighting I had, along with my companions, friend and fell—entered the castle, the gates signalling that they were closing behind us with a resumption of their groaning, whining, two-part motet.

With little trails of vapor still clinging tenaciously to our heels we proceeded down a long hallway. The timbered ceiling was covered with iron shields; the walls were adorned with spears, swords and axes. At its farthest end, where another set of doors was already yawning open to greet us, several more armor-clad girl-children stood at attention, a guard of honor who, standing aside as we walked past, proceeded to join the troupe who marched behind, ensuring our compliance. The measured concussion of their high-heeled jackboots against the flagstones contrasted with the three grown-ups syncopated, less enthusiastic steps.

The doors, once we were beneath them, seemed almost as big as the huge gates which had provided our entrance to the castle. Marshalled through them, we entered a chamber, the vast dimensions of which competed only with its barrenness; for apart from a dais and throne directly opposite, but located at the extreme, shadow-haunted limits of this great hall, apart from the musicians who had begun to saw at their violins and milk mellow melodies from their trombones the second we had entered, there was nothing else of note to be seen.

Without hesitation, Pocahontas walked ahead. The honor guard, if that was what it was, formed a line across the doorway, pre-empting any notions we might have had about offering the Queen of the Dead a raincheck and doubling back to seek whatever hospitality might be offered here at some remove. I looked askance at the orchestra. It was at least one hundred strong but, in the vastness of the hall, seemed of altogether more modest proportions. The musicians were all men—Nazi somatotypes who would not have seemed out of place beside the muscle-bound sculptures in Paul Ludwig Troost's Munich Art Gallery, circa 1939—and all were naked. Of course, they played Wagner, the high, timbered vault echoing to the sounds of "The Pilgrims' Chorus." Twitted by those ironic horns and strings (for no Venusberg was likely to snare us with delight on this pilgrimage) I clasped my hands over my ears and faltered.

"We have to go on," said Mr. Twist out of the side of his mouth, a hand sliding inside his jacket and finding its way to his hip. His gun had been taken from him shortly after we had been apprehended; he missed it sorely. My own weapon, which I had taken the opportunity of reloading when we had returned to the *Birdcage* the previous night, still lay undetected beneath my frock.

"Of course," I said, clenching my belly as if suffering from a stomach-ache, or stitch, in order to comfort myself that the derringer was, indeed, still in place. It was. I straightened myself. My light-headedness had gone, as suddenly unreal as my abdominal cramp. I increased my stride, keeping pace with Mr. Twist only with the greatest effort, his long legs clearing two or three flagstones with each step, mine struggling to clear the one.

The dais and she that sat on its throne separated itself from the shadows and came into focus, as did the figure seated below the queenly one, at the dais's foot. The weight of shadows lay heavily across the entire chamber, but was of particular thickness in the vicinity of the throne. Even so I felt, as we approached to within a range of fifteen to twenty feet, that I could have taken out both figures should I have dared to hoist my skirt and draw.

Pocahontas commanded us to stop. The Indian maid stood to one side, next to Mr. Twist. She made a slight bow toward the mysterious majesty whose face, cobwebbed with darkness, refused to resolve itself into its components. Mr. Twist seemed unconcerned; his attention had, all this time, been on one thing alone, that thing enjoying a resolution denied its royal counterpart. It had become evident even as we had approached that the girl who sat on the lowest step of the dais, her chin cupped in her hand, a girl attired in like manner to our female escort, was the proxy we were going to have to deal with.

The orchestra fell silent.

"I told you they would come," said Pocahontas, addressing the seated girl. The girl inspected us lazily, a faint smile disturbing the corpse-like equanimity of her mouth. Like Pocahontas, she seemed about the same age as me. But something old and terrible flickered behind her eyes. The smile widened. She crossed and then recrossed her legs.

The dais was set against the chamber's wall. A fabulous array of bookshelves rose to the ceiling, offset with ladders whose equally fabulous length suggested that they might have been originally designed for the use of steeplejacks whose job had been to service the foundations of heaven. The titles of some of the volumes seemed to burn away the surrounding gloom. The almost luminous gold-leaf, for instance, that emblazoned the spine of *Mein Kampf.* That tome was accompanied, almost inevitably it seemed, by a copy of Feuchtwanger's *Jew Süss*; and there were catalogues of films starring Zarah Leander and Ferdinand Marian; English-language texts with titles like *The Female Body Considered as an Alien Artefact*, *My Life in Joy Division—A Young Lady's Confessions* and *Unity—Her Struggle Against Terra Vitae*. But there were scholastic works, too: books on exobiology, genetics, alchemy, psychogeography; and racks of magazines, some of which included *Scientific American* and *Nature*.

I saw the girl freeze. The fricative music of the fidgety *crissare* of her legs had stopped as stockinged thighs were pressed jealously together as if in a convulsive fit of *frisson*-induced incontinence. "I'm really so glad you could make it, Cochise," she said. "And you too, Venusian. I'm not sure if you realize just how gratified I am to receive you. You have come to me in my hour of need, so to speak." The girl's beehive wobbled to and fro, threatening to untangle and smother her in black tresses.

Mr. Cochise pointed toward the throne's shadow-shrouded occupant. "I see you still have a sentimental regard for *that* thing." He moved forward. Pocahontas raised a hand to indicate that he should remain where he was. "Oh, please," he continued, "won't you tell your little friend that I'm quite capable of reducing her to ashes if I should choose?"

"Let him come," said the girl at the foot of the dais. "I think we all realize the virtues of restraint in the present situation, do we not, Cochise?"

Mr. Cochise did not reply. Instead, he ascended the dais; and then, with what seemed to me incredible audacity, put his hands upon the Queen of the Dead, grasping her about the back of the neck. Stepping to one side of the throne, with one hand still committing that act of gross impropriety, he played to the auditorium, like a ventriloquist about to introduce a grotesque mannequin to a new and incredulous audience.

"She's no queen," said Mr. Cochise, "no real queen. Not on Niflheim, and not anywhere else. She's just some renegade energy-form that's been corrupted by her diet." Obeying the urgings of her puppet-master, the queen leant forward, still masked by shadows, with only the glint of her eyes hinting at her face's no doubt hideous geography; and if her eyes had not been black as opals I would have thought that she had been the creature I had witnessed spying on us from the stone eyrie above the castle's gates. "You fed on too many souls from this planet's last big war, didn't you? And you developed a particular taste for the souls of Nazis. They were your loves, your paramours, no? And now you have come to Earth to fulfil their frustrated dreams."

Mr. Cochise, in a fit of nonchalant violence, pitched the queen's body off the throne. It tumbled down the steps, a bunch of rags and bones, a flour sack sending clouds of black dust into the air. The body lay spread and broken before us, the face visible now, its thin, creased parchment of skin like the sloughed-off integument of a serpent. Wisps of grey hair fell from a snood, a black piece of gossamer that recalled a spider's web in the same manner as the withered body to which it was attached recalled the ossified body of a famished spider. Yes, if my mother was a fat spider, here was her cousin, a spider thin and mean. The hair, steely bright and antique, was like hair that might have been discovered on a mummy, an embalmed arachnid miraculously preserved despite the whittling of the years.

"Fuck you, Cochise," said the girl, who hadn't shifted from her sulky pose. "I don't need a crone's body to be the Wicked Witch of the West. I decided upon that long ago."

Still with her chin in her hand, she had begun to play with a loose strand of hair, winding it about a little finger while surveying the four people who stood in front of her. Her gaze, after it had attempted silent communion with Mr. Twist and Miss Viva, settled upon me. "I did indeed have a sentimental attachment to that hoary old mansion of flesh. Still, it had to go *one* day." She ran her hands down the close-fitting armor, luxuriating in her boyish curves. "It's much better," she added, "to have a body such as *we* have, don't you think?" I found myself silently agreeing with the alien shape-shifter.

"Hey, something pretty damn *insanitary* is going on here," said Mr. Twist.

The alien's former body was melting, pink and putrescent, streams of gook running across the floor. It resembled, perhaps, that of a zany in the last stages of a chronically diseased life.

The queen, the real *soi-disant* Queen of the Dead got to her feet, hands still caressing the steel plates that adorned her torso. "It is for people like you," she said, still keeping her gaze upon me, "that I am going to build my Reich. Children are so animalistic. So amoral. It is a real delight to shape each little dough ball of chaos into the kind of disciplined urban soldier you see here—" She nodded toward Pocahontas. "A child who will serve me without question." For a Teutonic demon-queen, she possessed a surprisingly good command of English. There was even, buried in there, a trace of an American accent, as if she were taking polite account of present company. "You and your friends, of course, will stay here as surety until the Venusian provides me with what I desire. Of them, I care not a jot, but I must say I certainly look forward to having fun and games with *me*, my funny-looking little *Jungmädchen*. It shall perhaps be my pleasure to recruit you into my order of Valkyries."

"What do you want with *me*?" said Miss Viva.

"Her Majesty, it seems, wants to destroy all life on Earth," said Mr. Cochise, with a flat, in-your-face that's that. "We have walked into a trap. I'm sorry, Viva Venera. I have delivered you into the enemy's hands."

"I have no use for your *sorry*, Death," said Miss Viva.

I turned to Miss Viva. "She wants *you*," I said, finding that I understood the Queen of the Dead better, and more instinctively, than my companions (something I was far from comfortable with), "she wants you so that she might build her dream-empire, a Reich that will reach out into all the worlds of the living and claim their souls for her own."

"It is a concept," said the queen, walking up to Miss Viva, "that you, as a fellow Death, must surely find seductive?"

"You are no Death, Musidora of Niflheim. You have betrayed your world. Do not think you and I are the same. A Venusian does not murder or seek to colonize *any* planet."

"Oh, hypocrisy, thy name is Viva," said the queen. "Your exploits in the West are well documented. You're as much a murderer as I am." Two roses bloomed on Miss Viva's pale cheeks.

"I have made mistakes, Musidora. But if I have killed, I have not raped human bodies for their souls. I have murdered in the spirit of self-preservation, or rather, the preservation of the human who is most dear to me. We should take only what is given us. No more. You know that."

"For a long time I have been given very little, Viva Venera. I have grown hungry. And now I *will* take." The queen held up a hand to stay further discussion. "There are outsiders due to arrive soon who expect to purchase a fully functioning Q-bomb."

"CIA," said Mr. Cochise, looking down from the dais.

"Perhaps," said the queen, raising a coy, finely stencilled eyebrow. "But that is not an issue you need be concerned with. No. What you should be concerned with, Viva Venera, is assisting me to finish work on my bomb."

"So that the Americans can start World War III? That really would give you a feast of souls, wouldn't it, Musidora?"

"So that your friends may continue to exist," replied the queen. "Would you wish that the soul who is your beloved should find communion with *me*?"

Miss Viva looked at Mr. Twist, her face animated in a manner which was a revelation. Never had I seen her so unsettled, so bruised by emotions concomitant with life. The threat to my own existence seemed wholly forgotten.

"You will do as I wish, Venusian?"

"I suppose I will," said Miss Viva, numbly. She turned and gazed into the perspective provided by the phenomenal length of the hall, as if she could bear to meet neither my eyes nor those of Mr. Twist's; but especially, of course, Mr. Twist's. "You'll let them go free, so that we may travel into the frontier, if I use my knowledge and skills to perfect your wretched bomb?"

"I know that you have such skills, Venusian."

"And Earth?"

"I do not wish so much to destroy all life on Planet Earth," said the queen, "as to merely wipe out the human race. Unfortunately, the former extinction is a condition of the latter. But do not concern yourselves. Though we may expect even the West to be ransacked by the blast, you will be quite safe in its farther reaches. Desdichado will not, I am assured, be affected." The queen walked up the steps of the dais and sat down on the throne with a tintinnabulation of armor plating settling into place. Mr. Cochise drew back from her, his jaw set. "I hope you appreciate how much trouble I have taken to placate your anxieties, Viva Venera," she said. "Play ball with me and you'll get to have the wedding of your dreams. A big black wedding in beautiful Desdichado. The little girl," she said, smiling down at me, "can be your bridesmaid, yes?" Again, she turned her attention on Miss Viva. "But if you resist me I'll make sure that you never get to enjoy your precious Mr. Twist. You can't escape. I have hundreds of servants here. Besides, I think you can sense my power. I think you know that, even aided by Cochise, you would be no match for me." Miss Viva stared at the floor, acknowledging the truth of the queen's words.

I walked to Miss Viva's side. "But you *can't* help her, Miss Viva," I said. "You can't—"

"Be quiet, Nicky," said Mr. Twist. "Miss Viva knows what she's doing."

I half-turned and confronted him. "We can't be a party to destroying the whole planet," I said, incredulous at the surge of pleasurable excitement that rose from my loins into my brain to do battle with my conscience. "We can't," I said, feeling that dark thrill begin to prevail. "Can we?"

"It's true what Musidora says," said Miss Viva, "I am a murderer. I've killed humans before, and I can kill them again. But, of course, that's not really the point." She stared at Mr. Twist, holding his gaze long and pitifully. "Don't you know by now, Nicky, I would do anything so long as it ensured that I would be at long last together with Mr. Twist."

*

The cage—one of several that stood at the back of the

dungeon—seemed originally designed for the confinement of stray dogs. "Oh please, please let me be like her," I said to myself. "Please, God: change me into a Venusian." But God was dead, or so Mr. Nietzsche had averred. And maybe I would be dead soon, too. I would never be a necrobabe. "Never, never, *never*"—that last "never" a drawn-out heave that had me depositing another glob of puke into the growing pool on the cage's floor—"*neverrrrr.*" I needed a fix of whisky.

The hitherto silent girl who knelt in the cage next to mine slid herself into a corner, pushing her head violently into the junction of the cage's bars and the floor.

"So, how do you like the girl-coop?" she said. "How do you like the hen house?" I didn't like it at all. The dungeon—or, at least, the part of it we occupied—was a naked, high-ceilinged chamber with straw scattered over its flagstones and obligatory rings set in its walls. Every surface glistened with damp. "You'll be like me soon," she continued. I glanced at her. Her eyes were dead. And when she had spoken, it had been as if her voice had come from far away, reaching me by way of a tunnel lined with cork. Like the other Valkyries I had encountered, she could have been no older than eleven or twelve. "The Mistress took part of my soul, but disdained to consume the rest. She does that sometimes, if she wishes to punish her followers. I'm half-dead. Between worlds. In limbo." She stared into her lap. "It's not fair. Everyone on this planet has a Death waiting for them, whether on a nice world or a bad world. Everyone! And everyone eventually gets eaten. Not just nibbled on, or used as a snack, saved for later. No; eaten all up! Why should it be *me* that's neither here nor there?"

"I assure you," I said, with false bravado, "Musidora will not get to eat *me*." I turned my attention back to the task of springing myself, as—the bobby pin I had earlier plucked from my cell mate's hair poised between slippery fingers—I fumblingly resumed my struggle to pick the cage's lock. My locksmith's skills were considerable. They had been honed by years of escaping from one educational establishment after another. It was just as well. I could not use my derringer; the noise would surely have alerted the guards.

I had barely started lock-picking when the iron door that connected the cell with the corridor outside opened with such crepitation that I thought its hinges had cracked, like a jaw that has been unable to contain a particularly violent yawn. Surreptitiously, I deposited the bobby pin down the front of my blouse and shifted my legs so that I sat back on my heels, smoothing my hands over my skirt, its pleats bouncy upon a squab of stiff white petticoat, the picture of a submissive, respectful girl.

The Indian maid strode across the cell, keys jangling at the end of a chain that was looped about her waist. Ignoring the girl-next-door, and the several empty cages that extended to either side of us, she came to a halt opposite where I knelt.

"Good evening, chicken," she said. "I hope you put your day in the coop to good use by taking time to reflect on the coming destruction of the decadent West and its replacement by a New Order." My cell mate uncurled herself and sat up, reclining against the bars, the sullen pleasure with which she regarded me indicating that she anticipated my interrogation with some relish. "That brave new world," the maid continued, "will be led by a Death with whom we will all fall hopelessly in love."

"Give me a break, Pocahontas," I said. "You're not a Nazi. You don't even know what a Nazi is."

"I do too."

"Oh really? You know Wilhelm Reich? Reich says that Fascism is *'the basic emotional attitude of the suppressed man of our authoritarian machine civilization and its mechanistic-mystical conception of life'.*"

"Well, I always knew you were clever, Figgy. So many posh schools, I'll bet."

"Expelled from pretty near every one," I said. "But"—and I couldn't help but show off to the pretty child-warrior—"I'm what they call a prodigy."

"Really? How interesting. Okay, if you're so prodigious, what do *you* say I am? You may speak freely."

"Well, if you must have it: Fascism is a biopathic expression of the orgastically impotent man. Or woman," I said, excited now, unable to discipline myself, the surging joy of rebellion—a certain biopathic feedback informing my tongue—too great to contain. "Or girl. If you don't mind me saying so." Pocahontas waved a hand through the air to underline the latitudinarianism she had already avowed. "Suffice to say, what we're talking about here is a schoolgirl crush. You've gotten mixed up in all this simply because you've never been loved. *Verstehen?*"

Her nose wrinkled and she brushed a lank of hair over her shoulder with her hand, puffed air through her lips, as if she had suddenly grown hot, and tugged at the steel plates that hung about the tops of her spare, Minnie Mouse thighs. I gripped the bars of the cage with both hands, my cheeks flush against the iron palings, the metal pressing my lips into a sulky pout. Her eyes darted, avoiding contact with my own, to fasten, at last, with an abstracted glaze, upon the feed bowl and, next to it, the bucket in which I had been expected to relieve myself.

"Are you here because of your mother?" I said. The little Indian maid shrugged.

"S'pose so. She's always been so disgustingly faithful to Cochise. She really worships him, like she's praying that when the time comes it'll be him that eats her soul. I got so sick and tired of all that. Whenever I come down here and put on my uniform I feel as if I'm getting *away* from Ma. I really can't stand her any more. She makes my flesh creep."

"I hate my mother too," I said. Her eyes widened.

"Then you understand."

"Yes, I think I do." I leant away; reached into my frock pocket and found the piece of rock candy. I took it out and held it up, the light from the door passing through its glacial, black heart, so that it shone like a sticky, paste jewel. And then I placed it between my front teeth; pushed my face back against the bars. Without further prompting, Pocahontas knelt down, and then crawled toward me on all fours. Pressing her mouth against the cage, she sank her big, gravestone-sized incisors into the candy, her lips closing about the rock with slow, voluptuous delight, grazing my own lips so that I was left with an aftertaste, not merely of sugarplum, but of her own candied, sweet self.

The taste flowed down the back of my mouth. And then it rose, like the fumes of a burnt offering, aromatic and intent on appeasing the pleasure centers of my brain. My eyelids became heavy. Shaking my head, I swallowed, trying to resist the call that echoed through the byways of my skull, the seductive call urging me to sleep.

Pocahontas sat back on her heels, one side of her face distended with the swell of the rock candy. There was a crack, almost as tremendous as that which had accompanied the opening of the cell door; and then her jaw began to grind, sticky black juices spilling from the sides of her mouth.

"You could join us, Figgy," she said, thickly, as she paused from her heavy-duty chewing to draw breath. "We both, surely, recognize the deadly and insidious threat of Communism, especially with the Soviets putting rockets into space and the like. We must be thankful that, in addition to the prospective E-bomb, we will soon have a Q-bomb, too. Without the help of a Death like Queen Musidora the USA would be finished."

"Without the intervention of the Venusians," I said, "the Apache would be most likely extinct, or else living in those reservations that the government had planned for them." Pocahontas conceded a smile; it was like one painted onto a corpse by a jesting, apprentice undertaker. The determined, rapid motion of her jaw had slowed and she seemed to be as near to being overcome by sleep as me.

"All my life," she said, "I've been looking for, what? Utopia, I guess you'd call it. Been looking for that land all my life. I believe in"—her eyes misted and she looked into the distance, beyond the confines of the cell, beyond the West—"purity. That's why I believe in planting trees, why I believe in clean water and undiluted blood. So many evil things have polluted this nation since we decided to pussyfoot around with the Reds. Only a strong woman like Musidora can redeem us. Only another *Führer* can save us from ourselves. Oh how beautiful it will be! I can see it now. Won't you be my friend, Figgy Newton? Won't you come play with me in the new world that we are building?" She raised her eyes, so that those milky comfits with the delicious black chocolate-drop centers were half-occluded by red, sleep-starved orbits. Before I could decide if her expression indicated exhaustion, fatalism or extreme fright, or whether she had, like a Venusian *manqué*, simply chosen to feign death for the sheer pleasure of it, her head lolled forward; she rolled to one side, collapsing across the straw in the kind of graceful, becoming manner I would have expected of her.

As I fell against the bars I knew that our mutual predilection to sleep had not been coincidental; it had been precipitated by the rock candy. A vision dropped into place before my inner eye. No beautiful dreams, it seemed, if you resisted the Apache drug, but a real scarifying number from a Grand Guignol slide show involving my mother, an army of gigantic bugs and a two-week holiday in Camp Labor Via Joy. I slapped myself across the face. The hallucination burst like a boil and, though it had lost me some seconds, that brief, eidetic nightmare had had the fortuitous effect of freeing me from the soporific's noxious spell.

A tiny stream of liquorice-like drool trickled out of Pocahontas's mouth and soaked into the straw. It was my good fortune, I knew then, to have sampled no more than a taste of the candy, and it followed, no more than a microgram, perhaps, of the pharmaceutical that it had been impregnated with.

I spat onto the floor, trying to expectorate what was left of the taste in my mouth. And then I took the bobby pin out of my blouse; focused on freeing myself from the cage.

"You going to let me out too?" said my fellow prisoner.

"You're a Nazi," I said. The cage door sprang open. Feet tingling as a surge of blood filled erstwhile constricted veins, I unwound myself from myself and clambered out of the iron box.

I knelt down beside Pocahontas; ran a finger along her cheek. Her eyes were still open, and I contemplated, in a fit of *amour fou*, what it would be like to suck those toothsome eyes clean out of their sockets. I breathed deep; tried to ignore my churning stomach, my banging heart. I took the keys from Pocahontas's waist and walked to the cell door. "You shouldn't play games you don't understand," I said, briefly looking back at the caged girl. I pushed the key into the lock, turned it and pulled the door open, the iron hinges announcing my escape with a fanfare of overfamiliar cracks, groans and shrieks.

"I can take you where you want to go," she said. "I know the castle. I know it well." I turned and studied the one whose soul had been part drained, her face now pressed to the bars of her cage. "I want to get out of here as well, can't you see that?" It was true, I needed a guide. And I could think of no reason why the half-dead girl should betray me. I walked back across the cell, squatted by her cage and, with newly acquired familiarity, rapidly picked its lock. The cage door opened. The girl eased herself out and stood before me.

"My name's Drusilla. Drusilla X, Drusilla X. Oh what a bad girl *she* is," she said, reciting what was doubtless her hokey *nom de guerre* with nursery-like pleasure, relegating her assumed identity to the third person.

Tentatively, we both stepped into the passageway outside. The alert I had sounded by opening the cell's stentorian portal had not been answered. There were no guards to be seen. I scurried along in a claustrophobic embrace of fetid air, the fingers of one hand entwined with Drusilla's own, my other hand touching the curving wall so as to brace myself for whatever should present itself about the next bend.

*

I had been wise to make use of a guide. The castle had proved a maze of stairwells and galleries. Sometimes, to avoid detection, we had moved through passages that resembled priest holes, and sometimes between the castle's thick walls. After ascending several floors and taking too many turns I had quickly become disorientated, but Drusilla had assured me that we were on the right track. She had gained intelligence from the dungeon's guards of my friends' whereabouts; and, after passing though ever more obscure regions, between walls, over ceilings, through closets and under flagstones, her intelligence was proved to be correct.

The laboratory was situated in a spacious chamber deep within the castle's bowels. During the last hours of Miss Viva's labors—the hours during which I had kept it under surveillance—it had come to resemble less a workshop filled with familiar, if highly advanced technology, than the atelier of a charlatan, a quack. It followed that when Miss Viva—standing amid a chaos of bubbling jars, lights, generators, vats and test tubes—announced that the Q-bomb was ready, Mr. Twist and Mr. Cochise swapped dubious glances. The brass sphere that stood on the laboratory table was no larger than a baseball and seemed the prop of a sorcerer's apprentice, something from a charlatan's case of samples, a veritable quintessence of quackery. Queen Musidora, however, seemed to recognize that what Miss Viva had asserted was true, and she nodded appreciatively. The two besuited men in Raybans, who had not spoken since I had begun my vigil, took the queen's cue and inclined their heads as if submitting to her judgment. One was markedly older than the other, with grey hair and a goatee. The junior partner had a face covered with zits. I immediately decided to call them the Brooks Brothers. "Yes, it's finished," said Miss Viva, unbuttoning her lab coat, and then pointing to the innocuous-looking object in front of her.

"What's finished?" whispered Drusilla.

"Shhh!" I said. We were lying in an air vent, looking down through a grille situated in the bottom of its metal shaft. The vent, in keeping with the rest of this underground realm's monumental engineering, was big enough for an adult to stand up in. The grille itself was some six feet wide. Below, in the high-ceilinged chamber, the *dramatis personae* of good guys and bad guys (or more accurately, perhaps, bad guys and worse guys) stood among the theatrical machinery that suggested the classic mad scientist's den. Miss Viva threw the lab coat onto the floor and moved among the paraphernalia, her hands reaching out to touch the glass and metal surfaces that furnished the womb out of which the doomsday device had been born.

"Congratulations, Venusian," said the queen. She turned to the two suits. "This calls for a celebration, gentlemen. Would you care to join me in my private apartments so that we may conclude our deal?"

"We should be on our way," said Brooks Brother senior.

"We can supply you with E-devices too, of course," said the queen.

"The E-bomb will be as nothing compared to the Q-bomb."

"True."

"DARPA has been looking into the possibility of utilising electrospiritual technology to take out incoming Soviet missiles. There has already been progress with the so-called 'thunderbolt effect'."

"The death kiss?"

"The death kiss to the power of ten, twenty, a hundred, a thousand. A *blown* kiss, you might say. The surface temperature of the old v-2 we used as a target was raised to eight thousand degrees C."

"Instant vaporization?"

"Instant. Complete." An electrospiritual generator, I had heard, could be used to fire a plasmoid into the path of an incoming missile. The plasmoid would effectively ionize that region of space and thus disturb the aerodynamics of the missile's flight. Such a weapons system would provide protection against attack via space or the atmosphere. "It may well," continued the suit, as if completing my train of thoughts, "form the basis of an effective ABM system. But it is the Q-bomb"—he pulled back his shoulders—"it is the *bomb* that will bring us final victory over the Reds." Better Dead than Red, my mother used to say. But better Dead than Alive in that suburban quagmire in which I had grown up. "We can't rely on the Venusians any more. The Russians are wary of American superiority, but they're working on their own E-device. Then it might be a question of use it or lose it—attack NATO, that is, before NATO redresses the military balance in its own favor. No; we need something to settle things once and for all."

Miss Viva continued to wander among the exotic machines. "Explosively pumped Flux Compression Generators"— she muttered, stroking the bronze surface of a mysterious conglomeration of steel and cable—"explosive or propellant driven Magneto-Hydrodynamic generators"—she stroked the surface of another—"and a range of HPM devices, like that Virtual Cathode Oscillator, or Vircator, over there. You certainly have the ability, Musidora, to manufacture all manner of weapons."

The queen smiled. "We have here Relativistic Klystrons, Magnetrons, Slow Wave Devices, Reflex Triodes, Spark Gap Devices, as well as Vircators. From the perspective of a bomb or warhead designer, of course, the device of choice must be the Vircator, a one-shot device capable of producing a very powerful single pulse of radiation, yet mechanically simple, small and robust, one that can operate over a relatively broad band of microwave frequencies."

Drusilla tapped me playfully over the head with the knuckles of her index and middle fingers. "What is she *talking* about, Nicola?"

"She's talking," I whispered back, eager to silence the garrulous child with some sort of explanation, "she's talking about selling all kinds of horrible weapons to those two CIA spooks. Those guys think they're so clever. They think that they're circumventing Venus by going through this crazy Death. They think they're getting something that Venus would never let them have in a million years. And they think that the queen here is doing it just for money. But they're being set up. Outmaneuvered. The queen wants a war. Nothing more, nothing less! She wants the Americans and the Russians to blow each other up so that she can consume their souls!"

"That's terrible, Nicola," she said, her eyes swivelling to take in the sights below, unleashing a bead of inquiry that bore directly into the top of each player's head.

"So you see," concluded the queen, turning to the Brooks Brothers, "we really *are* able to supply you with weapons such as lightning-bolt howitzers—indeed, any other kind of electrospiritual weapon, should you so desire."

"The Q-bomb," said the senior spook, "will be quite suf-
ficient."

Drusilla again tapped me on the head. "Your friend, the
Venusian. She surely isn't part of this?" she said, not quite as
quietly as I would have wished.

"She has *some* morals," I said. And if something in me was
relieved at the confidence of my assertion, then something was
disappointed too. "She's entered into the queen's conspiracy in
order to ensure my freedom. I must *help* her."

Mr. Twist's fist crashed down on the table; the little brass
ball with the potential to annihilate a planet jumped into the
air, bounced and rolled against a sheaf of research papers. It
was unusual—almost unknown—for Mr. Twist to lose his tem-
per. He liked to project the configuration of an emperor of cool,
an emperor betrothed to an empress of ice-cream. But Queen
Musidora's silky sales-pitch was bringing him to the boil.

"For heaven's sake, John—" said Miss Viva. She folded her
arms across her chest, her ice-blue eyes flashing like those of
an Inuit scold.

"What about your end of the bargain, Musidora?" said Mr.
Twist. "What about letting us out of here?" He gave Miss Viva a
hard stare. "Lord knows, I never thought any of this was such
a good idea in the first place. Who the hell cares what happens in the outside world? This is the West. We have our own
concerns." He looked at Mr. Cochise. "And as for you, you've
just ended up making things worse, haven't you? You were
supposed to be cutting this whole thing in the bud, instead
you've been instrumental in bringing it to fruition. Dammit,
if we hadn't come here, these boys"—he pointed to the two
suits—"wouldn't have their precious Q-bomb."

"They would have had it soon enough, John Twist," said
Mr. Cochise. "Viva Venera has done little more than keep the
development of the device on schedule."

"For which I am infinitely grateful," said the queen.

"So how about releasing us," said Mr. Twist. "How about letting me see my friend Nicky?"

"I'm afraid that isn't going to be possible," said Miss Viva with a shrug and a nonchalant pursing of her lips. "I suppose"—she glanced at the queen—"it is time to reveal my true purpose." Her eyes had hardened. She was not as she had been in the queen's audience chamber, when she had seemed to surrender so readily to necessity. She was the Viva I had often dreamt of, an interplanetary renegade, her own woman, proud and unwilling to bend her knee. "It is true that I would do anything to be with Mr. Twist. Kill, maim, lie, cheat—anything so that I might at last consume him. But I am still a Venusian, Musidora. We are not of the same kidney. There are some things I simply *cannot* countenance. So listen up: I intend to redeem myself. For I *have* done things contrary to the Venusian way; in some respects, I'm as bad, perhaps worse, than you. And now I must put things right."

"Oh, the *hell* you're worse than her, Miss Viva," said Mr. Twist. "You're an angel, is what you are, a death-angel worth a hundred or more of the likes of ol' Queen Musidora here."

"Mr. Twist, we must not let these people destroy Earth."

"This is no time for moral absolutism."

"There can be no argument, Mr. Twist. If we leave this place intact, other weapons will be produced, and there will be other buyers. Next thing we know, there'll be a SUSY-bomb on the market. A supersymmetry device like that can switch on another Higgs field. The stars would stop shining. Electrons would flee from their atoms. A whole portion of the universe would disintegrate." Miss Viva turned through three-hundred-and-sixty degrees, surveying the laboratory. "No, no we can't let that happen, Mr. Twist. The whole caboodle is going to have to go up!"

"You talk nonsense, Viva Venera," said the queen, looking up at the Brooks Brothers, a child eager to calm a pair of over-anxious grown-ups who have yet to grasp the cruel, animal-istic rigors of the game she has elected them to play. "You can do nothing to harm me. Besides, your friends—"

"Forgive me, Mr. Twist," said Miss Viva.

"I don't like this, Miss Viva," he replied.

"I don't either, Mr. Twist. But it must be done." Miss Viva walked over to the table where the Q-bomb lay; picked it up; stared at the queen. "My friends will understand."

I shook my head. "I'm not sure *I* understand."

"Or like it," whispered Drusilla. "I don't care to be a sac-rificial pawn."

"Scared to die?"

"I'm half-dead already. But I wanted to stay on Earth a *little* while longer. Musidora promised us so much."

"Better to rule in Hell than serve in Heaven, eh?" I said, though as soon as I'd offered up my "thought for the day" I reflected that it was a sentiment that could as well be applied to me, given the infernal course my life had taken. But no; I wanted heaven, I told myself. It was the place that, finally, I would be prepared to give everything for, even what integrity and little conscience I had left. Was this the only way I would get there? I disposed of this uncomfortable meditation before it followed me into the darker corners of my mind and took advantage of me.

Miss Viva forced out a laugh between her tense, com-pressed lips. "I always said, Mr. Twist, that you would never escape me."

"I very much hope that I will not, Miss Viva."

"Consider yourself doomed, Mr. Twist."

"I do, I do, Miss Viva. But how do I know Musidora ain't gonna *consume* me instead of you?"

"Have faith, Mr. Twist. I do not believe you are her type."

Mr. Cochise took a step forward, then hesitated and stopped. "Don't you think, Viva Venera," he said, "that you are being somewhat rash? You and I, it is true, cannot die; but that device will not merely destroy this colony of Niflheim's, it will destroy the entire Earth."

"No, Cochise. I have modified the bomb so that it will unleash the *White Heat*."

"You're crazy, Venusian," said the queen, "it will imprison our energy-forms. For a Death, the Heat offers no escape."

My apocalyptic Venusian folded her arms across her chest, tapped a foot against the tiled floor and looked about her at the array of ionized glass tubes, filaments that crackled with electrostatic. "When you, so desperate for my compliance, gave me the run of this laboratory, you delivered yourself into my hands, Musidora. Now be quiet. You, me and Cochise are going to be together for an eternity, it seems. We'll have more than enough time to talk things over."

"What exactly *is* this White Heat, Viva darlin'?" said Mr. Twist.

"A release of energy on the scale of that contained here"— she tapped a fingernail against the bomb—"might not just destroy my adopted body, but commit the form beneath to a place, another dimension, from which it cannot return."

"Shit—" said Mr. Twist, not given to flights of rhetoric whenever a conversation might broach areas unfamiliar and arcane.

"Lost to another dimension. And one that not even a Venusian could walk out of. Just wouldn't *that* trim your wings," said the queen. "Be sensible, Viva Venera."

"Hey, we're not going to die in this rathole, are we?" said the junior spook, who seemed only just to have become cognizant of his likely fate. He sniffed disapprovingly at air tainted by Miss Viva's experimentation and the bodily emissions of people who had been slammed up in its chemical stew an hour too long. "Are we?" His partner put a hand inside his jacket and produced a snub-nosed handgun. He levelled it at Miss Viva.

"We're not going to die, I'll make sure of that," he said. He made a bow, his hand grazing the floor as the long, dramatic sweep of his arm silently proclaimed the laboratory and all its contents to be hers; until, that is, he should deem otherwise. "Put the bomb down, alien."

Miss Viva continued to refrain from making eye contact with either the grey-haired spook who had offered her two-cents' worth of tasteless sarcasm or his younger, somewhat effeminate confrère. And then, at last condescending to bring the two into her field of vision, she held the offending article at arm's-length, toward them. "You want to take it?" she said, idly juggling the doomsday bomb from one hand to the other. Her lips parted in a smile that revealed two bright rows of tightly clamped lipstick-stained teeth.

"The Venusian and her henchman will not prove any difficulty," said the queen, treating Miss Viva and Mr. Twist to a look of cool disdain. "Their reputation is overly inflated. Besides, the Venusian is mad. She is no match for me. I am older than her. Much older. I will tear her simulacrum apart, throw it to the four winds, and leave her naked." Miss Viva glared at her, the bomb held close to her chest, as if it were a baby-bomb demanding succor. Then she looked away, unable, seemingly, to any longer brook the sight of the queen's smug, sassy countenance.

"Catch," said Miss Viva. She slid back a panel on the bomb's casing, depressed a small button, slid the panel back into place and then tossed the bomb into the air, whereupon, transcribing a lazy arc, it fell toward the gunman. Brooks Brother senior dropped his weapon, ran forward, extended his hands and caught the brass projectile before it could hit the floor.

The queen clasped a hand to her flat little bosom, as if she were praying, or about to suffer a thrombosis.

"*No!*" cried Mr. Cochise.

"The bomb," said Miss Viva, formally announcing her interest in the complete annihilation of this new Reich and all its inhabitants, "is activated."

Brooks Brother senior gazed down at the Q-bomb, turning it over in his hands as if trying to solve its puzzle.

"Nervous? Better be careful—that thing's like me. It's got a short fuse."

Drusilla put her hand on my arm. Her grip tightened. "Musidora can't get herself imprisoned in this White Heat thing before she's finished eating me!" she said. I prised her hand off, my fingernails digging into the fleshy pad of her palm as she at first resisted and then gave way to my efforts.

Mr. Twist had put his arm about Miss Viva's waist. "Just how *much* of a short fuse," he said.

"We have sixty seconds, Mr. Twist."

"Oh, *nooooo!*" cried Drusilla.

Below us, six pairs of eyes looked up to where the scream of despair had originated.

"We're going to be killed if we stay here," I said. I drew myself up into a squat and got my fingers about the iron crosshatches of the grille. "Help me, Drusilla," I added, pulling. The Valkyrie lent her efforts to my own and the grille came away from its surround. Drusilla immediately slipped through the opening and plunged into the laboratory, bouncing off the table on which the Q-bomb had been displayed and tumbling across the floor. She snapped to her feet, springing at the queen. Her legs wrapped about Musidora's hips; her hands clawed at her hair. And all the while she screamed with laughter:

"'Why fight it?' you said. 'Why not give up the struggle and allow yourself to drown in a sweet, undifferentiated sea where your will shall become one with the *Führerprinzip*; a sweet, watery grave where you will always swim with the tide and where you won't have to make any more decisions?' But you never said anything, Musidora, you never said *anything* about having to live out my life as one of your half-dead slaves!" The queen struggled, but could not free herself from the clam-like attentions of her former devotee. Drusilla giggled and squealed, her animalistic cries reverberating about the laboratory, echoing down the air vent, even haunting, I imagined, the empty shells of tenement and warehouse in the underground city outside, filling all creation. "Oh, and I thought Fascism was so *fascinating*," continued Drusilla. "Especially after you said you loved me! Especially after you said you would give me a new life! Take me into you now, Musidora, before the bomb explodes. Take my soul, make me yours entire!"

"Miss Viva!" I called.

"Nicky, I'm so sorry, my sweet," said Miss Viva, peering up at me. "I had no other choice."

"The air vent," I said. "It must lead to the surface. Hurry. Please!"

"I suggest, Miss Viva," said Mr. Twist, "that we allow ourselves to believe that what Nicky says might in fact be true. Your willingness to sacrifice yourself is noble. But it would be nobler by far to take this soul of yours you so covet, that is, my good self, far, far away from here. John Twist does not wish to perish in the conflagration that is about to engulf present company. No, John Twist wishes to perish in other circumstances, in your sweet arms, and preferably in the far, far future. I appeal to you, Viva darlin': let's make tracks."

"Posthaste tracks," she said. "Nicky, you are *incorrigibly* on the side of life."

I found time to smile. "Sorry, Miss Viva."

Mr. Twist's arm snaked about his Death's waist. Slowly, he walked backwards, his gaze never leaving the spook who still held the bomb. Paralyzed with confusion, Brooks Brother senior absently stroked the bomb's brassy rind.

"Guards!" cried the queen. "Guards!" Drusilla had only just wrestled the queen to the floor when she flew into the air, her body hurled across the laboratory to land, in a ball of flame, against a generator. She lay, lifeless, her armor melted and pooling about her blackened flesh. A lick of electricity played about the queen's open mouth.

"Quickly," I said. "Over there. A stepladder!" Mr. Twist disengaged himself from Miss Viva, disappeared behind a hulk of metal and wires and re-emerged with the ladder in his hands. He opened it up and set it down beneath the aperture in the vent. The queen, meanwhile, had risen to her feet, and I feared she was about to visit the same harm upon my friends as she had upon Drusilla. With one arm extended, I urged them to join me.

The heavy doors that connected the laboratory with the passage outside rumbled open. Cool air crossed my face; and through the gaping portal I glimpsed a long, narrow stretch of tarmac: a tunnel whose curving lines displayed wall-lamps moulded in the shapes of swastikas. Some hundreds of yards distant, at a somewhat higher elevation than the lab, was a semicircle of night sky where an archway provided access to the city. But then I forgot all this; forgot that here, perhaps, was another and better route of escape. For through the doors came a sight that should have had me gagging and attempting to flee. Instead, my eyes merely opened and then opened some more, my blood freezing in my veins and transforming me into an ice-sculpture, shock-stunned not by the new or the unexpected, but by recognition. The horror that had appeared below had, one way or another, suggested itself to me ever since I had begun to fancy that my mother was a spider in human form. Ever since I had witnessed those red lights dotting the abyss of the aqueducts and known myself scrutinised by those red eyes that had appeared above the castle's gates.

Five armored Valkyries sat astride their mounts: spiders that were as gigantic as they were obscene. Green slime dripped from chelicerae as the spiders worried at their bits;

and, as their red eyes focused upon my friends, their black, wiry hair stiffened on their fat bodies, rising like the hackles of a dog or cat. The riders kept the monstrous arachnids on a tight rein as they assessed the situation; then, registering the fact that their queen was looking daggers in the direction of the absconding Miss Viva and Mr. Twist, they launched their attack, geeing their mounts across the chamber in a blur of black, skinny limbs. The spiders' barbed feet sent up a mad, symphonic clickety-clack that was like an accelerated sound effect of high heels in panicked flight.

Mr. Cochise ran and put himself between the charging infantry and my friends (Mr. Twist, putting his arm again about Miss Viva's waist, and all the while looking over his shoulder, as if he had put an automobile into reverse and was guiding it into a parking space, had moved steadily away from the enemy. Miss Viva also now turned her head to scrutinise the lay of the land to their rear, taking over from Mr. Twist as chief navigator as she steered them both onto the ladder's bottom rungs.). A jag of lightning issued from the manitou's open mouth, and one of the spiders exploded with such violence that it might have earlier that day been given a rubdown with paraffin.

"Let go of me, Mr. Twist," said Miss Viva, with urgency and not a little irritation. I empathised; I shared, at that moment, a wish for autonomy befitting one eager to get out of harm's way as smartly as possible. Mr. Twist complied, if reluctantly. Miss Viva broke free of his slackened embrace to race up the ladder, while he, with his long stride, rapidly followed. They pulled themselves over the lip of the vent, stood and looked down at what ensued below.

Brooks Brother senior ran across the room, his hands held out before him, proffering the bomb, as if he were an incompetent busboy delivering a covered dish to an impatient diner. Meanwhile, the queen knelt by the combusted spider, mourning her loss, and Brooks Brother junior held his hands to his head and jabbered like a lunatic. Mr. Cochise had climbed halfway up the ladder, the great arachnids snapping at him, themselves beginning to find purchase on the ladder's steps. Mr. Twist leant over and grabbed the Indian by his outstretched hand, pulling him into the vent. I tried to push the grille back into place, but a spider had already got its front legs through the aperture; I jumped back. And then we were all running down the shaft, the sound, the brittle, scuttling sound of massed stilettos behind us, informing us that the nightmarish beasts were in pursuit.

Mr. Cochise brought up our rear. "They breed in the depths beneath the desert," he gasped, sounding like an anxious, overworked tour guide. "They are mutants, like the creatures you call zanies. Musidora has learnt how to farm and train them."

With my attention either fixed on the dark perspective ahead or on the pursuant spiders, I had not immediately recognized that Miss Viva was no longer quite humanoid, that her arms had extended, were covered in diaphanous leather, and that her fingers had become claw-like pinions. When I at last took stock of her metamorphosis, I found myself praying it was no visual aberration. Trying to forget that the spiders were nearly upon us, some of them running along the shaft's ceiling, their riders suspended upside down with their short swords drawn, slashing at the shadows. Trying to forget I was near to being a giant arachnid's supper, I inspected Miss Viva more carefully.

Her metamorphosis was real. Presto! She was shape-shifting herself into something resembling a pterodactyl with pretensions to anthropomorphism. Or if one were to make a less kindly critique, an actress wearing a latex Godzilla suit. Her transformation achieved its end in a convulsive blur of protoplasm and feathers that suddenly congealed into a terrible vision of avian symmetry. Miss Viva's arms—a small set of arms, like those of a bipedal dinosaur—gathered Mr. Twist and me to her white, downy bosom. Then, her equine face looking impassively ahead, her wings beating fast, but with a smooth, untroubled action that belied the formal cause of our panic—the Valkyries were, by now, almost within plucking distance of her plumous tail—she became airborne.

We flew upward, and though the pitch blackness had closed about us, I knew we were ascending through a section of the air vent that rose out of the castle and into the great basement's vault. Something rushed to meet us and, as we left it behind in a jet of splinters, I realized that the spiders were never going to match our speed—for at that moment the air vent was irradiated, as if we had been transported into the heart of an exploding star.

A hot wind tossed us this way and that, Miss Viva's wings folding up as she impacted against the shaft's walls, then springing back as she stabilised and regained the momentum of her flight path. The trailing edge of her feathers caught fire, leaving a multitude of orange streamers snaking behind her, writhing like salamanders in the furnace that was roaring below.

Blind now, white light searing the center of my brain, my skin sore as if it had been blasted with hot sand, I felt another obstacle give way. For a few moments of grace, I could see again. We ascended through the stairwell of a house, Miss Viva's trajectory like that of a rocket. We were passing, I supposed, through Musidora's residence in Boot Hill. I had barely time to take in the Nazi flags draped across the various landings when darkness again closed in. There was a great boom. I was showered with plaster. And then we were high in the air, high above Tombstone.

It was daytime. Boot Hill's morbid skyline stretched out around me far below. What had been the turrets and campaniles of Musidora's house was now only smoke and combustion. The roof had completely disappeared, consumed by a gout of flame; its windows spat glass onto the streets as each casement exploded with light. And then we fell, leaving a signature of fire behind us, the arc we described in the ultramarine sky like that of a comet about to crash to earth. I spied the esplanade and its promenaders—hundreds of people who, putting their hands to their faces, were screaming in agony as the waterfront buildings dissolved like a strip of photographic negative exposed to the noonday sun. And what bodies then, melting like wax maquettes, gave up their souls? And to what planet might those souls be bound? Miss Viva had begun to reassume humanoid form. Icarus-like, clothes smouldering, hair singed, but otherwise intact, falling as if doomed never again to rise, the three of us crashed out of the cruel brilliance of the afternoon sky into the dark waters of the reservoir.

I felt a hand grab hold of my own, and let concern waft away for those that might be consigned to the big gridiron that, I assumed, was set to barbecue the planet. We had outshone ourselves, certainly, being party to a crime that would qualify as the greatest, and indeed last, example of mass murder in the history of mankind. Not that history, itself, had much of a future, except perhaps in the farthest reaches of the West.

My head broke the surface; I sucked hungrily at the hot air. Before me, a pall of smoke hung over Boot Hill, its thin, broken monuments the legs of a belly-up arachnid a boy had sported with by way of perpetrating half-hearted dismemberment before committing the disgusting, pathetic thing to the flames with the aid of a magnifying glass.

For a while, I floated on my back, half-in, half-out of consciousness. The stars twinkled above, careless of my fate. How many planets revolving about those multitudinous points of light were death worlds, I wondered? How many types of Death was it possible for humanity to know? The heads of Miss

Viva and then Mr. Twist, I noticed, were bobbing alongside my own. Viva was Viva again. She had put off her feathers, her avian tat, and reshaped herself into a woman. And then Mr. Cochise appeared. He too, in order to escape, had assumed the shape of a bird, but, unlike my Venusian, was still in the process of growing back his human body. His plumage fell away, flesh taking its place. I inspected him; he seemed to be having trouble with his reverse metamorphosis. Though he now had the form of a man, there was much about his corporeality that was unfamiliar. He trod water, black droplets streaming down his face; and then I saw that those droplets were mixed with sizzling gobs of fat. Involuntarily, I found myself drawing away. Mr. Cochise had suffered dreadful burns.

Not willing any longer to look into the Indian's pained eyes, I swam over to Miss Viva, disburdening myself of my frock as I did so. "Have we really destroyed the world?" I asked.

"No, Nicky. By modifying the Q-bomb so that it unleashes the White Heat, that is exactly what I have sought to avoid. Look!"

A great curtain of white light had risen over Tombstone. Hundreds of feet high, it extended on either side as far as the eye could see. It seemed palpable, as if the light were hard, a kind of luminous concrete. Set in its panorama I thought I could detect faces, hundreds, thousands of faces, straining to emerge from its white expanse. The wall of light seemed to be moving slowly, steadily toward us.

"We have only one hope," said Mr. Cochise. He dived beneath the surface.

"What the hell is it, Miss Viva?" said Mr. Twist, his eyes glowing with the reflected brilliance of the great wall.

"*That* is the White Heat, Mr. Twist. It is a tactical weapon. It is on the move now. It will destroy anything in its path."

"Anything?" I said. "Like, us?"

"Oh yes," said Miss Viva, "You can be assured of that."

"It would really have been better, I think," said Mr. Twist, "if you'd let those guys have their bomb. What the hell are we going to do now?"

The surface of the reservoir rippled, and then waves began to emanate from a point just a little way in front of us. With a burst of froth and black surf, a saucer-like flying machine that would not have been out of place in a Flash Gordon serial rose from the perturbed depths, water coursing off its silver airframe. Silently, it manoeuvred until it was directly above us. And then a trap opened in its glistening underside and a rope ladder unfurled, swaying from side to side, and then dangling in the water.

*

The saucer skimmed over the desert. As we had left Tombstone, the wall of light had threatened to envelop us; but, with the saucer rapidly gathering speed the threat had receded until we had left the White Heat far behind. Mr. Cochise complained that the ship was old, that it was liable to malfunction. I was loathe to hear it criticized. No human-built craft could have negotiated the West's airspace. We had been saved from the Heat only because the alien vessel in which we travelled possessed a dynamic that owed its being to the same laws that informed the parallel universe that connected Earth with Venus.

The four of us sat in the ship's compact bridge, a vibrant, flashing instrument panel before us. During the monotony of our flight I had amused myself by making a tally of my achievements to date: I had made new friends; found passage to the frontier; and, in being party to the unleashing of the White Heat, had also been party to the destruction of my biological family. Huzzah! I had, perhaps, even a claim to an involvement in the prospective destruction of the whole Wild West. I congratulated myself. Things had really turned out well.

Who could say now that I was just a silly little girl? No one. No one was, or would be, left. I remembered my speech to the mob when I had first entered Tombstone. "*I tell you*," I had said, "*if I live among you for much longer, then I shall either go mad or I shall* kill *you all*!" I had carried out my threat. I had seen them in their graves. All of them.

Yes, it seemed to me I had done pretty well. Though now I had at last time to think about what the future might bring I discovered that my stomach had started to perform flip-flops. I realized I had taken a path that, perhaps, led as much to something terrible as it did to joy.

We continued to fly low over the white sands. And we flew faster and faster. Through smoked glass, I watched the desert rush by, occasionally looking up at Mr. Cochise. Although he seemed about to renounce the fleshly shell that allowed him to walk among mortals at any moment, he was still issuing orders to the ship's computer, navigating us ever westward.

The sands and mesa blurred into pale streaks of speed, our vessel casting its shadow across the bleached, cactus-festooned nothingness beneath our feet. The desert's powdery white expanse, the rocks, the giant cacti, the hills, had become one anonymous sea of white. We travelled so fast now that I calculated that I should have seen the Pacific stretched out below; but then I remembered that, here in the transdimensional corridor, the West did not end with the eastern coastline, but extended over empty desert and plain for several million more miles. We passed over a region of America that had no counterpart in the quotidian world. This was nameless country, a part of the corridor made out of the stuff of wild, continental expanses such as the early settlers had known, but reshaped into something wholly new.

The saucer carried us westward for an hour before Mr. Cochise moaned, looked to the sky and discorporated.

"Nicky, look away!" cried Miss Viva. I did so; but not before I witnessed Mr. Cochise's body starting to melt. And as it melted, it shone with a weird light, a light like that which bathed the desert at sundown, a light such as informed the White Heat.

The light filled the bridge. Mr. Twist swore.

"He's going into primal state!" Miss Viva concluded. "Cover your eyes!" I obeyed. Miss Viva gathered my face into her bosom. When she released me and I dared peep between my fingers, I saw that Mr. Cochise had vanished and that the saucer was on fire. Both my friends jumped out of their seats, Mr. Twist desperately beating at the flames with his Stetson, Miss Viva punching the control panel and shouting at the computer in a bid to bring the ship under her control.

The airframe had been fatally compromised. The ship bucked and threatened to stall.

As we lost speed I saw that we no longer passed over white sand. The saucer had taken us beyond desert and mesa, taken us a million miles over the sweaty lands where the Pacific had once rolled and into the lands that marked the frontier. Thick jungle characterised this part of the West. We began to descend, the ship's skirt clipping the top of the jungle's emerald canopy.

I have no recollection of the impact.

*

Thanks to Miss Viva's piloting, we all escaped serious hurt. And we all escaped being marooned in the jungle. Miss Viva had ditched the saucer in a forest clearing near to a railroad town. There, we had eaten, drunk (oh yes, we had drunk), slept and bought provisions with the money that we had found in the saucer's strongbox.

On the morning of the next day, we stood on a platform, eyes trained along the die-straight line of the railroad tracks. Mr. Twist wore his new leather pants. And in his buttonhole was a dried flower, a hothouse bloom white as the desert that we had put far behind us. Miss Viva wore a black A-line dress by Christian Dior. A little pillbox hat was perched on her head, its veil down, covering half her face in sooty netting. I stood between them, holding their hands, as if I were a little sister, or even their child.

"I am resigned, I suppose," Miss Viva was saying, taking off her white gloves, for it had ceased raining some hours previously and the morning had begun to heat up, the humidity almost overpowering, "I am resigned to a long engagement. I'm a fool, I know. A lovesick fool. Not many women jilted at the altar would give their beaus a second chance. But someday all will be put right. Of this I am assured. Someday all will be…*heavenly*." I looked into the distance. I could hear the train's skirling carrying over the jungle's chittering roof. The sun was rising, shining obliquely through the treetops, an amethyst disk that radiated the sickly, neon glow that you might find in a morgue filled with livid, gangrenous bodies. Dawn to dusk, the whole world was a morgue. The whole of my world, that is. My new world. Cool. Ice-blue. And set with amethyst. Viva Venera! And viva Mr. Twist! And viva Nicola Venera! This is my paradise, I thought, out there, far out, beyond the plains where the zanies roamed. My paradise of ice and fire. Place beyond the borderlands of this world and the next. Place beyond all frontiers, all limits. And it would be a paradise indeed for murderers and thieves, aliens and truants, a paradise dedicated to gunslingers and little necrobabes, everywhere.

The train was coming. The soul train; the Zion train. Taking me to the promised land. Taking me deep into the West. Hoot-hoot! Hoot-hoot! Nothing could stop it. Things worked differently here. The laws of this universe weighed in my favor. It was a toy universe, designed just for me. I could sense its mind, its strange, alien mind immanent in the coconut-palms, the fronds and the monkey-song, in all the things that constituted its gorgeous lineaments. Nothing could survive in it which didn't allow the fulfilment of desire. Nothing could live in it, be of it, sing of it which didn't allow my rebirth. And nothing could prevent me boarding and following Death and her cheated prize out and over the limits of this world, to where my private universe dissolved and became all.

Goodbye Ma. Goodbye Pa.

I was free.

The low sun hurled splinters of light through the jungle, little vermilion, mauve and turquoise daggers that stabbed at my eyes and made them water.

I didn't care.

In fact, feeling hands tighten about my own, I laughed.

We were a family now.

Chapter Seven
Bound For Glory

We no longer travelled at the speed of sound, and, half-awake, I listened to the train's yackety-yack. For six days the lazy palaver of its steel wheels had been constant. Beyond the shuttered windows lay that jungle that had first spoken to me when I had stood in Miss Viva's room in Tombstone and she had tuned in her radio to a frequency whose chittering voices—a massed choir of chelicerae—had, she claimed, sometimes reminded her of Venus. Out there, despite being close to morning, the steaming land continued to radiate its nigh intolerable heat.

I was still a little drunk from the night before, and filled with melancholia. On this morning, as on others, I had had a certain dream. It was a recurring anxiety dream in which I imagined I was back in Boston, no chance of being free, no chance of travelling West. When I awoke it had taken several seconds before I realized that I was in fact in the borderlands, and that my earlier life had been sloughed off, along with the dead time and dead space that had formerly imprisoned my spirit. Lately, I had come to fear that one day the very opposite would prove to be true. That, one day, I would dream I was with Miss Viva and Mr. Twist, nearing the frontier, everything right, and waking, I would, shaking my head, come to realize that I had never left my bed back home, never left the East. Contemplating this prospect of cruel, ontological reversal, I would feel a bitter stab of despair transfix my heart. And I tried to console myself now, in case that latter dream stole up on me unawares, reducing my present life to a sham, telling myself that this land of half-waking, this drowsy world suggestive of death, had a counterpart out there, a real, solid counterpart waiting for me on the fast-approaching horizon of lucidity. At the West's limits, where the frontier melted into the beyond, there was another, supreme dream, a dream which would soon subsume me, one into which I would be able to completely disappear. It would be so good to disappear, for Nicola Newton not to be; to die, and become someone, something else.

But I could not disappear yet. Reality would not yield itself to me until I had crossed into the unknown, thrown myself over the edge, given myself up as lost and renounced not only the world, but myself.

Shutting my ears to the hypnotic music of wheels over track, I roused myself, eyelids opening with a gummy snap of cilia. Groping, I found and then raised the hip flask to my lips and let the familiar, burning comfort of its contents again warm my throat. Then I rolled over, pulled back the curtain and checked the corridor.

Some people had already stirred and a queue had formed in front of the bathroom at the end of the carriage. The rotary fan swivelled through its parabola. I lifted my chin, and let the fan cool my hot, sticky face. My hair was no longer plaited but hung loose, greasy and matted, over my eyes. I had, bar my shoes and top, slept in my clothes, as was common when travelling in a sleeperette where privacy is at a premium. I sat up and assumed a cross-legged position; scanned myself, appraising my creased, smelly wardrobe, both the clothes I wore and those that lay discarded in the tangle of sheets. Pedal-pushers. Big, stripy sweatshirt. Beret. Heel-less pumps. I had decided, lawless outsider that I was, to adopt the uniform of a beatnik. I pinched a roll of fat just above my hip-hugging jeans. I had of late begun to wonder, in long, unhealthy bouts of introspection, if I was doomed to share the same somatotype as my mother.

I yanked at the curtain. For a moment, its rings jammed on the rail, and then, with a shriek, the curtain yielded, furling and bringing the opposite berths into view. I brushed the hair from my face and blinked, my overexposed eyes acclimatising to the harsh, artificial glare of the overhead lighting.

Miss Viva and Mr. Twist had not yet stirred. The curtains of their berths remained drawn. I slipped on my shirt. Turning to the window, I grasped its security shutter in both hands and pushed upwards. The shutter gave, wobbling in its jambs, and settled in a half-open attitude, slanting a little from left to right. I was now able to open the window partway. Propping up a pillow against the berth's headboard, I lay back, luxuriating in the air that rushed in from outside, still nocturnally cool, but warming now that the sun had peeped over the horizon, drenching the countryside in soft light.

I had escaped from the East of my own country only to come to another East. Not the East of the world I had known in my Bostonian childhood, but an East that, even if I had not received a superlative education in such matters from Miss Viva, I would have known, and known instinctively, gave way onto the world of death. I looked out, now, over flooded rice fields that shimmered, empurpled by the rich imperial dye of the sun. A line of monks in black robes walked in file across the ridge of an irrigation ditch; a boy was riding atop a water buffalo, his little sister, running alongside, tapping at the muddy beast's hide with a stick. Far away, high above a small group of teak houses, a bald eagle circled, its altitude extreme enough to reduce it to the size of a kite or toy ornithopter. The air was filled with the distinct and overpowering perfume of tropical plenitude and decay. Goodbye El Paso, Roswell, Durango, Flagstaff, Salt Lake City, Reno, Eureka, Deadwood, goodbye you deserts, you plateaus of sagebrush, you canyons and dusty trails—you were memories of a bent, whacked, unreal Earth, but an Earth nonetheless, not a land such as the limbo I had entered upon.

I rested my chin on the windowsill, my teeth chattering at each bump and sway of the carriage. There it was; there it had been for a handful of long, hot days. See, I told myself, take it all in, feel it in your blood and the reptilian depths of your brain; for here, at last, is the place you had always meant to arrive at. Look. Behold. Desdichado.

A hand grasped my shoulder. "You got a drink?" Without looking I reached behind to the shelf that had been created by the conversion of seat into bed and picked up a plastic bottle, brought it onto my lap, eased off its cap with a thumb, and then, turning, handed it to Mr. Twist. He had drunk a lot last night; we all had, keeping the bar from shutting until a guard had had to be called to announce that we either went back to our carriage or slept under the tables. We had complied, reluctantly. Travelling second class, as our impoverished circumstances forced us to do (the money we had retrieved from the saucer had been quite modest), we begrudged sharing our sleeping arrangements with the fifty or so others who populated our section of the train, gamblers, charlatans, whores, adventurers and scoundrels of every kind.

I quit my window gazing, leant back and regarded my friend. Mr. Twist sat down on the edge of my bunk, lifted the bottle, put his lips to its neck and tipped it with the wanton panache that characterised his life. Grimacing, he turned his head to one side; spat. "Water," he said, a violent cough threatening the disemboguement of his lungs. "How could you? And spring water, effervescent *spring* water at that. I didn't expect an act of gratuitous cruelty from my own sweet Nicky on such a dark, dark morning as this, my poor head fit to explode from a simply *gargantuan* hangover."

"I'm sorry," I said, taking the bottle from his hand and substituting it with another, "my mistake." He swigged at what remained of last night's liquor, brown, syrupy dregs staining his stubbly chin and dripping onto his unbuttoned shirt and smooth, suntanned chest. "The swollen brain, oh crapulous one: is it really so painful?"

"It's the last trump. The seventh seal. It's atomic."

He looked pretty rough, to be sure. The years had been untender; he had taken his rough joy of them and they had determined, now, to pay him back in kind. After each heavy session, each long audience granted by Lord Alcohol, he looked as if he'd just crawled back from a fight with old man mortality, a fight, to his credit, he always avoided losing, even if each bout left him nearer to the final, inevitable kayo. "Is Viva awake yet?" I said.

"Miss Viva is indeed awake. Miss Viva is making herself presentable. And well *might* she. For I suspect that she'll soon be escorting me to the midnight ball. She has the smell of victory in her nostrils does my *belle dame sans merci*, the smell of my imminent demise. I must say, Nicky, I'd never supposed I would have made it to the frontier just *yet* awhile. Goddamn that flying saucer."

"You've got a good many years left to you yet, Mr. Twist."

"Ah, you sweet-talking apprentice stealer of souls, Miss Nicola, you flatterer, you Venusian epigone you."

"Not nice, Mr. Twist. I am, it is true, an admirer of all things Venusian. But that does not mean I am any the less loyal to you. You should treat yourself a little more kindly. Cut down on the booze."

"Rich, coming from you, girl."

"I'm younger. I can party all night." I eased myself forward and kissed him lightly on his damp, whisky-branded mouth. Withdrew, licked the liquor off my lips, and, getting the taste, took the bottle off of him and breakfasted on what was left of its contents. "I need you, Mr. Twist. So does Miss Viva. Slow down. We're at the end of the line now. Nowhere else to run. I don't want it all to end too soon. I've only just got to know you."

He stood up, pulling his suspenders over his shoulders, then snapped them; ran both hands down his grimy, flannel shirt and the tops of his worn, chamois pants, and then slicked back his threadbare, salt-and-pepper quiff with the grease and sweat that had rubbed off the filthy leather.

A pair of legs, encased in the same kind of pedal-pushers as I wore, but tailored from plastic, not denim—a black vinyl that might have been dredged from a soup made out of boiled down seven-inch singles—dangled over the edge of the upper berth that was twinned with Mr. Twist's sleeping quarters. And then Miss Viva emerged, fussing with her lacquer-buttressed hair.

I averted my face from her scrutiny and stared down to where my pumps lay, their toes turned inward and jutting out from beneath my bunk. I reached out and plucked them up. There was a sound that was like a recalcitrant zip being unfastened as their soles were separated from mucilaginous contact with the floor, its surface vile with a patina of spilt, soft drinks and hard liquor.

Miss Viva leant forward as Mr. Twist handed her the bottle so that she too might slake the terrible, alcohol-induced thirst which was one more downside of occupying the flesh house of the human spirit.

"Water, Mr. Twist?"

"Rotgut, Miss Viva."

"Capital, Mr. Twist."

She drained the last of the whisky, smacked her lips with

appreciation, and then again stared down at me, her keen gaze penetrating my bedraggled, mousy fringe, burrowing into my skull, the interior walls of which resonated with the scrapes and bangs of my alcohol-shrunken brain, a calcified sponge tossed about by the dark, pulsating currents of an undersea cavern.

"I used to live in these parts," said Miss Viva, breaking off her intra-cepahlic inspection to spread her arms, as if she meant to embrace the territory outside. "Did you know that? Lots of Venusians live here, in human form, at the end of the line. My people, these days, sometimes like to spend time in Desdichado listening to the distant heartbeat of their loved ones, those to whom their own hearts perpetually call."

"And humans?" I said.

"Plenty of *real* humans here, too," she said. "Humans come here to die."

"To die? They can do that anywhere."

"To die *romantically*."

"Oh," I said, a little shamed by the dullness of my early-morning wit.

The rice fields, which had been slowly obscured by track-side hovels, now disappeared entirely, to be superseded by tenements—high walls of banal sandstone, stained with coal-tar and pocked with barred windows from which protruded poles festooned with ragged laundry. Beside the track ran a canal, its turbid surface covered with green scum and lily pads. There was *Dracaena* there, too, that tropical plant related to the lily that yields a resin known as dragon's-blood; and there were many, many other flowers, some grotesque, but all bearing a semblance to blooms that you would expect to find at a graveside. As if cued by my meditation, another procession of monks flashed by the window, those cowled acolytes of the gods and goddesses of death holding alms bowls filled with black orchids and other votary plants bestowed by the faithful whom they had passed on their morning round.

Exiles, outcasts, solitaries of all kinds, from all over this world and the next, that was Desdichado. That was what you found, they said, at the end of the line, the grand terminus of the known universe.

Mr. Twist had sat down again on my bunk. He was looking out of the window across the faintly lit countryside and into the violet sky. I let my gaze follow his own. I knew for what he was looking and soon catalogued, adding to observations taken over the course of the years, the ice-bright celestial body to which so many of the souls of the departed, the dead, past, present and future, had, were now and would be emigrating, taken into the bosom of love's alienness, there to reside forever. Those, at least, whom, among the dead, were fortunate enough to be loved by that planet's indigents. Mr. Twist spoke:

> *"Thou rainbow on the tearful lash of doomsday's morning star*
> *Rise quick, and let me gaze into that planet deep and far..."*

I looked at him. He had taken out his dog-eared, pocket edition of Beddoes and placed it on his knee while he set to work lighting his meerschaum pipe. "Shouldn't Venus look bigger by now," I said, "after all the miles we've travelled?"

"Of course not," said Miss Viva, with a Gioconda-like smile. "Psychogeography doesn't work that way. A few miles ahead lies the river. You only have to cross it to discover that the *dérive* has delivered you up unto the shores of the planet of love."

"So we definitely *are* going to Venus?" I asked.

"Of course. We have more than lawmen and bounty hunters at our heels now. We have the White Heat. There is nowhere else left to run." Miss Viva avoided my eyes. I had pressed her on several occasions about whether I too would be accompanying my friends off-world, and had never received anything more than an ambiguity or two for my troubles. Still, I pressed my case again.

"And I will be coming with you?"

"Eventually," said Miss Viva.

"Eventually, but not just yet, if I may petition for myself," said Mr. Twist, "not just yet, eh, darlin'? Give a man a little time to get a look at the new town, play a little faro, enjoy a little mischief." Mr. Twist was struggling to ignite a match, his hands shaking with what might have been his numerous debts to dissipation, excitement, or even perhaps fear.

"We shall leave when you are ready, Mr. Twist."

"Thank you, Miss Viva."

"I am a *patient* psychopomp, Mr. Twist."

"I know, Miss Viva. But patient or not, you'll soon be conducting me to the other side. There's no use denying it."

I tried to conceal the anxiety and disappointment I felt at Miss Viva's continued failure to bring me into her confidence, to reassure me that I would not be left alone in this bad, cruel world.

A cloud of smoke, its bouquet redolent of hot toffee, floated across the carriage and entertained my nostrils with its sweetly aromatic high jinks. Mr. Twist took the pipe from his mouth and gazed down meditatively into its smouldering bowl.

"It's recently occurred to me that I'll soon be forty-six." He blew out another cloud of smoke. "Forty-six," he continued. "That's the same age as Beddoes when he died."

"Superstitious, Mr. Twist?" said Miss Viva. "Don't be. You might walk under a ladder, spill salt, have a black cat walk across your path—and all those things would be as nothing compared to the lethal fatefulness of my love."

"Strange thing about Thomas Lovell," said Mr. Twist, pretending he hadn't attended to Miss Viva's somewhat minacious commentary, "given his propensity for the poetry of the grave, that is."

"What is?" I said.

"Yes, tell, Mr. Twist."

"His father was the man who discovered laughing gas."

But with only a whiff of pipe smoke to intoxicate me, and still viciously hungover, I did not laugh; and neither did the sepulchral Miss Viva.

"The planet of love," I said, wistfully, again looking out at the lightening sky. "Are love and death really the same thing, Miss Viva?"

"This world and the next interpenetrate only where there is love, my little butterball. Or else"—Miss Viva paused to roll her tongue about her gums as if trying to sluice away an unpleasant taste—"where there is hate."

"It must be funny," I said, still staring out the window, even though the sky was by now largely obscured by bricks, mortar and black rendering, "living on a world where people don't have permanent form, where faces are forever shifting from one mask into another."

"In death, we forget who we are and become many things," she said.

The track bifurcated, then fanned into a network of lines, idle rolling stock replacing the dreary rows of tenements as principle backdrop and announcement of our arrival.

"Get your bags, Nicky," said Miss Viva, "we're nearly there."

"No bunting," said Mr. Twist, peering out at the tangle of track and trains. "Neither balloons nor streamers were they greeted by. Oh lackaday."

"If the telegraph is still working, Desdichado might be forewarned about us," said Miss Viva. "To hell with bunting; let's hope we don't see no wanted posters." I wondered at Miss Viva's ingenuousness, this town representing a homecoming

for her, of sorts, the nearest to home, at least, that she could
expect to come to without giving up her mortal body. I wondered also if her nights now might be spent in more than
usually earnest, dreamy longings of Mr. Twist dead, his heart
drilled through with bullets, his soul hers at last to consume.
"The only reception *we* ever get is hot, nasty and brutish," she
concluded with, perhaps, only my fancy confusing her tone
with that of a woman who prayed that this town would prove
unexceptional; that her lover would be delivered up unto evil,
that her jealous embrace would no longer have to share him
with life.

I clambered out of the berth, collecting clothes, accoutre-
ments and valuables and giving Mr. Twist a sidelong inspection as I moved some of my bags off of the luggage rack. For
a moment, he seemed confused. He was looking down the
corridor, as if down that other, transcendental corridor, that
corridor of light that had manifested itself to him when, as a
twelve-year-old, he had fallen toward eternity, a noose about
his neck. And then the confusion left him and he too fell to
preparing for our disembarkation.

The train's wheels began to groan and keen as they negotiated the chaos of interlaced rails that served notice that we
were pulling into Desdichado Grand Central. Porters began to
run alongside, calling through the windows in their attempts
to procure custom. Miss Viva climbed down from her perch
and situated herself by a window. Having taken her beret from
her back pocket, she waved with it to gain a porter's attention;
and then, when the boy's grinning face signalled that he had
understood, she placed it on her head, set at the requisite jaun-
ty angle, with the silver brooch, that spelled out RIP, displayed
to coquettish effect. I put on my own beret which, though sans
jewellery, was, I hoped, a fashion statement that brought me
into the sisterhood of the honorary necrobabe.

People deluged the corridor as they fought to be the first

ones to leave the train. Miss Viva was caught up in the flood. Mr. Twist, grabbing two handfuls of luggage and swimming with the current, quickly sought to catch her up. The crowd gave way compliantly to his looming, dangerous presence. I followed them both, lethargically at first, but soon, fortified by the fear of being lost, with a panting enthusiasm that soon approached panic. In less than a minute the three of us had left our uncouth fellow travellers behind and stood in the space dividing one carriage from the next. The door had already been flung open, its handle banging against the outside coachwork. Our porter drew level with us, taking some of our bags even before we had come to a complete halt. As soon as there was that shudder indicating that the engine had drawn flush against the buffers, Mr. Twist leapt onto the platform and, quickly turning, put his hands under Miss Viva's arms and lifted her off of the train. After depositing her on the ground, he next awarded me the same service, hoisting the somewhat heavier burden of my rotund little frame into the air—those gold-encrusted teeth of his seemed to gnash a little—and then gently dropping me, my deposition so much less graceful than Miss Viva's, by his side.

"Yes, yes," said Miss Viva, "oh, how this brings it all back. Memories. Sweet memories! We must stay at a hotel by the river. The river is the most beautiful thing in town. The same hotel I stayed in, perhaps, the last time I was here." She turned to the porter. "The *Hotel Terminus*—is it still standing?"

"It is," said the boy, briefly scratching himself through a tear in his dirty, torn pants before hefting the last of our bags onto his trolley. "But much decayed, ma'am," he continued. "I guess, though, that that is as you would expect it, eh?" His accent was Western, but not of a kind I had heard before. It had a nasal inflection that I had only heard before in Chinamen, or some of the other, unidentifiable Asians who worked the railroad as coolies, cooks or loan sharks.

"Indeed," said Miss Viva, "that is as I would expect it and *want* it." I looked around at my new surroundings. Grand Central Station rose above me, its glass roof, criss-crossed with vines and other tropical vegetation, like the dome of a big hothouse, and we, crawling about on its floor, among the press of humanity that swarmed the platforms and the concourse, a chittering, scuttling army of bugs.

"You'd like me to get you a cab, ma'am?" said the boy. But Miss Viva was distracted by the sounds and scents of Desdichado.

"Lead on," said Mr. Twist. We followed the porter down the platform, through the gates and into the ferment of the crowd. We found ourselves, then, in a concrete arena, caught between the early sun and the hard white ground as between a hammer and an anvil. Everywhere, travellers who had disembarked upon land that was to be their last foothold on this world were gaily met by Venusian lovers—I saw men and women, young and old, running into the arms of those whose beauty was conspicuously alien. But some remained alone, looking about furtively as if seeking an assignation that would take them beyond doubt, beyond sorrow, into the lands of blessedness.

"Sort of reminds me of when I ran away from home for the first time," said Mr. Twist, scanning the crowd. "Last time, too, as it happens. Found my way to the railroad and took the first train that came in. Didn't care where it went, just so long as it would take me as far away from *home* as I could get."

"And where *did* the train take you?" I said.

"Into the West, of course," said Miss Viva. "Where else?"

"Perdition," said Mr. Twist, "that's where it took me."

"And was it so bad?" I said. "Your home, I mean?"

"Well, my Ma and Pa weren't *Nazis*, Miss Nicky, but—"

"Theirs was a more sophisticated cruelty," said Miss Viva.

"They were a pharisaical bunch, for sure, and as you say, *sophisticated,* at least as far as white trash goes. Concordia Parish, it was, by the swampwater of the Cocodrie, that was my natal homeland. Cold and lonely, my boyhood was, if you'll all permit me a little self-pity, this poor ol' boy having so little else to soothe his frayed spirit these days. There were the whuppings, of course; but it's the loneliness I remember. The cold, empty days with no one to speak to. That boy, my father would say, the venom dripping off of his tongue, that boy's a *dreamer.* He'll end up on the end of a noose. And so it was. I was never really part of the family."

"Poor baby Twist," said Miss Viva.

He squinted and looked about him, as if alerted to a threat.

"People don't ignore you *now*, Mr. Twist," I said.

"For sure, Nicky," he said. "I've seen to that." His stride lengthened, so that he began to outpace our porter. Miss Viva and I struggled to keep up. "I learnt my first lesson real quick," he continued, "that people usually do foul things for no other reason than that they can, because they believe that they can get away with it. I learnt my second lesson, the most important lesson of my life, straight after. Despite my cold, but relatively pacific childhood, I came to greatly respect violence, for I realized that it was just about the only thing such people as do foul things—quiet, cunning, subtle foul things—would themselves respect."

"Mr. Twist has yet to learn the full import of lesson number three."

"That I should submit to a Death rather than be a slave to the banal?"

"Quite, Mr. Twist."

"But, oh, I do submit."

"Not nearly enough. Not with nearly enough *absoluteness*."

"Well," he said, his mouth contorted into a crooked grin, "I *am* still around."

"You are *bloody-mindedly* incarnate, Mr. Twist."

"That I am. Put it down to my emotionally impoverished childhood, Viva dear, breeding ground of the irrepressibly vital psychopath."

We passed out of the station's forecourt and into the street, a queue of hansom cabs awaiting our pleasure. Touts eeled through the milling bodies, grabbing arms and urging their prospective customers toward a fare, their eyes flashing as they offered assurance that the price they quoted could not be bettered, that their ride was the best in town. Mr. Twist shook off a hand that had dared to touch him and, as another tout tried his luck, I saw his own hand fall to his side. His fingers twitched, as if, indulging himself in a gesture I had grown familiar with—the smell of cordite and death ingrained, like trail dust, in my clothes—he was momentarily tempted to fling back the skirt of his coat and place the barrel of his pistol to the importunate one's head. But, biting down on his pipe with a vehemence that I thought was about to snap its meerschaum stem in two, he desisted, using his height to shoulder his way through the mob and impose his authority in a manner more restrained, if no less certain. Selecting a hansom, and pushing aside a young couple and their child who were about to board, he curtly ordered our porter to load our luggage, issued orders to the driver and climbed inside. We followed, giggling.

I sat between my two friends, snug, enjoying the comforting warmth of their bodies. It was pleasant to be so close to Miss Viva and Mr. Twist, my only friends, as we passed through Desdichado. It was good, because despite of the tropical heat, a chill had goose-pimpled my flesh. I leant my head against my favorite Venusian's shoulder; and I might have been the child I had been several weeks ago, when those two desperadoes, if not the only family I had known, had become the only family I had ever cared for.

"Will I go to heaven, Miss Viva?" I said. She was about to fob me off with more of her shilly-shallying when an expression of pain transformed her vacant face. She had come to some kind of decision, like a mother who was about to disabuse her little daughter that, though Santa Claus existed, he would not be visiting her. At least, not that year.

"I can't take you with me, Nicky. But don't fret. You have your own Death waiting for you, somewhere. She'll take you when the time comes, I can vouch for that. She'll take you—"

"To heaven?" I said, a sob catching in my throat.

"Yes, darling, to heaven."

I looked imploringly into Miss Viva's ice-blue eyes. "But I go where you go, don't I?"

"I said I can't take you, Nicky. It's just not possible. I'm not your Death. But yes—" Her eyes, their surfaces of frozen blue ink too thin for my own eyes to skate over without crashing through into their stark, cold depths, held onto my attention unflinchingly. I kept still, unwilling to chance drowning. It was, I apprehended, as she had said: I was not yet ready to cross the border. "Yes, we will all be together at last," she continued, "I think at least I can tell you that."

"I suppose you know best," I said, gulping back my anguish.

"We all have to sometimes learn to wait," said Miss Viva. "Lord knows, *I've* had to wait long enough. I tell you: this Venusian is hungry."

Turning my face to conceal my tears, I looked out at the town. It had been constructed in the same style as Boot Hill, but entropy, here, at the edge of things, meant that there was nothing maniacal or even grand about its design. The suburbs we had passed through when we had arrived on the train constituted an elevation circling the town that resembled the lip of a huge crater. But here, away from the town's outskirts, the skyline was modest, the tombs and mausolea in which people lived and conducted their business of the dimensions, not of a scaled-up Père Lachaise, but a Père Lachaise that might have been an exact replica, so much did it evoke the verisimilitude of moving through one of Europe's great urban cemeteries. Apart from the occasional office building, or temple, or hotel, or bar, sparse examples of which were scattered among the headstones and tombs, Desdichado, this *reductio ad absurdum* of Western township, *was* a cemetery. A cemetery infested with vines, creepers and other strangulating forms of tropical vegetation. A big, overgrown, fetid, steaming grave.

"The river!" cried Miss Viva. "The last river across which lies my home. Behold!" The river, the chthonian river—don't call it the Styx or the Jordan; call it, in hushed wonder, or while choking back a sob, call it only "the river"—lay before us, a mile-wide, infinitely long and sparkling like dark, mellow wine shot through with violent sunlight. The hansom turned onto the riverfront. On one side, rows of headstones scrolled past; on the other, people strolled through the gardens of re- membrance that led down to the river.

It was low and flowing gently, I noticed, and not like I had heard Miss Viva describe it when, bloated with mon- soon rains, it rushed by carrying timber and flotsam from the distant mountains—not its source, for the river had no source—rushed by so torrentially that it sometimes precipi- tated flash floods. The early morning strollers—they brought to mind those whom I had seen promenading alongside Tombstone's reservoir—looked across the stretch of water at the mist-enshrouded bank opposite, a panoply of coconut palms occasionally protruding above the white coverlet of swirling, scudding cloud. It seemed to me that those wist- ful ones might have been praying for such a flood, a sudden, preternatural sundering of the skies that would unleash a monumental downpour to fill and then burst the river's banks and engulf the town and them. For they, I think, longed to be bound for glory as much as I.

The hansom pulled up. Solitary among the headstones— at least for a stretch of several hundred yards—stood a decrepit, forlorn three-storey building, a sign above its portico proclaiming *Hotel Terminus*. The hotel, I thought, was distinguished by a certain charm and—standing alone as it did—the privacy our little gang valued.

"Does it have a gaming table?" said Mr. Twist.

"There'll be time enough for all that," said Miss Viva. "We need to rest."

"Rest? We need money, darlin'. Now listen: I've been casting an appraising eye over this town and in my honest opinion we can rob it blind."

"And what then?" said Miss Viva.

"There's always a "then" Miss Viva." But Mr. Twist was grimacing, as if he saw through his own mocked-up sense of conviction.

"End of the line, Mr. Twist," said Miss Viva. "How long before you understand that? How long before you digest what that really means?" Mr. Twist pulled his shoulders up into his ears, opened the carriage door and stepped out. He immediately headed toward the hotel. "Oh dear," said Miss Viva, "I've put him in a huff. The poor man's been quite frazzled, lately, knowing that he won't get to enjoy his vices for much longer. Perhaps I should indulge him."

"Perhaps," I said, getting out as the hotel's porters ran up to our hansom to relieve it of our luggage, "perhaps you should let him have one last gunfight."

"That's what I was thinking," she said, following me onto the sidewalk, bestowing a knowing wink that recruited me as a co-conspirator.

"No, no, Miss Viva," I said, "I didn't mean *that*. I meant, well, it might make him feel *better*."

"Yes, you did mean that. You meant you would like to see him killed."

"No I didn't."

"Yes you did, you did, you little apprentice necrobabe, you, oh yes, yes you *did*." I walked after Mr. Twist, keeping my lips closed, conscious that Miss Viva might be correct. I had learnt that I didn't understand my own desires as well as I often thought I did.

The doorman took off his top hat and gave a little bow; and, acknowledging him less than the two marble angels that flanked the door and that seemed, with their prayerful countenances and long, folded wings, to be like the guardians of a noble infant's last resting place, I nodded and then entered, holding my breath as if about to be reinterred in the family vault.

*

My room was simple, but adequate. I unpacked. I had not slept well on the train and so decided to treat myself to an early siesta. I have always found sleep a great benison. The back of one hand placed over my perspiring brow, I fought to attract its grace, like some hooker working the fringes of a desert who sees the mirage of Mr. Big Time over the horizon. But sleep would not come; I was working Hypnagogiaville's dusty streets without prospect of pity or pay. Stop it, I said to the cavalcade of images percolating through my mind. Stop it. Don't carnival. This is a place of mourning. A bleached-out, desert place. Haven't you heard? The West is dying. But the faces still came, spinning out of the darkness, the faces of my mother, my father, indeed, of all the dead. Their faces peered out from the luminous wall of the White Heat. And they all stared at me: Nicola, they said, Nicola, how *could* you.

Chapter Eight

My Very Own Dark Night
Of The Soul

Six months passed. And if in all that time my dreams were haunted by images of the White Heat, they were also haunted by images, terrible images, of Miss Viva. That recurring dream that I had had on the train after first arriving in the frontier, a dream of being back in Boston, with no hope of escape, had been replaced by one in which I ran from the Heat, and finding refuge in Miss Viva's arms, had looked up only to see her lovely face transformed into a grinning skull. *It is all a lie*, she seemed to whisper. *Death can never be beautiful. It can never be a release. Death, Nicola, is always ugly.*

I rarely left the hotel. Neither did Mr. Twist and Miss Viva. Rumors of our arrival had begun to circulate. When the three of us had first hit town we had had our share of the vapors; but we had been happy, too, often spending whole nights carousing in Desdichado's bars. But the melancholia had deepened. And it didn't seem to be merely because we had an apprehension of ourselves as hunted prey. For me, the blue mood seemed intimately connected to my growing doubts about the path I had chosen, a path that had initially seemed to offer redemption, but which now seemed to offer only the cold comfort of the void.

I told myself that I had no reason to be blue. I told myself that I had got everything I wanted: friends and a substitute family, the incarceration of my progenitors in a wall of quantum fire, and the promise that I would one day, and perhaps one day soon, travel beyond this world and arrive on Venus, there to be united with my friends forever. But still doubt knotted my stomach. And doubt began to beget despair.

I tried to find solace in routine. I would get up, shower, slip into a nice, long cheesecloth smock—perfect for aeration in such a torpid climate as this—and decamp onto the balcony. With a bottle of champagne supplied by room service at hand, I found it possible to sit, feet up, staring past my pretty pink espadrilles to survey the river and the people who passed below, and pretend, for a while at least, that I had not a care in the world.

Despite the relentless sunlight, the populace were an etiolated bunch of wretches. A casual slap of the hand might have easily knocked any one of them to the ground. Miss Viva had told me that no human lasted long in Desdichado, that physical and mental well-being could not long endure submersion in this far-flung region's sickly environment. Its malarial slums, the melancholia of its grand piazzas, made this town the Earthman's grave. This, Miss Viva had explained, was central to the town's charm, and for those who came here, waiting for death, its chief merit.

But routine has limited efficacy. I tired of gazing down at the promenaders, tired also of gazing out over the river; and one day, the blue mood became almost too much to bear.

I got up. The sun was directly overhead. Those who walked below—those temperamentally given to coveting the darkness—continued to stare across the river it was their overriding ambition to cross, their eyes looking out from beneath the brims of panamas and parasols toward the farther side, where they would be cleansed, the too bright, too insistent years washed away by the balm of oblivion.

I plucked the half-empty bottle of champagne from its bucket of slush and left my room, padding down the corridor to where the stairs led to the roof garden. Emerging onto the hotel's roof I walked over to where Mr. Twist and Miss Viva sat under a sunshade, their table crowded with bottles similar to my own, magnums half-empty, empty, or still unopened and protruding from freshly-delivered ice.

"Good afternoon, Miss Nicola E. Newton," said Miss Viva, thickly, as if her tongue had grown too big for her mouth. I walked past them and stood by one of the embrasures of the garden wall, looking away from the river and out over the town to where the jungle began, a baize tapestry sown with emeralds stretching out to the line where coruscating textile met pale horizon. The air rippled, convective, and a shiver coursed through my body in sympathy.

"I never knew Venusians could get so drunk," I said.

"When we have a mind to it," she said, "when there's the rationale. Like: trying to forget I'm an interplanetary criminal. A heartless killer of men, women and children!" Mr. Twist put his arm about her.

"It was the only way of shutting down Musidora's operation," he said. "Nobody knows what happened back there, except us."

"I suppose," said Miss Viva, "I suppose it was for the best. I configured the White Heat to bring the West's souls this way, to Venus. Better they die and be consumed by my home planet than the whole Earth be eaten by Niflheim."

"Of course, darlin'. It's a qualitatively different death. Even I know that."

"The West will be swept clean," she said. "Perhaps it will even collapse upon itself. That might not be so bad. My people have always fudged things. I mean, when we found out the damage we were doing when we first came to Earth, we should have left. Instead, we started giving away death-toys. Gave them away like candy. And then, to try to absolve ourselves, we turned the corridor into a place where we hoped humans, while still having free will, could live in peace. Fat chance. We should never have turned the *dérive* into matter. Let us Deaths stay on Venus, and let humans come to us as they did in the old days, via a *dérive* that is non-material and metaphysical. There has been too much alien interference in Earth's affairs."

I put a hand over my eyes, bringing my gaze to bear on the white glow that rose from beyond the horizon, staining the lower sky with a brilliance that had stripped it of its color, leaving a pale, jagged band of light in its stead.

"To hell with it," I said. "I don't give a damn about killing my Ma. Give yourself a break, Miss Viva. Care less about mass destruction."

"Well put, Nicky," said Mr. Twist.

The horizon's skirtlet of light flickered as if some terrific electrical storm were raging just beyond the limits of perception. The people who fled the White Heat's progress said it had grown; it was now, apparently, some thousands of feet in height, and its breadth such that none could escape it. The Heat razed all that it passed over in a westwards journey that gathered pace with every day. People also told of the terrible faces they had seen within its curtain of destruction, millions of faces, they said, each one sucked into the white prison of its luminous wall, each one set in a rictus of ecstasy.

"Well," I said, "at least your people won't be going hungry, Miss Viva. They seem to have a banquet in store." I focused on the train station at the edge of town. In the plaza in front of Grand Central I spied a fresh contingent of refugees. "It may be paradoxical, but I suspect, Miss Viva, that *you* don't think about death very much. I mean, you're not mortal in the way *we're* mortal. You don't fear oblivion." There were cowboys among the newcomers, and there were Indians, sodbusters and townspeople too; there were even zanies, on their best behavior, natch, those slimy cannibals having struck up a kind of truce with their fellow travellers, foraging for them in return for safe passage. There were all kinds of vermin. They had been arriving for weeks now, these fugitives from the lands of the frontier, their ears still buzzing with reports about the fate of the territories east of California. Even here, at the West's limits, where we had supposed we and others would find sanctuary, there had been concern that Desdichado itself might not be safe.

"I don't think much about death? A dreadful thing to say. I can't decide, Mr. Twist. Is she a person cruel, or merely vulgar?"

"Miss Viva *is* Death, Nicky. A Death, at least."

"An ambassador, that's what I am."

"So you should get to ask your employer sometime, Old Man Death himself, you should get to ask him what's to become of the likes of me and Mr. Twist if even creatures like you can be sucked into this *White Heat*. What, after everything we've been through, everything we've done, the sublime death you promise turns out to be an illusion?" I turned; leant against the embrasure and looked my alien friend in the eye. "What if death turns out to be just nothing at all?"

Miss Viva let the flute of champagne she was lifting to her lips slip from her hand and fall to the floor. She looked down at her feet, at their perimeter of glittering shards, and groped blindly for another glass, another magnum.

"Why did you run away, Nicky?" she said.

I thought of the time, back in Boston, when, one day, I had awoken to discover that everybody was talking in advertisement jingles. When the television seemed always turned on, blathering about getting and spending. When I had discovered that I was surrounded by cheaply made robots who forever barked *barf, barf, barf, barf, barf.* I had known that if I did not get out, and get out quick, I was going to be smothered beneath an avalanche of dead time.

"I wanted to—" I hesitated; I was suddenly unsure. "I wanted to disappear."

"You mean you wanted to escape from your parents?"

"Yes." I chewed my lip. "No. I mean I wanted to *disappear.* That's something more than escape. I wanted to leave everything behind. I wanted to run away from myself."

"And you thought you could do that with me?"

"I did, yes; but now—" I ground my knuckles into the concrete of the parapet. "Tell me it'll be all right, Miss Viva. Tell me it'll all be all right."

"I can't tell you that, Nicky. I've never *promised* you anything, have I?"

"You promised Mr. Twist." She shrugged.

"You must understand, Nicky: I don't really understand what happens to a human when they are taken by one such as me. I don't have a subjective grasp of that experience. I am the consumer, not the consumed." Miss Viva poured herself another glass of champagne. She drank, her eyes averted from my own.

"But it's good, isn't it. Oh, tell me it's *something.* Tell me it's not just the void."

"Nicky, I'm sorry. Don't ask me these questions."

She didn't have to give answers. I could tell she didn't have them. For us three—for everybody perhaps—the edge had become more precipitous, more so than anybody, no matter how long they had courted death, could have wished.

It was coming for us. It was coming for us all, mortal and immortal alike.

White Heat.

White Death.

*

I tore the wanted poster off the lamppost and scrunched it in my fist. Then, with a concession to the obsessive-compulsive behavior that, of late, had had me double-checking whether I had locked a door, fastened a window, stashed my money in a safe place, I relented; opened my hand and, with some difficulty, smoothed out the poster's creases against the lamppost's fluted iron. The likeness was still there, of course; like any neurotic I had known deep inside that it really hadn't gone away.

Posing us as if for a family photograph, the artist had drawn me sitting in front of my two confederates, dressed in a little girl's party dress and sporting the plaits that I had forsaken some months previously. It was fortunate that this draughtsman had a sentimental streak and had taken his inspiration from Miss Pears rather than the mug shots of juvenile delinquents that he could have found at the local sheriff's office. It had meant that, since the posters had gone up a few days ago, I was able to walk the streets with little fear of arrest. In contrast, Mr. Twist and Miss Viva—standing behind the chair on which I sat hugging my porcelain doll—stared out boldly at John Citizen, their faces sketched with considerable mimetic skill. No one, I thought, could possibly mistake them.

News of Mr. Twist and Miss Viva's exploits, as well as news of my association with the pair, had been disseminated throughout Desdichado by way of the refugees, each one of whom carried reports out of the doomed West. But none, I believe, had suspected the full nature of our crimes: that we had been the ones who had engineered the very doom they fled.

I let my fingers again scrunch the poster into a ball; and this time, with a nervous flick, I tossed it into the gutter.

I walked across the street to the saloon. I had come to this part of Desdichado—a slick district of parvenu wealth that had a vicious underbelly—to sound out whether there were any bounty hunters in town. Mr. Twist and Miss Viva could not remain secreted in our hotel much longer. The proprietor, whom they had tied, gagged and imprisoned in their room, would sooner or later be called on to settle bills, or to otherwise account himself to relatives, friends or guests. A hansom bisected my path, showering me with dust. I stepped aside, my beatnik clothes allowing me, I hoped, to blend with the other teenagers who strolled by. Desdichado's tenderloin had become a fashionable haunt for bums and generic freaks who had travelled West, and then farther West, in search of "spiritual enlightenment". Peace was hardly something I could expect. I sensed a showdown loomed, a private Armageddon.

I pressed on. A sign above the saloon's swing doors read *The Catafalque*. I entered and descended. A series of stone steps took me into a crypt.

The tables were stone sarcophagi, or cists; the customized piano was styled after a gun carriage; and the bar was set into the length of a black marble wall, like the sepulchre of a man who had been stretched on a rack until he were some twenty-feet from toe to head. At the back of the saloon, concealed behind a heavy, velvet curtain, was, I presumed, a small theatre, though what entertainment it promised could only be guessed at. The curtain could, in keeping with the rest of the saloon's décor, as well have hidden a small crematorium or charnel house.

Only a handful of customers sat about the tables, a handful more sitting at the bar, staring into the wishing-wells of their beers and whiskies, and all of them characterised by a monolithic silence, as if they were this crypt's long-time inhabitants, embalmed mummies quietly rotting away. A mansard window, high above, provided the only source of illumination, a shaft of mote-filled sunlight—so malapropos, here—pooling in the saloon's empty, central arena, and leaving the outskirts of this haunt, its tables, bars and sullen men, to the shadows.

I sat down on a stool at some remove from those who, drinking themselves to death—or rather, dead and not knowing it—seemed like ghosts doomed to act out the habit of a lifetime, and pushed a few dollars across the cool, stone bar. "Bottle," I whispered, myself infected with the spirit of desuetude that festered in this place of lost souls. The bartender drifted from the farther end of the bar to where I awaited service; a man recruited, I would hazard, for reasons of adding a final, morbid embellishment to the saloon's funereal atmospherics, rather than for his celerity or his wish to please the patrons. With a gravedigger's cheerlessness he took my money and conceded me the honor of pouring my own drink. I filled the grimy tumbler he had left and downed a magisterial four fingers of instant cirrhosis. A small electric fan nestled on a nearby shelf below the cobweb-festooned optics. I turned my face into its lazy, rattling orbit, enjoying, for a moment, the movement of air against my sweat-bemired skin; and then, with eyes closed, spoke out, as hushed yet as distinctly as I was able. "Seems there's some real money to be had for anyone who can bring in that Twist Gang."

My voice echoed about the stark interior. The living corpses continued to stare into the bottoms of their glasses, deaf to my conversational gambit; and then, as I was about to try to rephrase my words, the man nearest to me, an elderly man in checked shirt and Bermuda shorts, spoke, the loose folds of skin on his neck tremulous with the exertion of proving himself more than nominally alive.

"*Pro forma,*" he croaked.

"*Pro forma*? What do you mean?"

"The wanted poster. It's *pro forma*. The judge wants the Twist for himself. He won't let no bounty hunter spoil his day."

"Oh? And what judge might that be?" The man lifted his head and looked at me. As he did so, several of the other patrons, as if cued by my outrageous ignorance, also chose to examine the one who had come to disturb their rest.

"Only one judge in Desdichado," said the old-timer. "Least, only one judge worth that name. I'm talking about the one we call the Sexton."

"Oh, yeah, yeah," said another voice from an unidentifiable source, rising up *de profundis* as if through a mountain of damp rags, a high-piled swelter of sighs. "The Sexton. Yeah. The Sexton'll bury that *Twist* bunch for sure."

"That bunch'll be *wishing* for a bounty hunter."

I refilled my glass and summarily glug-glugged my tipple. Finished, I wiped my lips with the back of my hand and slammed the tumbler back onto the bar, a splinter of crystal skittering across its black marble top. The assembly line, mechanically, almost unconsciously, it seemed, resumed their duties at the factory for drunks, determined, this day, to up productivity. And as they all, to a man, raised their drinks to their mouths, draining their glasses as if in a toast to the early demise of outlaws and the coming deification of The Twist Gang's nemesis—cheers, said their thoughts, so loud with vindictiveness I could almost decipher them, cheers, Sexton—I eased myself off my stool and made my way out into the daylight, blinking furiously as I passed through the swing doors and up *The Catafalque's* steps to leave the crypt and its dark hinterland behind.

I stood on the boardwalk. In front of me a tethered horse lapped at a trough. A black marble trough. And across the street there were black marble tombs. I raised my eyes, half-expecting to discover a black marble heaven above. The prospect of death militant was everywhere, consuming my vision with black foreboding. Unusually high for Desdichado's skyline, the tombs rose, imposing their columns, their stone angels, their flutes and arabesques upon the cruelly bright, ultramarine sky. From far away, audible by virtue of the un-natural stillness that permeated these streets, interrupted only by the occasional passing carriage, came the sounds of river life. Slicking back a kiss-curl of recently hennaed hair, I began my walk back to the hotel.

*

The recently-widowed manager of the *Hotel Terminus* drooled like an infant. Miss Viva forcibly inserted the dessert spoon into his mouth, and then, believing that he had had more than enough stewed prunes than was good for either him or us, pulled the gag back into place and got up from the sofa where, bound with ropes, he reclined. I walked over to him, took out a handkerchief and wiped the poor sap's eyes. We constantly subjected him to loud deliberations as to his fate, and he knew that until such time as we chose to free him or dispose of him, he would remain trussed up, his limbs stiffening into agony.

Mr. Twist sat at the card-table by the window, its drapes pulled until only a chink of light remained, a slat to which he would periodically fix his eye to survey the street below. And then he would return to his game of solitaire. On the table was a box, open and displaying velvet-lined concavities. It was the gilded box in which he had kept his matching set of Colts. Ever since he had had one of his beloved firearms confiscated by Queen Musidora, one of those concavities had remained empty. Unable to resettle himself into his game, he took to running a digit forlornly about the contours where his favorite pistol had often rested when we had travelled through customs posts that frowned on a too blatant, too naked advertisement of one's personal arsenal. He made a fist and banged it on the table, losing patience with himself for conceding so easily to this nostalgic interlude; took his other pistol out of its snug place of repose and, plucking a handful of cartridges from his belt, began to load it.

It was good to see Mr. Twist thus employed, just as it was good to see him looking so dignified, clothed as he was in a new frock coat and leather pants. His Stetson, one so chic it might be kept aside for villainy on a Sunday, hung by its brim from the back of his chair. He was an object-lesson in black magnificence, his wardrobe providing, as well as a tutorial in gunslinger's aesthetics, a lecture on what constituted "perfect camouflage" for waging low-intensity warfare on the streets of Desdichado.

Miss Viva placed the opened tin of prunes on the floor and wiped her hands on her faded jeans. "I'm not at all sure that we're doing the right thing, waiting here, brooding on what's going or not going to happen. We should be more decisive. We should be taking the fight to *him*."

"We should be getting ourselves killed, eh, darlin'?" said Mr. Twist. "I appreciate your position. I understand your rationale. You are, after all, Miss Viva, a Death. *My* death. But, by your leave, this errant soul you so long to consume wants to whack a few of his enemies, and whack 'em good, before ending up face downwards in the dirt." He tucked the loaded gun into his holster, and then, removing a segment of velvet-lined wood from the gilded box, began to refill his cartridge belt with the ammunition he kept in reserve, secreted in the box's false bottom. "Out there"—he pulled the drape a little to one side and looked down the street, first one way and then the other—"out there we're going to be wide open. We'd end up walking straight into a trap."

"Is it so much better to be cooped up here? Here we don't have the element of surprise," I said. I was leaning against the door frame that connected the bedroom with the bathroom, fingers of one hand stroking the pearl handle of the derringer that protruded from my hip pocket. "Here we could be placed under siege, starved out, smoked out, subjected to mockery loud and gross. I think Miss Viva's maybe right. We should take the initiative."

"Right? Yes, I believe I *am* right," said Miss Viva. "We should march down to the courthouse, show that Sexton fella just how much he bit off when he decided to put *us* away."

"Sure, sure, keep on talking, Viva darlin', you almost have me convinced. I *don't* think."

"You are reluctant perhaps to show this man how much you love me, Mr. Twist?"

"Meaning, how much I want to die, Miss Viva?"

"Same thing, Mr. Twist. You should know that by now. Love. Death. Same thing."

The banter that characterised my friends" relationship no longer exerted quite the same charm as formerly. So often, these days, such talk seemed no more than an attempt to fill a meaningless void with desperate noise. But I knew I had a part to play; and I knew I would have to play it to the end. Rousing myself from the lethargy of my months-long depression, I got into role.

"Just think, Mr. Twist," I said, "there's this ruffian, this arrogant ruffian, who presumes he's going to be the one to tie the knot. You want a *ruffian* to be your priest? You want his deputy to be your best man? The only way you can really be sure he's not going to be the one to do the honors is to kill him first."

"Oh, oh," said Mr. Twist, "the sophistry." He got up and rubbed his thigh at the spot where leather concealed the scar left by an old gunshot wound, a wound that, healed or no, still had the power to elicit nervous caresses; turned toward the pier-glass and evaluated the work of his tailor. He had discovered him during the course of a furious drinking spree. Many a night had I heard that sartor praised. Now, as then, Mr.

Twist silently announced by way of a crooked, auric grin that the stitch and weave of his brand-new clothes were examples of unparalleled workmanship. "I suppose it's a pretty enough winding-sheet," he continued, letting his hands descend over the moleskin lapels, and then over the black frock coat's seams. The coat's skirts were of a particularly generous cut, reaching almost to mid-calf. He picked up his hat and set it on his head; stroked his cleanly shaven chin. Then, suddenly, spinning about—rehearsing his shootist's *pas seul*—one hand throwing back the swishy fabric that obscured his pistol as he went into his crouch, he put a hand on the Colt's ebon butt, ready to draw. "But I guess a man has to be reduced to his constituent atoms and be blown away by the wind of chance *sometime*."

"He surely does, Mr. Twist," said Miss Viva.

"And goddamn it, darlin', nobody's gonna spoil *our* wedding!"

He straightened. His eyes never left his reflection in the mirror, chin tilted haughtily toward the ceiling in what appeared to be an attempt to consolidate his *amour propre*. "I'll kill him. Kill 'em all. *You* know I'm no coward, don't you, Nicky?"

"Yes, Mr. Twist, I do know."

"I just get so—"

Miss Viva smiled. "You get so excited, Mr. Twist."

"Indeed I do, Miss Viva. Sometimes, *paralytically* so. Been anticipating the end for so many years now, ever since I got my neck stretched, but not broken, by a certain, accursed length of hemp. Long ago when just out of Arcadia I was, been anticipating so long it's true to say I'm a just a little bit frazzled. But no more paralysis of thought or action for me, darlin'. I do think I've been reborn. Reborn as the Antichrist! The bane of Desdichado!"

Miss Viva held her head to one side and let her tongue loll out of her mouth, a charade suggestive of a hanging.

"Condemned, Mr. Twist. But they had no right to condemn you."

Mr. Twist spun about to face us and struck a pose. "Condemned! God knows I wish I had a piano. I feel a hellrai-sin' rock 'n' rollin' mood comin' on. A pure piece of rockabilly! A jivin', screaming, jug-full of pure *Liebestod* swamp-stomp thrash!" He held his right hand over his chest, as if he were swearing the oath of allegiance. His left hand was held high, so that he looked like an old-time gospel preacher in his pulpit, a bible raised aloft, or else a man given to mockery of such conventions, that heaven-raised hand having one digit pointing up at the cornicing with obscene, caddish glee, as if God had shrunk and taken to hiding there. "Condemned! he cried, even from the gallows, though not by you, but by the abracadabras of angels, by the intervention of a Death! I main-tain I have always been but half alive, a sullen child dressed in black, sentenced for some sin against the skies! Sentenced to exile, to rediscover eternity in the dregs of a leftover life, to commit crimes which were no crimes in *my* world! Not by you, burghers, *judges*, other would-be executioners, but by her, *her*"—his raised hand descended in a slow, deliberate arc; the accusatory index finger was now levelled at Miss Viva—"will I consent to be *condemned*!" Miss Viva clapped with enthusi-asm; and I, a little belatedly, joined in, an awareness that Mr. Twist's hammy performance contained, that afternoon, a un-usually spontaneous depth of sentiment, overriding the irony filters through which I had grown accustomed to appreciating his theatrics, both on and off stage.

"Well said, Mr. Twist," said Miss Viva.

I walked to the door. "I'll be glad to no longer have to share a room with that prune-eating, smelly old man," I said, casting a last look at our hotelier. He returned my stare, his eyes pleading for his life, as if I were about to draw my gun and violently dispossess his body of its soul. But, in truth, my friends and I had forgotten our plans to despatch or, indeed, to release him. His fate was now in the hands of whomsoever would be next to enter this room, or to the strength of his heart, how much water he had at his disposal, or else some other contingency. The Twist Gang was going into battle, perhaps its last. We had no time to worry about hostages. "Are we ready?"

"We're ready," said Mr. Twist, always one to bounce back, his disposition one-part phlegm diluted with two-parts vim, his ego made of titanium.

"Then," I said, "let's do the town."

*

The riverfront was deserted, word of our approach having preceded us. The rumors had begun almost as soon as we had decamped from the hotel; and they had gone before like a tidal wave until all human life had been swept off the street. With Mr. Twist striding down the center of the road, frock coat swept back, his Colt in full view, and with his two women flanking him, the gang that had been muttered about for some time wherever two or three citizens met to talk gaily of mortality had been readily identified.

We marched on, commanding the whole street with hip-rolling contempt for pedestrian etiquette, our swagger a definitive announcement of *trouble*. I kicked an empty Coca-Cola bottle to one side, its brittle trajectory terminating in a brilliant tinkling as it struck the curb. And then I looked askance, concerned that the rows of headstones might harbor snipers. The pressure of a small and somewhat ineffectual firearm against my hip refused to give adequate comfort. In fact, I could almost detect a tiny ironic laugh escaping the derringer's throat, like the hiss of acid poured over metal, like the thin sound of someone mocking our progress by whistling Laurel and Hardy's theme tune. We passed a few buildings that, like the *Hotel Terminus*, punctuated the interminable lines of graves. I scanned their windows, each one of which seemed to have had its black drapes pulled tight; but neither rifle barrel, nor the glint of an assassin's eye, yielded itself to my scrutiny. The thin, ironic whistle again started up, deep within my ears, the conceit that my derringer had been laughing at me replaced by a conviction that I was about to pass out. I ripped my gaze from the drawn curtains and closed doors and forced myself to again look straight ahead. I didn't want to take a bullet. I didn't *not* want to take a bullet. I wanted to be merely with Mr. Twist and Miss Viva, no matter where this walk alongside the river of dreams would take them. Let the road unfold, I told myself. Let the bullets fly, the wheel turn. No more hedging your bets, gentleman, ladies. This afternoon we're playing for keeps.

We passed a temple. It belonged to the cult of the black monks. Attired like Benedictines, these cenobites worshipped no other gods other than those mortals they chose to deify, mortals they deemed had served Death. A line of black-robed figures, their cowls pulled down to hide their faces, stood like a crowd who were there to watch three envoys of a conquering army enter their city, knowing that those arrogant fools would themselves soon fall victim to the conqueror worm. They were weighing each of us up, I knew, for shrouds and the lead petticoats of coffins. The glazed tiles of death-sanctified spires sparkled above the palings of the temple gates.

"Damn vultures," said Mr. Twist, not deigning to divert his attention from the prospect of the deserted riverfront. But, as it transpired, those monks were less vultures, and less voyeuristic crowd than reception committee; for as they began to chant—a low, rhythmic hum that, if it were not for the words, which I recognized as I back-translated into the original German, would have seemed like a Buddhist man-tra—a group of men walked into our path from an adjoining street, a swift, fluid motion of bodies that solidified about a broad-shouldered, top-hatted figure who took up a position that blocked our path. Standing about one hundred yards distant, his feet wide apart, his thumbs hooked in a belt that was dislocated by the great swag of his belly, he seemed to have chosen his ground. The monks continued to rhapsodise, conferring on us their metaphysical ramblings, heads bowed as they contemplated the vanity of existence.

"*Should I tell him that the value of life lies precisely in this, that it teaches him not to want it? For this supreme initiation life itself must prepare him.*"

"What are they gabbing about?" said Mr. Twist. Even though his monolingualism had been catered for, he still seemed incapable of apprehending that that gloomy line of ascetics had referenced him.

"Schopenhauer," I said.

"Schopenhauer," echoed Miss Viva, a keen student of Earthly philosophy. "Mmm. Wasn't he the gay dog."

"He lived to a ripe old age," I said. "Be reassured, Mr. Twist, to come to an appreciation of the futility of life does not necessarily preclude renouncing one's vitality."

"Thank you, Nicky. I am reassured, since *you* say so. It's just that those monkish crooners sound as if they know something I don't. And sound mighty *pleased* about the knowing."

"*For the world is Hell, and men are on the one hand the tormented souls and on the other the devils in it.*"

"Do you think you might blow them a kiss and vaporise a few of their number, Viva darlin'?"

"The very thought, Mr. Twist. How blasphemous!"

"But these people don't believe in God, Miss Viva," I said, my early Catholic training, before it had been subverted by my mother's new-found faith in the sanctity of consumer durables, briefly surfacing, gasping for breath.

"They believe in me," said Miss Viva, curtly. "Isn't that enough?"

"*Unjust or wicked actions are, in regard to him who per-*

forms them, signs of the strength of his affirmation of the will to live, and thus how far he still is from true salvation," chanted the monks. Some of their number had raised their heads so that their overshadowed faces—only the shiny knobs of their noses were illuminated by the strong afternoon light—were turned after us. They seemed to be remonstrating with our collective conscience, taking us to task for not detouring into the temple to be ordained, renounce existence and by so doing thus save our souls.

"Do you have unjust or wicked actions in mind, Mr. Twist?" I said.

"Of course," he said, as curt as Miss Viva had been. My heart boomed, as if there were a Flamenco dancer trapped within its fibres and ligaments, stamping across the stage of its big, cavernous chambers in her effort to break free. The group of men were nearer and it was good to hear Mr. Twist affirm his faith in his own wicked, wicked ways, good to hear him affirm his will to live. For though his confidence did not placate the crazed Spaniard who had by now whipped herself up into a furious tarantella, it gave me the thrill, the cold thrill I always felt, when confronting mortality in his presence.

Mr. Twist eased his cock-of-the-walk legs into stasis, his spurs giving a final jingle as he came to a halt. The men who blocked our path were separated from us by a distance of about twenty to thirty steps, the distance that two gunslingers might choose in a face-off, in concession to the most hackneyed of cinematic conventions. Mr. Twist, I reminded myself, was nothing if not a man who rejoiced in the clichés of the West.

The man in the top hat seemed to be their leader. A tightly knotted cravat forced his chin into a disdainful elevation; but even without that cantilever of a necktie he would, if toe to toe, had had to have thrown back his head to look at Mr. Twist. For all his brawny obeseness—imagine a Henry

VIII lookalike in dusty, but expensive, late nineteenth-century threads—this vertically-compromised lawman, sans headgear, would have only come up to my lanky hero's pecs. He cradled a sawn-off splattergun in his hands. On either side of him his posse shifted uneasily, as if the hot concrete beneath them had seared through the soles of their boots. Somewhat over-dressed for the climate, as was Mr. Twist (only Miss Viva and I, in our sweatshirts and pedal-pushers, were sensibly attired), they seemed to have sacrificed personal comfort to a sense of grand occasion. Mopping at the perspiration that streamed down from beneath their derbys, boaters and panamas and fidgeting within the tight confines of floral waistcoats and frock coats that, like Mr. Twist's, were all of a funereal black, I sensed each member of the posse prepare to draw a bead on us, their trigger fingers twitchy as cut worms. They were a cosmo-politan bunch. I saw an Indian among their number, cowboys, of course, and even—oh horror—a few zanies. The latter's flesh, roasted by the overhead sun, was seemingly more plastic than usual, and strips of burnt fat hung from their cheeks and lips (lips which they constantly licked, as if offering themselves a salve, or indulging in auto-cannibalism). The zanies, of course, were the oddest of the bunch, made odder by their conform-ing to their human brethren's dress code. Mucous dripped from their long, spindly hands like molasses; and even at this remove, I could smell their breath, the corruption bubbling in their bowels wafting up through their oesophagi, to be then expelled through contemptuously gritted teeth. It was a reek that made me think of slugs, cockroaches and all other foul, crawling things.

"You the one they call the Sexton?" called Mr. Twist.

"I am," called back the reincarnation of the Tudor uxori-cide. "And you are the one they call the Twist?" The Sexton dropped his arms to his side, the splattergun pointed to the ground. "I've been looking for you, John Twist. And for your friends, too." He nodded at me, and then at Miss Viva. "I regret one of our guests from Venus has had to be involved in this affair. And you, young lady," he said, looking back at me, "You are the *enfant terrible* I've heard so much about, are you not?"

"That's correct," I said. "But I'm *not* a little girl. I've put away childish things."

"Nevertheless, I've no wish to harm you, either. Why don't you two ladies just step aside?"

"We're the notorious Twist Gang," I said. "We don't step aside for anyone. Isn't that right, Miss Viva?"

"It is most certainly right, Nicky."

"And I have most certainly been apprised of your reputation," said the Sexton. "Tell me: how does a Venusian come to get involved in so much depravity and bloodshed? I've always taken you aliens to be *peaceful* folk."

"It's true: we are peaceful. But we are also capable of great passion."

"The killing and the thieving," said Mr. Twist, a cruel grin distorting his deadpan face, "It was *lurve*."

"No cynicism, please, Mr. Twist," said Miss Viva.

"Me? Not cynical, Miss Viva. Tired. Just tired."

"You'll rest soon, Mr. Twist."

"Promise, Miss Viva?"

"Promise, Mr. Twist. You'll rest for all eternity."

"But not quite yet, Miss Viva."

"No, no, Mr. Twist. Not quite yet. Not *quite* yet. How could I let you take your well-earned sleep before attending to the latest collection of upstarts, know-nothing guttersnipes and hobbledehoys to dare to upbraid you for your chosen way of life?"

"I thank you, Miss Viva. Care to begin the proceedings?"

"Let us not be precipitate, Mr. Twist."

I felt giddy. Their relentless banter, which had earlier lost its charm, now began to perilously resemble that *barf, barf, barf, barf, barf*—idiot song, perhaps, of not just a senseless life, but an equally senseless death. Had I been spoilt? Had intimacy with a death-angel engendered a contempt for things that had once caused me to wonder and marvel? The Sexton, who had begun to shake his head wearily at the beginning of Mr. Twist and Miss Viva's colloquy, was, to go by his appearance, feeling as vexed as was I. He held a hand aloft in a bid to have them pause and let him have his own say.

"*Wait*!" Mr. Twist and Miss Viva seemed, for the moment, to be willing to humor him.

"We're waiting, Sexton," said Mr. Twist.

"Can't you see you're hopelessly outgunned? I'm going to take you in, John Twist—either that, or I'm going to kill you."

"Either/or, eh?" said Mr. Twist. "Sounds more like my young friend's line. What do you say, Nicky? I was never much of a one for logic."

I rallied. I would not put my fear and trembling on public display. "Either he's a fool or he's a fool, Mr. Twist, there ain't no two ways about it. That's *my* logical analysis."

"Yeah, I reckon so. Show the fool, Viva darlin'. Go on, *be* precipitate."

"Unsupervised testing, Mr. Twist? You surprise me."

"Don't be the tease, Miss Viva."

"There's an interplanetary treaty that says—"

"Miss Viva, be good now and just show this gentleman what you can do."

As I had witnessed on that previous occasion in the *Birdcage*, Miss Viva filled her lungs with air, puffed out her cheeks, and then pouted, as if she were about to blow someone a kiss. Instead of a stream of air a jagged streamer of lightning was disembogued, an effect that might to the casual onlooker be dismissed as a magician's trick, if, at the next moment, the section of the riverfront we found ourselves sharing with our enemies had not part exploded with human flesh and screams.

"Oh, you little E-bomb you, Miss Viva!" said Mr. Twist.

The Sexton looked down at the cowboy who had stood next to him. Face down on the road, a smoky hole in the center of his back, the man lay motionless. The Sexton half-turned and checked out the member of the posse who stood behind the dead man. Still on his legs, but only just, Miss Viva's second victim was forlornly studying a similarly-shaped hole blown through the front of his shirt. A lick of flame played about its edges. The wounded one fell, covering his dead companion with his own already stiffening body.

"I left the leader-man for you, Mr. Twist. I know how much store you place in your gunslinger's pride. I don't want to babysit you, now do I?"

"You are, Miss Viva, the personification of considerateness."

"Considerate? I am selfish, Mr. Twist. Your pride, your precious pride, will, as I have long averred, be your undoing."

Several things happened then. Several things had to have happened. But all I can remember of them is that I was suddenly running in a traverse direction down the street. I fired my derringer; found a target. The young cowboy I took out reminded me of one of the little Nazi thugs who had accosted me in Tombstone, a resemblance that had no doubt reflexively conditioned my aim. Of other events I recall only this: that the Sexton's top hat flew off his head, a bullet hole dead center; that Mr. Twist, going into his crouch, had merrily fanned his Colt; and that several of the posse, engaged in a bloody terpsichorean display, had taken to hopping, jiving and screaming. And there too, but fainter, is the recollection of Miss Viva casually walking clear of the firefight, walking to the railing that separated road from river, there to lean upon its bar and gaze down the embankment at the dark water"s imperceptibly rippling, sun-glazed edge.

I clove to a wall. A barrage of bullets ricocheted off its surface. Head down, I felt my way ahead, an unexpected opening allowing me a momentary respite.

Ducking through, I found myself in a garden, a small quadrangle cloistered with lilies and orchids. Climbing plants hung from a canopy formed by a pergola. I made a quick recce of the garden"s inhabitants—two startled women who sat on a bench with richly illuminated books held on their laps—and concluded that this was the temple's nunnery where female counterparts to the black monks had dedicated their own lives to the service of Death.

I pointed my empty weapon at the astonished nuns and then, collecting myself, looked about for cover, for I had felt my nape prickle, as if it were already in the sights of those guns that surely followed. I darted through a colonnade, and then through an open door, reloading my derringer as I did so.

I found myself in a long, white gallery. I walked ahead, holding my gun behind my back, distracted, for a moment, from the prospect of being drilled through, by a percussive music that immediately gave way to a chorale, the import of which my loins acknowledged before my powers of analysis could dissect. For preceded by a brittle overture of high heels on tessellated stone, a distant confusion of voices, increasing in volume, and becoming almost intelligible, assaulted me with a fanfare of brute girlishness.

Some way ahead, bursting through the doors that stood at the end of the gallery—like *belles sauvages* surprising an explorer who has breached the dark heart of a perilous, gynocratic land—a gaggle of novices emerged to give that shrill commotion form, the staccato of stilettos punctuating the clicks, whistles and squeals of their pure, if abstract dithyramb. A flock of frenzied blackbirds, they seemed. A bedraggled, slatternly, avian fivesome who were a paroxysm of whip-lashing hair, agitated limbs and frisky habits that fluttered about their ankles in a paroxysm of pleats, glimpses of frayed, black stockings alternating with displays of white, strappy mules. I walked toward them. Their chatter, even as they neared, oblivious to my head-on trajectory, though it taunted the ear with almost recognisable cognates, never rose above an id-like babble. It mattered little; the girls" kinesic energy articulated their thoughts in a way human language could never match, and I shuddered with immoderate pleasure as I determined the signification of that silent, blatantly sexual tongue, its celibate cry of *want*. The girl-gaggle broke formation to allow me to pass—bye-bye, little blackbirds—a few of their number brushing insouciantly against me, little demonstrations of simulated carelessness that each elicited a mock penance, the offenders lisping *"'scuse me's"* and *"pardons"* as they looked up, polite yet coy, their eyes dark and hot beneath long, black lashes. I hurried on.

Giggles turned to squeals and I knew, without having had to turn and look, that my pursuers had entered the building. Knew, likewise, that only that wall of novices protected me from a bullet, and that that wall, to go by the novices' cries, was even then being demolished. All the same, I did look, and knowledge was confirmed; two zanies were leaping over the hunched scrum of the nuns, their fried-up faces contorted into masks of mucous malevolence, as if their flesh, newly poured from a Halloween jelly mould, had not quite set.

I started to sprint, my head arrested in its position by fear, so that I continued to look over my shoulder, running blind. My reflexes, however, conditioned by months of practise (for Mr. Twist really *had* taught me how to shoot) meant that my pistol was now situated under my left armpit, where I pointed it at the forehead of the loping figure that was closing on me, its arms extended with gastronomic ardor. "You want fast food, try elsewhere," I gasped, squeezing the derringer's trigger. The slug implanted itself in the thing's skull just as it was in mid-stride, the hot, leaden seed at once sprouting tendrils of blood and brain matter. It took a few more loping steps toward me, its eyes suddenly veined with scarlet, bulging out of the sockets like fertilised eggs squeezed from the rumps of two scalded hens. Then, with a wet slap of diseased flesh against stone, the thing fell spreadeagled on the floor, momentum carrying it forward over the marble tiles, the corpse leaving behind it a trail of slime.

The other zany jumped over its companion's body, a hiss issuing from between broken teeth, as if its mouth were an ancient tin of meat that had been wantonly punctured to re-lease a pressurised, steam-like jet of miasma. My pistol spent, I put my hopes in adrenaline and thanked the Lord that zanies were never entrusted with firearms. My head turned forward, backward, then forward again, sought a door, a stairway, a trap, indeed anywhere that might put some temporary hin-drance between me and the monster that wished to make me its lunch.

The zany had approached to within a hair's-breadth of raking its claws down my back when I spotted an elevator. I threw myself through its opening just in time to see the zany fly past, unable to copy my emergency stop, its inertia carrying it down the gallery. I pulled the reticulated metal gates shut and stabbed at a button—any button—with my finger. The el-evator groaned, and then began to descend just as the zany put its face against the latticework of the cage's guard, the rusted metal impressing its ugly visage with lozenges, rhomboid seals pressed into hot wax.

I panted, my throat aching with exertion, my hands fum-bling as I struggled to reload my gun. The cartridge refused to obey my trembling fingers. Cursing, I watched it fall to the cage's floor. The elevator juddered; came to rest. I looked up. Lit by a beam of light from the corridor above that fell diagonally across the elevator shaft, I could see the mutant. The thing had torn off its clothes in what must have been frustration with the civilized trappings imposed on its ignoble savagery. Naked, it banged its fists against the diamond-patterned grid. In disbelief, I watched as it squeezed its spare torso through a lozenge, its red eyes never leaving me as it stared down from high above.

I reached out, drew back the gates, ears ringing with the oxidised metal's squeal of protest, and found myself in a wine cellar.

Tentatively—for it was dark, with only the light that fell through the elevator shaft offering illumination—I ventured into the shadows, past racks of dust-fogged vintages, through veils of cobwebs, penetrating the cellar's maze of masonry and urgently seeking an exit.

The zany must have wriggled through the guard and fallen the fifteen or so feet that separated the cellar from the corridor above, for I heard something flop onto a steel floor. Heard, concomitantly, the elevator shake, like a birdcage restless with a sick budgerigar's tantrums. A very un-birdlike noise ensued, my ears perking to the sibilant imprecations of the one who stalked me; a noise more like that of a cat that had swallowed its mistress's pretty caged pet, and that was now set on consuming the mistress. Bird, cat—the thing that I saw as I took refuge behind a wine rack, peering through a space left by whomever had failed in her duties to keep the cellar fully stocked, that thing was not animal, nor was it human. It was pure, distilled malice, a *vin extraordinaire* that might have been pressed out of grapes straight from Hell's vineyard.

The vision threatened to incapacitate me with terror. No, I told myself, get a grip of yourself. You've seen zanies before; you just killed one. They're not supernatural. But ever since first seeing such creatures they had inspired in me an irrational sense of helplessness.

I stilled my hands by a sudden, bravura act of will and forced another cartridge into my derringer, summoning up those precious memories, those eternal memories of when Mr. Twist had shot-up the war party that had attacked our stagecoach, leaving a half-dozen or so zanies dead. Reloaded, I rested the derringer's barrel on the edge of the rack, sighted, and waited for the mutant to come within view. My ears strained to locate a betraying sound: a stubbed toe, the thing's hoarse breath. My eyelids peeled themselves into attitudes of extreme wakefulness, eager as I was to absorb the cellar's every stray photon. I suppressed a sneeze—a bead of sweat had run down my forehead, paused in the bridge of my nose, and then trickled down the length of my plain girl's proboscis to hang, then drip onto my miniature pistol, the gunmetal of which I could almost taste, so close was it to my lips, my chin.

My nape prickled. For the second time that afternoon my intuition served me well. Without having to turn and look, I knew that the mutant had doubled back and had crept up behind me. Did not have to look? I did not want to look, did not want to have knowledge confirmed. But this was no time for prevarication. I whipped myself about.

Fate, dumb fate had it that my gun-hand, automatically extended to fend off my stalker by way of a bullet to the brain, pointed merely into dark, inane space. I looked down just as the zany sprang up from where it lurked, rising on its hind legs like a mangy dog and then jumping into the air, as if to snatch a tidbit offered to encourage the performance of a particularly odious trick. The thing's head collided with my outstretched arm, knocking the derringer out of my grasp. Its jaws snapped, as if to devour the gunmetal treat. Then, as the weapon clattered onto the stone floor, it turned its face full on mine. Its teeth were bared, ready to snap again.

I hadn't appreciated before just how small zanies were. But then I had never been this close to a zany. We gazed into each other's eyes, Nicola E. Newton and the thing that had been born in the electrospiritual wastes of the desert. Its face resembled a pasticcio of Goya, Munch and Bacon. Green drool, like masticated avocado, flecked my adversary's long, pointed chin and collected in its cracks and rills. It was as if that horror-house visage were criss-crossed with a miniature system of blocked drains. It smelt like a drain, and it was a smell far worse than that which I had sampled when I had stood outside, the whiff of decay that had carried across the riverfront as nothing compared to the olfactory experience of being so close to the mutant breed. And then, surprising myself, I began to cry.

It wasn't self-pity; it wasn't fear—though fear I felt. No, it was a kind of wretchedness that inspired that fit of sobbing, my throat knotting with a surge of memories that all served to taunt me about how I had chosen to throw my life away. As I observed the corners of the zany's mouth lift themselves into a lipless smirk, the wretchedness transmuted itself into anger.

I grabbed the mutant by its skinny neck, snarling, pushing it backwards, using my superior weight to carry it across the passageway between the wine racks until its head crashed against the rows of bottles opposite. But as I attempted to consolidate my hold on the thing's windpipe, my fingers seeking to find a more deadly purchase on the slippery skin, the zany got its leg behind mine, hooked it behind my knee and jerked. We fell to one side, hitting the stones.

Battle has many reversals. Twisting as I fell, I had landed with my knee on the thing's crisp, pulpy chest, pinning it to the ground. Its arms and legs flailed, but I held it fast. It writhed, gasped, expectorated huge wads of sputum, its chest caving in about my knee like a badly cooked pastry with a thick, pink, gooey center, a disgusting sweetmeat that flaked and begrimed my pedal-pushers with raspberry-coated scales.

"My life is a mess," I shouted, great hiccups of rage and

sorrow and agony shaking my bones, inflaming my cheeks. "A complete fucking mess! Why did my parents have to be such bastards, eh? Tell me *that* you vile streak of mutant shit! If they hadn't been so unfeeling, if they'd given me some respect, some freedom, if they hadn't been just so fucking *annoying*, maybe I wouldn't be here, on the edge of the world, waiting to be snuffed out of existence. Maybe I wouldn't have the blood of innocent people on my hands. Maybe I wouldn't have been party to the destruction of the whole fucking West. Maybe—" I choked on the great fluff balls of pain that had stuck in my craw. And then the zany did something that quite astonished me, for, giving up the struggle, and looking up at me with eyes that had suddenly ignited with intelligence, it spoke.

"Go ahead. Take my life. You think I want it? Go on, take it, take it. Hanging on to the paltry, squalid thing has been more trouble than it's worth. Why bother? I mean, you think *you* got problems? You didn't get on with your Mom and Dad. Huh. Big deal. I was born in the badlands, sister. Smack in the eldritch middle of the fucked-up U.S. of A. The West they call it, and it's supposed to be like some wonderland. Oh thank you very much, manifest destiny. Thank you very much, Venus. The desert was a spiritual and physical enclave of the alien, they said. They said that, even though the West was still nominally part of America, the big sky under which I was hatched belonged to the goddess of love. Huh. I was a *child* of love, they said. Yeah, well fuck that. What have Venusians given me except a mouldy body, a bad dose of halitosis and the ability to inspire chronic social antipathy wherever I show my slimy face? Eh? *You* tell *me* that, you sad sack of concentrated carbohydrate."

His thin voice gave out; his eyes closed and his chest ceased its labored breathing. The zany's rant had so surprised me that the quietus that followed added little to the effect already produced by the unexpected eruption of words, namely, the suspension of all my efforts to throttle it.

Thus mesmerised I quickly discovered that however sincere that speech might have been, its purpose had been ulterior to its *cri de cœur*. With a spasm of wiry limbs, the zany returned to the world of the living—the world it had only pretended to leave—and, catching me off guard, was able to bring up a leg and dislodge me from my perch. With rat-like alacrity, the thing freed itself from my clutches and scurried on all-fours into the shadows. Almost immediately following its eclipse by the darkness, it reappeared, walking upright, and moving slowly toward me, brandishing the retrieved derringer. Its mouth was open in what resembled a terrible war wound, to either suck in the oxygen that had been too long denied it, or else to give notice of a howl of triumph, a howl which, though it never came, was all the more ghastly for being silent.

I rolled to one side, so that I was partly shielded by a heavy, oaken cask. Then, knowing that such cover would not long preclude being picked off with my own weapon, I staggered to my feet and, weaving through the lanes demarcated by the wine racks, ran back toward the elevator before the zany could cut off what I knew now to be my only means of escape.

I half-fell into the cage. It rattled and swayed with my headlong flight, alerting my adversary that I had attained my goal. Grasping the concertinaed outer door, I unfurled it and secured its latch, performed the same operation with the inner door, and punched a button, on this occasion taking care that I selected one that would ferry me directly to the gallery above. The noise of gunfire resounded down the shaft, the elevator giving off a sympathetic vibration, like the soundboard of an eviscerated piano struck viciously by a steel pipe. I looked up, but as I did so, another sound, as distinct but, in timbre, the obverse of the sharp detonations overhead—a thin, bronchitic whine—immediately distracted me. The zany, even as the elevator began its ascent, was charging the cage, its red eyes brilliant against the dim backdrop of the cellar.

Before the cage could clear the guard, the zany had leapt, launching itself at the latticework, pushing its small, rubbery head through one of the metal lozenges. I expected the elevator to decapitate the thing as the cage rose past the cellar's ceiling. I involuntarily averted my face in disgust but, hearing no telltale scream or noise of steel slicing through vertebrae, I refastened my gaze upon the intruder. I saw that, with preternatural speed, it had somehow been able to get its shoulders, and then the rest of its body through the cruelly small aperture, oozing onto the floor like a boneless chicken that miraculously seemed able to dispose and then reclaim its skeleton at will. The zany, recovering from its contortionist's trick, swiftly rose to its feet and confronted me.

I pressed myself against the back of the cage, my gaze darting from the thing's fiery eyes to the derringer, and then again to the eyes, seeking to know its thoughts, its purpose. I was not given time to indulge in further speculation. The mutant's hand shot out and encircled my throat, pulling me toward it; and then it snared me about the windpipe with its forearm, like a shepherd might do with a crook, turning me about and securing me in a stranglehold, my own gun pressed to the side of my head as I, poor lambkin, was brought into the thing's clammy fold.

"Taking you in, Miss Nicola E. Newton," it said, its words rustling like rice paper against my ear, its breath, with its bouquet redolent of meat left out in the midday sun, overpowering. "I'm taking you in to claim my bounty. Don't struggle, bitch. It's easier for me if you're alive—desert folk like me like our victuals *fresh*—and the good folk of Desdichado wouldn't want to be deprived of a hanging. But don't tempt me. Hear?" I nodded, spluttering a little as I shifted within his embrace, his stranglehold horribly suggestive of a noose. "Good," he concluded, "this mutant boy is surely glad to know it."

The elevator slowed; stopped, shivering like a wind chime made out of old car parts. The sound of gunfire had ceased.

We had returned to where I had taken my detour. The zany slid back the gates and urged me forward and, with its arm like an iron bar across my throat, I was forced to acquiesce.

I stumbled into the gallery. Several bodies—they all looked like those that had once harbored the souls of the posse—were lying along the route that led to the garden and the world outside. We came to a halt as the zany paused to evaluate the nature and meaning of the carnage.

"Let the girl go," said a voice behind us. I struggled to breathe. The black dots that speckled my field of vision, like an inverted star field, grew larger. "*Let her go.*" It was Mr. Twist.

The zany turned about, placing my body between his own and that of the dark avenger who occupied the perspective where the gallery terminated in a set of big, closed doors. Mr. Twist winked at me. The brim of his Stetson was pulled down, though not as to obscure his line of sight, I knew, only to intensify it as one does when improvising a telescope with an incompletely fisted hand. "Do it, Mr. Twist," I said. "Kill this piece of animate slime." My body stiffened, and I clenched my eyes shut, not wanting to flinch when—my acquaintance with his ways bestowing a certain prescience—he would throw back the skirt of his frock coat, go into his crouch, and draw. And no sooner had I closed my eyes than there was indeed that familiar *crack*! of his Colt. I felt the zany tighten and then straightaway loosen its grip. Breaking free, I opened my eyes just in time to see the mutant stumble forwards and then crash onto the stones, a single hole in the back of its hairless skull where a bullet had passed through its brain and then exited.

Mr. Twist now stood near where the gallery led into the garden, having somehow transported himself to a spot diametrically opposite to that from which he had fired at and killed the zany. Framed by the light falling in from the open doorway, he unbent himself and stood tall, his Colt still smoking.

"Oh no," he said. "Oh, no, no—not yet, darlin'. Please, not yet."

But Mr. Twist had not opened his mouth; the words had emanated from behind me where he had originally stood before he had made his impossible dash from one end of the corridor to the other.

I turned. Mr. Twist had a double, it seemed, for there he stood, as before. He had not moved an inch. "Does this mean what I think it means?" said the Mr. Twist I labelled—since he was the first Twist I had seen after emerging from the wine cellar—Twist 1.

"I believe it does, Mr. Twist," said Twist 2.

"I thought it was like, a story. I thought it was legend. That seeing your double is a portent of imminent death—oh say it *is* mere legend, Miss Viva."

"I happen to enjoy the stuff of legend, Mr. Twist."

"You are something of a legend yourself, Miss Viva."

"Thank you, Mr. Twist. Let's just say that I've saved your life for the last time. I'm calling in my debt."

I looked down at the dead zany and saw, then, that what I had taken to be an exit wound was in fact an entry wound. Twist 2, that is, Miss Viva, had blasted the thing from behind.

Another blast. A roar like that of a great wind, and the doors behind Twist 1 ruptured, a fist-sized vomitory opening up and disgorging a plume of blood-like flame, as if the wooden panels had sustained a mortal wound. But the doors were brute matter, not like the man in black who had been showered with splinters and peppered with shot. Twist 1—ah, and it was *Mr.* Twist, of course, my real, one and only John— Mr. Twist shuffled forward, a haemorrhage filling his mouth and leaking from between his lips; yes, now he was the very *picture* of mortality. He sidestepped, slouched against a wall, a hand reaching inside his waistcoat, as if fumbling for a few cents of change. Retracting his fingers, he studied the red pool coagulating in his palm, as if debating with himself whether it would suffice as a tip for his executioner. The fractured doors crashed open and the Sexton was revealed, his squat, powerful body dominating the black void that lay at the center of the ruined architrave. Smiling, he levelled his splattergun at his indisposed quarry.

I was about to spit a torrent of abuse and imprecation in his fat, smug face, but a groan from my dying friend took my words and scattered them like chaff before I could get them past my lips.

"Congratulations, darlin'," said Mr. Twist, sliding down to the floor and leaving the white plaster smeared with his blood. "You finally got what you wanted."

I threw myself onto the floor, groping for the derringer that lay near the trepanned skull of the mutant that Miss Viva had used for target practice. Finding it, I aimed square at the Sexton's generous figure and fired. Mr. Twist's murderer snorted, his feet shuffling as if he were a drunk that had been ordered to walk down a painted line. Over my prone body came a clipped, no-nonsense fusillade that put my own gun's dirty work to shame. More to the point, it put the Sexton, whose thick hide seemed to have absorbed my pipsqueak round with complacency, on his back and, prospectively, in his box. I feared Mr. Twist had been likewise served. I tossed my puny weapon aside, got up and hurried to where my friend, no longer able to sit, lay, in the formal pose of the sculpture of a medieval knight resting atop a sarcophagus. His arms were folded across his chest in what may have been an attempt to keep his soul within the confines of its blasted husk. Or it may, perhaps, have been simply a rehearsal, a getting-in-character exercise for the reality of his next port of call, that generic box which, like the Sexton, he would soon be confined to until, paid for, stamped and mailed, he would be shipped-out to cross the river of dreams. Embarkation was to come sooner than I thought.

I bent over the dying Twist.

"Where is she?" he murmured. "I want her, Nicky. I have to see her." Miss Viva, a tear flowing down the masculine cheek of her metamorphic flesh, stood at the end of the gallery, her Colt still smoking from its fit of retribution. "Where is she? Oh Lord, don't tell me she's left me here, alone. I need her. I need my psychopomp." I reached out for his Stetson. It had hooped itself over the toe of his right boot and still spun lazily on its scuffed leather axis. I picked it up, folded it, and used it as a pillow to prop up his head.

"Damn. I won't ever get around to it now," he continued. "I won't ever get to set my favorite piece of Beddoes to that tune that's been partying with my soul."

"Miss Viva," I called softly, unable to project my voice.

She no longer appropriated the semblance of her lover, but nor had she reverted to her previous aspect of dust-blown, roadhouse adventuress. The Viva that floated down the white gallery—that whiteness like a manufacturing flaw in an urban landscape that was otherwise immaculately black—the Viva I had always known would reveal herself in this place that was the end of the world, and for so many, the end of time, this Viva was pale and beautiful and unearthly, and she was clothed in mourning weave, a billowing full-length gown of night-black bombazine. Her bonnet had its veil pulled down, and her face shone through its smoky gauze like the moon through clouds. In her hands she held a wreath of black lilies.

"Belle dame," said Mr. Twist, his mouth bubbling with blood, his glazed eyes struggling to focus on his Death, "it's like you said, there was no escaping you. Even when I was a boy and you were a little girl—that was clever, darlin', to first come to me as someone my own age—yeah, even then I knew my soul was yours. We grew up together didn't we, darlin', a boy and his girl from the stars, though you stopped growing long before I did. Was that Venusian vanity? I don't know. But for me you were always ageless. I was blessed. I think I was always waiting for you, darlin', right from when I was knee-high, wandering among the deer and coon, or swimming in the Mississippi. But after you did arrive, it was you who were really the patient one, to wait as you did and to put up with all of my wicked ways, even going so far as to take up some of those ways yourself. We've both been waiting, though, haven't we, Viva? One of us patient, the other trying to put the brakes on time. I figure we've both been waiting too long. I'm glad it's finally come to this."

Miss Viva drew up to him and knelt down, her dress belling out on all sides so that she seemed to be squatting in an oil slick, or else rising from a shimmering midnight lake, according on whether your take on things, at that moment, was cynical or heartbreakingly romantic. My take? I am a romantic; always have been since first seeing my terrific two-some in a stagecoach thundering through the Wild Whacky West. They converted me; they saved me; they redeemed me from cynicism; for they, then and now, were, and always will be *vastly* romantic. And so it was: Miss Viva was a lady of the lake indeed, risen from her black, watery home to bestow flowers on the brave, fallen warrior. The lilies, strewn across Mr. Twist's bloody torso, had waited for that moment to release their perfume into the air, a cloying, sickly but wholly seductive odor that perked my nostrils and burnt my eyes. It told me, that rhetorical scent, it told me that now was the time for tears to again fall, but soft, and not as some minutes before, when my body had shaken with pain and I had rained blows down on the zany that had taunted me. No, not as then did I go weepie-weepie; but soft, soft flowed those tears, so quiet my grief that it went unattended as Miss Viva put her arms under Mr. Twist's body and, standing, lifted him, effortlessly, cradling his head to her breast with one hand and supporting his weight with the other.

And then it was not just my grief but Nicola E. Newton herself who went unattended as Miss Viva, looking down into her lover's face, her brow creasing with concern and satisfaction, walked back down the gallery, that pair lost to each other and, I knew at once, lost to me. I followed, like a child who cannot believe that her parents have forgotten her and are about to go on a long trip abroad and leave her. Have said goodbye to relatives, friends, bank managers, bill collectors, indeed everyone but her, who will have to learn to live without them now, until the unspecified day when she would be called to join them. I stepped over corpses, detritus of the last battle that there would be for our little gang, and strode toward the oblique fantail of light that cast a gossamery, multihued aura about the receding figures of my friends.

It was only after we had proceeded into the garden that I heard the plangent tolling of the convent's bells. The nuns whom I had encountered when I had entered the convent were huddled behind the bench on which they had formerly sat. Their wimples were snagging on its slatted uprights as they peered out, like heretics in a makeshift prison, at the cortège that passed by. Were they censorious? Or would they have congratulated us, if their piety had conferred upon them the necessary aplomb? I gave a perfunctory salute to the bust of Schopenhauer that stood on a plinth on the far side of a pond. We had, today, given that deified mortal, as we had given all the gods of Desdichado, a rash of souls. Did I then detect, in the nuns' apprehensive visages, a hint of joy? I felt no such emotion, but an unheralded peace seemed to have descended, as if this garden was Gethsemane, all agony gone from its arbors, the Mount of Olives beckoning from beyond a deep blue sky that was like a vast stained-glass window.

Miss Viva walked onto the riverfront. Once again, the dark architecture stretched to either side, the whitewashed spaces of the walled garden and the cool, white hacienda-like interior of the convent a bone-bright vein in the cityscape's ubiquitous black marble. I dawdled—it was only for a moment—out of step with our little funeral procession as I was out of space and time, the garden's white oasis promising a balm to my throbbing head, my distracted sense of reality.

Miss Viva carried her man, her lover, her son, her brother across the street—more dead bodies, here, where my friends had acquitted themselves with deadly effect in the brief battle that had settled our collective, personal history—and moved on toward a gap in the barrier that ran alongside the riverbank. She passed through, descended the steps that led down to the dark, lapping water. Momentarily, she disappeared. I ran after her and, as I reached the steps, saw that she had already laid Mr. Twist in a small boat that was anchored in the shallows. She stood gazing down at him, up to her knees, her dress borne up and undulating in the current, its distended fabric becoming, as she ventured a few more steps into the purling, inky depths, a black lily pad encircling her waist, the pale face that shone out from beneath her bonnet's veil, that lily's single white flower. It was the last lily she was to offer my hero.

"Wait!" I called. "Miss Viva, wait! Wait for me!" I hurried down to the water's edge.

"Stay where you are, Nicky," said Miss Viva. She grabbed the gunwale and pulled herself into the boat, the bombazine sluicing what seemed gallons of river water from its countless niches and folds. "You can't come where we're going. Not yet."

"But you *promised*." But I knew she never had. I was losing her; I was losing both of them.

Miss Viva smiled her ice-cold smile. "You're a manipulative child, Nicola E. Newton. I sometimes think that, for the last half-year or so, Mr. Twist and I have been dancing to your tune. Have you got what you want now? We helped you escape from your family, we even destroyed the world you hated so much, and we have taken you to the very edge of the frontier. Can you really ask for any more?"

"I want you to love me," I said. "That's all." Miss Viva's smile vanished.

"Then I promise you one thing, Nicky. I'll always be with you. Until the end of time." She cast off, lifted the oars, slotted them in the rowlocks and situated herself so that she was ready to captain her little vessel from this world to the next.

"Miss Viva, come back! You can't leave me. You're my friend. My family. How am I going to get by? What am I going to do without you?"

"It's a cruel world I leave you in, Nicky. I'm sorry. But there is a better. Be assured. We will be waiting for you. Goodbye."

Ah, I thought, always the bridesmaid, never the bride. I called after her many times after that, but those were the last words I was fated to hear Miss Viva say in this world, this life. After a while, when the boat had got to mid-river, carried somewhat downstream by the water's powerful ebb and flow, I fell silent. And I would have stood there, silent, watching my friends until they reached the farther bank if the town had remained equally as quiet. But I soon began to detect a susurration of discontent on the street above, a medley that was to grow loud, the voices all descanting, in a multitude of different tongues, so that the rogue female, the junior outlaw, the delinquent with a heart of brimstone, was to be had for the asking. My reputation was such that it was still several minutes before I heard a vanguard of outraged citizens cautiously pad down the embankment. The boat, by then, was but a dot, a toy that moved against the backdrop of coconut palms that lined the demarcation zone. Beyond those palms lay the thin strip of land that segued into the country of the dead. Venus, the jungle planet—or so it had always seemed in my imagination—its hot, wet clime ready to anoint those who were about to come home, called to me. Its spirit filled the trees, the water, the sky; it dwelt within the chitter of insects and the cries of monkeys and birds. But inevitably I was to feel the hand on my shoulder that alerted me that I—unlike Mr. Twist, adrift, now, in his *longeur* of forgetfulness, the concerns of this world disappearing as he himself was to disappear, soon to be no more than a silly, tender dream—I was to be called to a less glorious account. The days ahead gave a prospect, not of dreamily melting into another country as I felt water gently lap against my barque, but of arrest, interrogation, trial, conviction, imprisonment and a long drop into a nothingness more brutal, and, I feared, less real. But to follow was my only hope.

Chapter Nine
Crossing The Bar

I had been lucky, of course, not to have been lynched by that irate mob. Not that my reprieve from summary justice had altered the course of fate. Each morning, the shadow of the gallows criss-crossed my cell as sunlight poured through its single barred window. The shadow of the hangman, who was also jailer and confessor, fell—less poetically, perhaps—at dusk, when he, in whom decency vied with an implacable regard for the law, would pass by outside, his appearance as regular as the path of the sun.

Captain Harrison Hollander—that was my hangman-cum-jailer-cum-confessor's name—leant back in his chair, sipping his Jack Daniels. The night shift had just begun; the Captain would be with me till morning.

"Still coming in," he said, laying his newspaper on the davenport. "Folks from all over the West. Still coming, yessiree. And what tales they tell, Miss Nicola. Tales of a great wall of light moving over the territories, coursing through the frontier like some crazy bush fire."

"It's moving fast now," I said. "It must be eager to cross the river. I helped make it, you know. I guess that's another thing I should have been arraigned for: the destruction of all life in the West from Tombstone to Desdichado. Perhaps of all life in the West, period, if the corridor actually collapses." He looked at me, his lips puckering, as if concerned for my mental competence. He put his feet up on the davenport and stared at his glass of Jack.

"You really think it'll reach Desdichado?"

"I think it will, Captain. I think you might soon be taking the same journey as me."

"Guess we all might, Miss Nicola."

"I'd like to buy you a drink. If we ever meet up Venus-side, that is."

"That'd be nice. I suppose, being a citizen of Desdichado, I should say I'd be looking forward to it. But I'm not sure if I'm willing to renounce existence just yet awhile." The Captain drained his glass and refilled it. "No, not yet awhile," he chuckled. "Still got me some living to do." He was a good-humored man, I've always found that confidence is rarely misplaced in those who are bibulous. The Captain it had been who had saved me from the mob. There might have been many who, disgruntled at being the only deputy to survive the slaughter on the riverfront—that gun battle was quickly passing into legend—would have treated me with cold indifference, if not cruelty. But the Captain, sot that he was, had befriended the doomed kid left to his charge with warmth and enthusiasm. And I had returned his affection. Yes, we got on real well, even if we both knew that our relationship, unequal that it was, was due to end with him at one end of a rope and me at the other.

"It's not the end of the world," I said, by way of offering comfort. "Just the end of *our* world, the West." I looked down at my untouched meal. The food was good here, but I had lost my appetite. Using my foot, I shoved the supper tray under the bars, and, taking out my clasp knife, again took up the task of inscribing my obituary on the cell wall, a traditional practice tolerated by other jailers as well as my own, as the wealth of graffiti scored into the bleak plaster testified. "Miss Viva knew that the Heat would not stray beyond the *dérive*," I said as I worked, musing to myself as much as addressing the Captain. "Even though the West is physical, it only interacts with the Earth where it shades into the continental USA east of Colorado. And she made sure the Heat came *thisaway*. The Earth owes a debt to Miss Viva. She isn't cruel. No Venusian is. They take our souls because they're lonely. And because they love us. And because they do not want us to despair." Had Miss Viva redeemed herself? She had ended up killing an awful lot of people—millions had been sucked into the White Heat. But the Earth was safe, and the West's dead were on their way to Venus, and not the hell world that would otherwise have been their lot. Viva Venera! was all *I* could say.

"Well, I suppose we should all be thankful for that, Miss Nicola, even if with this White Heat business the end seems to be coming just a little too soon. *Personally* speaking, that is. But folks *do* say not everyone gets to go Venus-side."

"I know it to be true, Captain. Too true. But I'm sure you'll be all right. You have 'Venus' written right across your heart."

"It's kind of you to say so, Miss Nicola."

It was getting dark and I could no longer easily see the marks I had carved in the wall. But my work was, at last, finished.

> Sunset and evening star,
> And one clear call for me!
> And may there be no moaning of the bar
> When I put out to sea.

The Captain lit the oil lamp on his desk; rose from his chair, picked the lamp up and walked over to my cell. "It's pretty," he said, his eyes studying the inscription, "but without recourse to sentimentality. I approve. *Tennyson was not Tennysonian.*"

"Why, Captain, you really are full of surprises. That's Henry James, isn't it?"

"I read no other author, Miss Nicola. My daddy was a Jamesian. A precious old fool. But he taught me that the most important thing is to *have a life*, even if the having means embracing oblivion." He held the lamp high, inspecting my austere confines, his brow creasing with solicitude. He became, then, like a father himself about to bid goodnight to a beloved, if troublesome daughter. "You have enough books?"

"I believe I do, Captain. Thank you, anyway."

"I have to leave you, now. I'll just be next door attending to some paperwork. You'll call if you need anything, okay?"

"Okay."

The Captain walked across the office and through the door that led into the adjoining room. The darkness coalesced. I stretched out on my pallet, another sleepless night in store for me, my only entertainment the buzz and flitter of my thoughts, worrying at my peace like insects whirling and battering themselves against a light bulb in an otherwise abandoned house.

Thoughts, thoughts. There had always been too many thoughts. Why not give up? I had thought back in Boston. Why not be like them? Why not dive, careless into the insensate sea of *barf, barf, barf, barf, barf,* that loud cradle song of crassness that had played incessantly in my ear, the song of damned America? But I had refused that death; I had chosen to run away, to find another, more transformative oblivion, a dying that opened the way to life. I was near to fulfilling the purpose of that long journey, a journey that had begun in the Rockies and had carried on over the parched soil where the Pacific had once boomed, to terminate here on the jungly edge of things. My quest had been, not to arrive, but to go, to endlessly go; to escape. Now I found myself on the threshold of the ultimate escape. It was another home that beckoned, a new home that promised compensation for a home I had never known. There was only one more crossing left and I would be there. And then, though I had not sought it, I *would* arrive. My quest would, unwittingly, have been realized and the world's moronic song be at last put to rest. And oh, how I longed for that silence!

Gone West, they would say when people told the tale of Nicola E. Newton. Gone West. Bound for glory, for the Promised Land. Bound for Desdichado and beyond. Disappeared straight off the face of the Earth, unmade, stripped bare, taken like Enoch, gone to an unknown place, no forwarding address.

I turned my head to one side. A Venusian stood outside my cell, her body encircled with a nimbus of multihued light that was like the fanned plumage of a bird of paradise. She was like one of the many angels that perched on headstones and stood guard at the portals of family vaults, real and ornamental, that decorated the city's environs, in the same manner that wooden false fronts and wagon wheels decorated other, less absolute Western towns. Her presence evoked—I fell prey to a quixotic conceit—Flaubert's vulgarly brilliant bird. Perched on nothingness—her toes were an inch or so above the floor—she was ready to transport my tired soul to heaven. Her gown was black, or perhaps merely diaphanous and revealing the ebony complexion of her slim body. But that aura, that white light flecked with reds, violets and pinks, radiated from her *négritude* to create a corona that made one long to reach out and immerse oneself in its paradisaical down. And I did reach out, turning on my side and bringing up my legs, my other arm clasping my knees in a foetal spasm.

"Miss Viva?" I asked, softly.

"No, Nicola," said the Venusian. "You can't see Viva Venera yet. You will, though, soon. Wait. Have patience."

"Then who are you?"

"I am Death, Nicola. Your Death."

"You're beautiful," I said. She moved nearer to my cell, the light that emanated from her like the paradoxical rays from that black sun which featured in Desdichado's territorial flag. The effulgence radiated through the bars and spilt across the floor.

"That which is most beautiful is also that which is most true."

"Oh ho, so you're real, eh? Give me a break, sister." The cell door, with neither a creak nor a moan, yawned open. "Some trick," I said, a little light-headed, feeling that I had just downed what remained of the bottle of Jack that the Captain had taken with him to his rooms. "Some hallucination." But liquor had not passed my lips, alas, for nearly a month. Lord Alcohol had deserted me for some other, less demanding lush. I sat up. The Venusian held out a hand.

"Are you ready, Nicola?"

"Ready and waiting."

"You won't keep *me* waiting. I know that." Her face, dark as it was, seemed to darken further. "You won't," she added, anxiously, "will you, Nicola?" Well, I thought, I was due to get my neck broken pretty damn soon now, but indeed, why wait for that? This invitation to the voyage was certainly less gruesome than that which I could expect from a baying crowd. It was, in fact, an invitation as charming as the belle who had extended it.

I rose and, on bare feet, walked to where she stood, passing, in a moment, from imprisonment to a freedom that, if qualified by my being still a girl condemned for a capital crime in the heart of a hostile city, tasted like the first course of a banquet of hope. "No, I guess I won't keep you waiting," I said, chowing down. "Why should I?"

I looked into her face, able to discriminate, now that I had drawn close, the planes of her high cheekbones, the more than pleasing arrangement of eyes, nose and mouth. I saw that she was not a creature of darkness after all. It had been her aura and its brightness that had had the effect of occluding what was—and I made a detailed inspection—a complexion amber and warm and beautiful, so very, very beautiful, more beautiful, far more beautiful than I, rushing to judgment, had at first supposed. I reached out to her, seized by an urge to place a finger on that golden neck, to feel the blood I could see pulsing in the ca- rotid artery; to feel that she was real. But I desisted. Assuredness could wait; I wanted at that moment to relish uncertainty and the solemn promise that I sensed was intrinsic to my vertigo. I let my hand fall to my side. "Take me," I said. "Take me and I'll never keep you waiting again." The Venusian smiled, grasped the hand that had been about to test her quiddity, pressed it, and by so doing conferred on me proof-positive of her presence. My vertigo remained; it was no less wonderful.

Without a sound, the door to the sheriff's office shot its bolt. We walked out into the tropical night. The street outside was empty, as if a curfew had been frantically improvised. More than people had disappeared. The buildings directly op- posite the jailhouse had been spirited away, and in their place was the mouth of a tunnel. That gaping, black hole that seemed carved out of the air was high, as high as the row of mausolea it had displaced. It seemed to go on forever, its tubular walls swirling as if they had been made out of mist, composing a perspective that sparkled like a tiny diamond lodged at the end of a massive, insubstantial cone.

Hand in hand, we walked into the tunnel's dark mouth. As we stepped over the white, swirling lip—like children dain- tily circumventing a gentle, foamy wave as they ventured into a sea notorious for its deadly undertow—I no longer felt the sting of the sidewalk's gritty surface against the soles of my feet. I looked down, and then, as I felt something tugging me forward, immediately corrected my vision. The Venusian and I were flying along the tunnel's length, still standing, but lifted an inch or so from the mist-strewn floor, in the manner in which my alien visitor had appeared to me in the sheriff's office.

Our toes trailed through the pale vapor as, frictionless, like ice skaters on point sliding across a gossamer sheet of ice, we each carved our own groove, two parallel lines that threatened to meet at the pinpoint of infinity that rushed impossibly toward us. Gazing through the tunnel's ethereal shell I descried the ghostly forms of monstrous examples of vegetation, smudges of ground-up, liquefied emeralds staining the otherwise immaculate gauze surround. But I knew instinctively that that jungle cover, its steam and convection, was not as the tropical lands from which I had just departed. Out there, it was cool, and, beneath the canopy was a region that, despite its lushness, was more extreme, a ground zero as chill as a morgue. This was where the certainties of Earth melted into the divine presence. This was the demarcation zone. The light that shone at the end of the tunnel was morgue-cold, it now seemed to me, a diamond lodged at the bottom of a bright, white mineshaft that lay beneath the North Pole. The pinpoint had begun to twirl; and as it revolved, it emitted darts of color like that which radiated from my Venusian guide. Without getting bigger, that lode at extreme perspective now dominated my field of vision, burning into my retinae like a cigarette butt sucked to white intensity by a slick young thug and then stubbed out in my eyes. Soon I could no longer see the tunnel, the one who held my hand or anything but the monotony of light that pinked at me, as if that floodlit corridor were sentient and had judged that I should suffer death by a thousand cuts.

I was falling into silence. I knew the silence was what I wanted, what I had always yearned for. But it terrified me, it terrified me more than the soul-shattering light. I was falling into a realm where I was being called on to renounce myself, to discard all that had made Nicola E. Newton the person she had been. And I knew that unless I surrendered to that imperious demand to strip bare and go naked into the silence, the light, unless I allowed myself to be extinguished, then I would not be admitted into the mansion that awaited me; and, more, so much more than that—I would not *be*.

I cried out.

"No," I said, "I can't stand it! Do something! Help me! Please!"

I held my free arm over my face in an attempt to shield myself from the radiance that persisted in skewering me with needles of light. I closed my eyes, tight, tighter; but I saw through the lids, saw through my arm—its bones translucent, like the flesh—the light tearing through my body with such force that I thought I would be atomised. I felt the Venusian draw me close to her side, and then, as a gentle hand grasped the back of my head, I was enfolded in her arms and lost to her embrace, my face buried in her bosom.

The light went out, as if whatever massive source that had supplied its power had been suddenly turned off, afterimages of sheeted effulgence bursting in clusters, spiralling like galaxies, behind my still clenched eyelids. The afterimages, dying, became specked with darkness; and as the black snowflakes settled, filled and then overcame their backdrop of white, I allowed my right eyelid to unseam and discovered, somewhat to my surprise, that I had not been permanently blinded.

I lay on the harsh, concrete floor of my cell, a ray of the morning sun falling through the high, barred window. The Captain knelt over me, my limp torso gathered up in his arms, my head against his grubby vest.

"Miss Nicola, Miss Nicola, are you all right? You've hit your head. You're bleeding."

"Where is she?" I said.

"Who, Miss Nicola? There's no one here."

The cell's reality was insistent. I knew I was waking from a dream.

"I have epilepsy," I murmured. "I must have had a *grand mal* in the night." He rocked me, gently. "I thought I saw what they looked like in primal state."

"There, there. You've had a bad turn."

"I thought I saw what a Death is really like." For theirs, I almost added, is the beauty that mercilessly blinds you until, at the extremity of that passion, you finally see. Or did I see? Perhaps that light at the tunnel's end had not been the naked sublimity of Venus, but a prophetic vision of the last days, the days of the White Heat. I did not know. Or rather, knew only this: that I longed to be so blinded again. "I want to be destroyed by that light," I said. "I want to be part of the world that swoons and faints when it is embraced by Death."

"Don't excite yourself. I have you now, Miss Nicola."

"But Death is your name too, isn't it, Captain? You are the one who will take my life."

"And I embrace you too. Death will come gentle, Miss Nicola. I will see to that." He lifted me and placed me on the pallet. I sat there, a hand to my forehead, my legs drawn up beneath my chin.

"She was very beautiful," I said. "My Death, I mean. My Venusian." I thought of Pocahontas. She had been beautiful, too. She had been my Baptist. She had prepared me for the coming of the one who was greater than her: a Venusian who would be my very own. A friend who would be with me to the end of time. My private Miss Heaven. My personal Love Supreme. Ah. I didn't even know her name. Would it be Veronica, which means "true image"? Would it be Vivian, which means "quick and lively"? Or would it be Valentine, most fitting for one whose valentine I longed to be. Whatever her first name, her last, of course, would be Venera, as mine would soon be too. I looked into the Captain's whisky-reddened eyes. "You know what, Captain? I think I'm in love."

"Oh, Miss Nicola, by all the stars in the sky, I'm sure that your Venusian loves *you*. Rest now. I'll go and make us both some breakfast." He stood, took a folded newspaper out of his back pocket and tossed it onto the mattress. "Something for you to pass the time with."

He left the cell, closed its door and turned the key in the

lock. Then he retired to the rooms where he had his other life. One, perhaps, where there was a photograph of a wife and children, something to remind him of a world where there was no talk of nooses and gallows, a world of beneficent forgetfulness of times spent away from his family's company, times occupied by executing the full constraint of the law.

I sat down on the edge of the pallet and picked up the newspaper. Unfolding it, I scanned its headline: WHITE HEAT: LATEST AMAZING PHOTOS. Turning the pages, I came upon a set of images telegraphed back to Desdichado by a photojournalist just before he had been consumed by the march of the relentless curtain of fire. They were the first close-ups I had seen. The telephoto lens that the hapless journalist had used had picked out the multitudinous faces that swarmed in the searing froth of quantum energy.

The headline was correct, these were amazing pictures. For among those faces that looked out from that prison of boiling yet limpid mist were many whom I recognized. Musidora was there, and so were some of her Valkyries, but so were many other children, children I had briefly known in Mademoiselle Moutarde's establishment; and their faces reminded me of my own when, in school and playing field in days gone by, I did not think so fondly about death. I knew, if only I had had a magnifying glass, I might well have spotted the faces of Ma and Pa, too.

Children and adults—they were all going to Venus. They were all being ferried across a cruel terrain so that they might at last cross the river of dreams. They were all going to where, at last, on the edge of things, their spirit would merge with that spirit of alienness that loved them and would make them whole.

Studying those newspaper photographs, I didn't feel so bad about destroying the West. I really didn't. Not any more. The West had had to be destroyed for it to merge with the East.

West and East, like Life and Death, were one now. And I could tell, by the expressions of those consigned to the flames, that that's the way those pilgrims riding inside the great wave of the White Heat would have wanted it. That great, opalescent wall, that slow, immaculate surf, that luminous vehicle had moved across desert and jungle with its millions of faces set in aspects of longing.

We were a family now. The Living and the Dead. We were one, or at least we soon would be. I wasn't sure if it was the family I had always wanted. But it was, I knew, the only family I was ever going to have.

I refolded the newspaper and placed it on the floor. And then I stretched out on the pallet. I lay there, then, as the smell of frying bacon drifted into my cell.

The Twist. Everything had happened the way it had because of the Twist. And I asked myself then: what exactly *is* the twist? Is it that, in expecting nothing, I will discover that everything is given? Or that hoping for everything, I will receive only the void? Was there an afterlife? Or had my visions of life-after-death, of divine consummation, been no more than a dream? What, I asked myself, would be the twist in the story of Nicola E. Newton?

A familiar darkness invaded my soul. I tried to imagine myself already in the privacy of the tomb. Yes, I decided, grasping at hope, a tomb really could be a fine and private place, even if it should prove not to lead to Venus. Oh, for a world empty of people, oh, for a world of emptiness. That would be *some* kind of peace. But there would be no peace, I knew, until I was gathered into the arms of my Death. And if she did not exist? If she had been merely a figment generated by my *grand mal*? I had begun my life in the East, in the living death of Boston, in the bosom of a family who suckled me on viciousness. Wanting to lose that life, I had travelled West, so far West that the West had become the East, another East, one that portended the New

Life. And now I waited for the sun to rise, the black sun into whose midnight rays I shall myself rise, at such time as I shall be transported from this world to the next. But transported to what exactly? Perhaps Venusians are cosmic liars. Should I believe anything that Miss Viva had said?

No, no; I could not bear to venture an answer. Still my brain teemed, it would not be stilled. I was again the victim of my own mentation.

A wind blows in from the west. A great light, a great heat, to burn away the veil of this existence; a wind that has travelled across desert and jungle. It portends the unleashing of a spirit, of an energy marking the end of the world. I hear their distant voices, those who have died in fire and brightness, those misfits, rebels, those mad and beautiful, those blessed by joy and those in pain. And they say: we are glad life has come to an end. We are glad. Glad.

And, despite my anxieties, I too am glad of the end. And I am glad that I will meet my end here, in Desdichado. Desdichado, where West becomes East, the sun setting at the same point at which it rises, where past, present and future are as one and this world melts into the next. Desdichado, my last stop before home.

I hear music outside. It is coming, I know, from a juke-box in a nearby café. The workmen who are constructing the scaffold—the little theatre in which I have star billing and on whose boards I will soon make my bow—the workmen feed it with their nickels so that they might have their morning's gloomy labors sweetened by an aubade. It is a Spanish melody, and its refrain is indeed sweet. It soothes my nerves.

Que esta vida no la quiero;
Que muero porque no muero.

But overlaying those plaintive notes comes another song,

a song that builds in intensity until it drowns the jukebox out.

I hear a pounding piano, a rock 'n' roll vocal that combines the dryness of Carl Perkins with the raw, hysterical whooping of Jerry Lee. All apprehension of the end, about whither my soul is bound, all doubt and anxiety, evaporates like steam rising from the jungle canopy of the planet which will soon take me and never let me go. It is then that I hear Mr. Twist's gravelly laugh. And I know that he has at last set his life to music. He has at last done justice to Thomas Lovell's vision of the grave.

Listen: I have a last wish. That road I trod down last night, the road that leads to and from death, that road which is most *real*; it should, I believe, be named *The Twist*. Not because I pretend to know what will exactly happen to me, not because I have resolved the twist in the tale of my own small life, but because that psychogeographic way from life to death, death to life, really is as crazy as my own dear, sweet John. It is a trail, a hard, dusty trail for exiles, solitaries and misfits—the twisted, in other words; leastways, certainly not the normal. And unless you're twisted, boy, you ain't going far. Yes, call that road over the river of dreams, call it *The Twist*. That's what I will petition for when I mount the scaffold. Desdichado, I'll cry, grant me, if you please, this one thing, this boon by which I may commemorate my friends and which you may look to as Death's surety. Call this thing, my life, my death, *The Twist*.

My mind is still. I am content. I know, now, know for sure that what is true is that which is most beautiful. Nothing else. For Mr. Twist sings, like all the world is singing in these latter days, of consummation. Yes, sir! John Twist is beating his piano black and blue. He is singing of how he and Miss Viva are one and of how they eagerly await my arrival. He is singing of how Venus shines in the morning sky.

He is singing just for me!

Chapter Ten
Dream-Pedlary

If there were dreams to sell,
    What would you buy?
Some cost a passing bell;
Some a light sigh,
That shakes from Life's fresh crown
Only a rose-leaf down.
If there were dreams to sell,
Merry and sad to tell,
And the crier rung the bell,
    What would you buy?

A cottage lone and still,
    With bowers nigh,
Shadowy, my woes to still,
    Until I die.
Such pearl from Life's fresh crown
Fain would I shake me down.
Were dreams to have at will,
This would best heal my ill,
    This would I buy.
But there were dreams to sell,

Ill didst thou buy;
Life is a dream, they tell,
　　Waking, to die.
Dreaming a dream to prize,
Is wishing ghosts to rise;
　　And, if I had the spell
　　To call the buried, well,
　　　Which one would I?

If there are ghosts to raise,
　　What shall I call,
Out of hell's murky haze,
　　Heaven's blue hall?
Raise my loved longlost boy
To lead me to his joy.
　　There are no ghosts to raise;
　　Out of death lead no ways;
　　　Vain is the call.

Know'st thou not ghosts to sue?
　　No love thou hast.
Else lie, as I will do,
　　And breathe thy last.
So out of Life's fresh crown
Fall like a rose-leaf down.
　　Thus are the ghosts to woo;
　　Thus are all dreams made true,
　　　Ever to last!

Thomas Lovell Beddoes, Germany, 1829–44
Richard Calder, England, 1997–98